April Showers

A P R I L

Showers

Briana Swann

First Printing, 2020

ISBN 13: 978-1-64921-832-2

TO MY YOUNGER SELF

You are worthy of love.

AUTHOR'S NOTE

Mental health is a serious topic, and no one struggles with it perfectly. Some of the characters in this book might react to things differently than the reader would expect. This fictional story is not meant to diagnose any of my readers. However, I do hope to shine a light on some of the internal battle's humans might fight, even against ourselves.

Therapy can be a step towards healing. It takes humility and vulnerability. Medication can be a step towards healthy recovery. It takes discipline and commitment. Making good choices for yourself should not be something to be ashamed of. It takes boldness and bravery. There is healing far beyond what you can even imagine awaiting you. It takes courage to begin the process of recovery. It is your choice alone to make, but you do not have to go through it alone.

April

December 2017

"On three," Preston's voice was calm and steady. His skin was tan, glistening with saltwater under the Caribbean sun. April found it fascinating how with each place she traveled, the sun always felt different. Here, in the Bahamas, the rays felt sweeter, colors looked fresher. But still, it was the same yellow star that followed her no matter where she went.

"You've got this, April!" Scarlet whistled from behind. Her long, brown hair was shimmering with natural highlights, tucked back into a French braid that fell halfway down her spine. Green eyes, black bikini, phone in hand recording video footage of the event so that weeks from now they could look back on these moments as more than just blurry memories.

Sweet sweat and salty scents stung April's nostrils like bleach to an open wound as she stood in anticipation on the edge of the top deck of the rented boat. Her dark brown to violet ombre hair was placed in two French braids behind each ear, just barely long enough for the purple ends to brush against her tan collarbone that peeked out from her black halter one piece.

The blinding light of the sun above them reflected off the expensive white flooring of the deck. So excruciatingly bright, April struggled against her instincts to keep her eyes open. The metal railing to her left sizzled under the heat like a hot skillet. Shiny and slick, the stability it offered her shaking hands seemed to be worth the burning sensation against her skin.

"There's nothing to be scared of!" April's slightly younger sister yelled over the pop track playing in the background. "Just think of it as a rollercoaster. You love rollercoasters!"

April gripped the railing with two hands as she looked back at Harper who was casually resting on the leather white bench. Her light, freckled skin was already revealing the earlier signs of a painful sunburn. With pink sunglasses propped on top of her perky cheekbones, the curly frizzes of her blonde hair were sticking up in all directions to say hello. She was stunning. A natural, carefree vibe to her look.

Christopher sat beside the blonde girl. Her brother's rich, tan skin completely contrasted the pasty white of Harper's appearance next to him. He fiddled with his fingers, completely disinterested in the entire moment.

"Roller Coasters have *seat belts!*" April argued with her sister out of panic.

How can jumping off a boat be the same as a rollercoaster? There are no safety precautions here. What if my wet feet slip on the slick deck as I try to launch myself, inflicting pain and bruises to my body on the way down? What if I miscalculate my jump and accidentally

land on one of my parents that are swimming in the ocean below?
What if the person in charge of the excursion is unaware that there
are *actually dangerous creatures secretly swimming under us? I*
could die. I might die. What if I die? Is this how I die?

"Hey," Preston's voice rumbled under all the commotion.
His tone was smooth and rich, like music. He opened his
steady palm to April, offering to take her hand. Preston's arms
were strong and welcoming. They were her safety precautions;
her seatbelt of sorts so she wouldn't have to fear any miscalcu-
lations.

"You can trust me," he smirked. Preston's stunning hazel
eyes glowed gold in the sunlight. His dark brown hair was wet
and sleek. April's heart continued to race faster as his eyes trick-
led down to her lips. His hand was still extended, waiting to
lead her into their jump into the sea that danced beneath them.
She felt as if she were in some alternate reality. Some sort of
fairytale or romantic movie where everything was magical and
beautiful and perfect. Celebrating her sixteenth birthday with
her family, best friend, and dream boy on a Caribbean cruise
for three days? What could possibly be more of a dream come
true?

Entranced by Preston's charm, April slowly released her
right hand from the burning hot railing. She glanced at the
cool ocean glittering below her. Turquoise and green. Wild
and refreshing. Dancing and swirling with excitement and
momentum.

"I've got you," he leaned close and whispered. "You can
trust me."

April glanced back at Preston's hand, wanting to lace her thin fingers through his. Adrenaline was pumping through her veins like a drug. The excitement and thrill of the moment made her feel like she was loopy. Preston was here. He was promising to protect her and keep her safe.

Then why am I still so afraid?

April's palm slowly reached out to take his hand, her fingers just inches from connecting with his before she looked up into his golden eyes once more. Glowing and gleaming, whispering secrets his lips wouldn't reveal. Her eyes searched his for a long moment. Her heart raced as her mind flew like a VCR tape spinning on rewind.

April's mind flashed to dinner the night before. Preston sat close to her side at the elegant dining table tasting exotic foods with her family. The type of dinner where they ate foods she never could have imagined eating back in Indiana. Swordfish, frog legs; she remembered her father and Preston laughing with amusement as they teased April on what a big baby she was being when the tough ox tongue was placed in front of her. She couldn't recall exactly what their comments had been, but she could vividly still see her dad and boyfriend exchanging looks of approval from each other at their clever remarks.

Looking into his eyes, April's memories followed the laughter that took place after dinner. Walking across the outdoor deck, live salsa music had flooded the atmosphere. She remembered watching her parents follow the basic three-step routine for salsa. Scarlet and Harper joined in on the fun by starting their own dance circle while trying to force Christopher to have some fun. And Preston.

He had swooped April up without missing a beat. He placed her right hand in his, and her other behind his neck. They salsa danced with ease, following the basic steps April had been taught since the age of 6. Her Hispanic blood practically required it of her. She remembered giggling hysterically after missing a step and crushing his toe with her pointy high heel. But instead of flinching, Preston pulled her closer and wrapped both arms around her waist.

"Hey, hey, hey. Watch it," Mrs. Lyndon had teasingly interjected. Preston and April exchanged an embarrassed glance with each other before smiling and returning to their original form of dancing. His hand inched its way further and further down her back as the song continued. He always thought he was so sneaky.

April's throat tightened as her memories took control, fast-forwarding deeper into the night. She felt like she was unable to breathe. As if a knife were just held to her side. The blade sharp and cold. Pressing further against her skin, but not strong enough to draw blood yet. As if any sudden movement would trigger its full effects. Her body stayed still.

She didn't want to think about the drama that came after that lighthearted dance routine. Still, she could see the dimly lit hallway. She could vividly hear the aggressive pounding of club music blasting behind the doors of the event April had just stormed out of. Her mind completely livid. Enraged. Her hands flailing about as she boiled with anger. Her insides on fire as she yelled over the meaningless songs at Preston. Clever, sneaky, Preston Schuyler.

"Ready?" The deep voice snapped her out of her daydream, his eyes intense and focused. But it was too late. April's mood had switched like the flip of a light switch, completely taking over her body, making her physically unable to move past the anger.

Why was she even here with him right now? Wasn't she supposed to be upset with him? Then why was she standing on this boat about to take his hand like everything was okay? As if last night were erased from her brain. All was forgiven and the two could move on like it didn't happen. After all, April had apologized. She wasn't sure why or what even for, but according to Preston, she was the one in the wrong.

Then why am I the one hurting so bad?

Standing on the blinding boat, in the middle of the Caribbean Sea with the dream boy she had loved for three years now, April still somehow felt alone. Her best friend and family were still only within a shouts reach, ready to reach out and intervene at any moment. All she had to do was say the word. If only they could hear her internal screaming.

April pulled her eyes away from Preston's hand and took a deep breath in through her nose. She dropped both arms at her sides, turning towards the never-ending ocean in front of her.

Exhaling deeply through her mouth, she shouted back at her friend. "Count me down, Scar!"

Preston retracted his hand quickly, pretending not to notice her change of mind as he faced forward.

"Ready?" He forced a smile, but April closed her eyes and pretended she couldn't hear him. Swallowing her fear with one big gulp, she inhaled a second deep breath through her nostrils.

Harper cheered and whooped behind them. "Let's go! You've got this!"

April repositioned her feet to get a good balance. Her hands aggressively shaking, heart aggressively pounding.

You can do this, April.

"Three!" Scarlet shouted as loud as her vocal cords could scream. "Two—"

Before Scarlet could say, 'one,' April bent her knees and launched herself from the deck. Wind rushing through her braids, stomach dropping to her feet, the blue water zoomed towards her.

Closer...

Closer...

Her body crashed into the concrete-like surface of the water, knocking her unconscious.

April's eyelids flew open. Lying on her side, hugging a grey pillow close to her chest in the dark. The only light was a red glowing **4:47 am** on her desk across from the bed. Her heart was still beating loudly. Her puffy brown eyes stung sore from sleep. She took a deep breath in through her nose and exhaled slowly through her swollen lips. She stared off into the darkness, trying to convince her livid brain to go back to sleep. Begging her mind to quiet down.

Shhhh. You're okay.

Her cheeks felt moist. She wasn't sure if it was from tears or drool that could have very possibly saturated her pillowcase in her sleep. The outer corners of her eyes were leaking clear liquid. But that could have been from sleep.

'It's okay,' she told her screaming mind. 'You're okay.'

5:18 am

It had been almost half an hour of April replaying her dream over and over again in her mind. A dream or a memory. Seven months of different variations of the same scenario was starting to all blur together for April. She was starting to question how many of the details of her summer memories were accurate, and which were embellished.

After another 30 minutes of staring blankly at the ceiling, it was becoming clear her brain was not going to shut up long enough for her to doze off again. Her body had already been kicked awake with adrenaline, but her sadness left her with no motivation to get out of bed and start the day. She would have been perfectly fine with lying in bed all day without having to interact with people. Without having to drag her heavy heart out of the walls of her room where it would be prone to more damage and bruises. It was Christmas break anyway. She didn't even have to go to school. Why leave her bedroom at all for the next week and a half? What was the point of even being awake?

6:30 am

The faint sound of birds chirping arrived before the sun did, illuminating the December sky with a cold, blue tint, slowing growing and streaming through the white sheer curtains that dressed the simple windows of April's room.

It wasn't quite 7 am yet. April thought she might be able to sneak downstairs to the kitchen to steal some sort of food to shove in her stomach before any of her family was up to irritate her even more than she already was. If she was quick enough, she might avoid having to talk to them at all until she came back home from work in the afternoon.

April tossed her heavy white comforter off herself and tiptoed her way out of her room and down the stairs to the kitchen pantry. Her heart jumped when she turned the corner to find Harper already awake, eating a bowl of granola at the granite island in the center of the kitchen. She was scrolling through something on her phone, already dressed in her clothes for the day. A red superhero graphic T-shirt, dark wash skinny jeans and black vans with the left shoelace untied. Her blonde curly hair hung casually around her shoulders. An everyday look for the 15-year-old.

Harper looked up from her phone seeming to be just as startled by the sudden encounter as April had been. April had never came downstairs before 10 o'clock. Sometimes 9:30 if she could smell breakfast being made. Harper watched her sister with a look of caution as April walked into the pantry and emerged with a massive slice of lemon cake on a paper plate.

"Why are *you* up so early?" She whispered as she watched April cram a large bite of cake in her mouth. "Are you sleep-walking? Or... sleep... eating?"

April glared at Harper with disgust. "I'm not 'sleep eating,'" she barked. Her voice was still raspy. "I had a bad dream."

Harper knew it was best to steer clear of April in the mornings. April was definitely not a morning person and used it as an excuse to justify any rude thing that she might 'accidentally' blurt out. 'Not a morning person' was like a free pass for April. 'Stay back, or else.' Harper slurped her orange juice, loudly, intentionally trying to get on April's nerves.

"What are you doing?" April hissed.

"Just waiting for you to tell me what the dream was. I assume that's why you're still standing in the kitchen instead of taking your plate to your room."

April was confused for a moment, trying to understand what her sister meant.

"It was the boat one... Again," she crammed another chunk of yellow bread into her mouth with her fingers. Mumbling with food still in her mouth, she continued. "It was my fault. I should just delete that video off my phone. I keep watching it randomly and then I complain that it gets into my dreams."

April found it weird how some people, like herself, could relive memories in their dreams still feeling the same feelings, smelling the same smells. Her dreams always breathed in such extreme details. It was almost like being transported back in time. Trapped in the past. Like the real thing but more exaggerated and intense.

April's mom strolled into the kitchen in a full day outfit. Her daughter's look-alike. Or, the other way around. Everyone who met them always said April was the identical clone of her mother. Besides the artificial purple hair, people often got the two of them mixed up. April never complained though. Her mother was naturally gorgeous. Young looking and mesmerizing. "Mi reina hermosa de Puerto Rico," as April and Harper liked to tease.

"Good morning, mami," her mother kissed April's forehead who ignored the gesture and shoved another chunk of lemon cake in her mouth.

The sleep-deprived girl walked back into the pantry as her mom began making herself a morning coffee. April grabbed another large slice of cake and dragged her feet back into the middle of the kitchen, pinching thick chunks of cake into her mouth with her fingers.

"April," her mom looked at her with disapproval as she watched her daughter desperately scarf down the sugary treat. "Are you eating poorly again?"

April froze, her fingers still pinching a clump of cake.

"You can't use food to cope," Harper chimed in.

"I'm not using food to cope!" April exclaimed defensively.

Harper frowned. "Food isn't going to make you feel better, April."

"So what?" April crammed an even larger piece of food in her mouth for dramatic effect. She chewed loudly. The muffled sound of her voice was raspy.

Harper sighed loudly. She really didn't deserve to start her morning off with April's tantrums. April knew that. But she was too upset to care about anyone other than herself today.

"April," Harper rubbed her eyelids with her fingertips. Her freckled covered cheeks flushed red with subtle frustration. "Look, I think it's great that you're finally eating again—"

"Eating again?" The girls' mom snapped her head around as if she had been pretending not to listen to the previous conversation before. But of course, she could never keep to herself. She stirred her silver spoon around in her full coffee mug. Careful not to spill the hot drink over the edges. "April, have you not been eating?"

April shot Harper a nasty glare. It wasn't entirely her fault. Ever since the breakup, she felt like she had no control over her body anymore. Not since the cruise. It had been 7 months of headaches, sleep deprivation and feeling completely lost and distracted. Gone. Detached.

When it came to food, some days she had no appetite, no desire to eat at all. She'd take one bite of bread and her stomach would shut down. She thought maybe if she kept her stomach numb, everything else would follow too. Maybe not eating anything would help her forget about the rock in her chest. She'd rather her body go completely hollow.

Other days, her body felt so tight and heavy, she felt the only thing she could do was gorge herself. Pints of ice cream straight from the carton. Massive gooey cheeseburgers. Family-sized chip bags. French fries. And an odd craving for blueberry pancakes. Her stomach would keep stretching and stretching as if food could somehow fill up the emptiness inside her. But instead of comfort, she was always left with bellyaches and self-loathing. Both habits were unhealthy, but April didn't have the motivation to control herself. What difference did it make?

"Oh my gosh," April still had a mouth full of food. She tossed her paper plate on the counter. "First you get mad at me for not eating. Now I'm literally eating right in front of you and you're giving me a hard time about it."

"You're sixteen years old, April. You need to take care of your body," Mrs. Lyndon scolded. "Even when you don't feel like it. You have to take care of yourself physically. You can't just skip over that part and expect everything to get better."

April rolled her eyes. She knew her mom was probably right. But she brushed it off anyway. She didn't want another stupid lecture.

April just wanted to be alone. She just wanted to listen to sad songs all day and stare at her ceiling for hours upon hours. Today was one of those days where she wanted to stretch her stomach with food to somehow try and fill the emptiness inside of her chest. The fast beating of her heart that echoed through her body like an empty, abandoned warehouse was enough for today.

So what if it had been seven months? She deserved time to mourn the past three years that were gone. Three years of loving someone so deeply were now just expected to be erased. Forgotten. Hidden like it never even happened. How could that be the end?

Throwing her imaginary 'not a morning person' pass down, April started to clear her breakfast mess to head back to her room to be alone. She was seriously regretting coming downstairs this morning. This had been a mistake. She knew she should have stayed in her room today.

"April, I know you're sad," her mother was incredibly understanding, her tone calm and sympathetic. "But you can't just be sad forever."

Her throat tightened. Her hands kept her balance against the cold, slick countertop as her fingers traced patterns of swirls on top of the glossy surface. April's voice cracked.

"But what if I was wrong, Mom?" She stopped hiding for a moment, revealing again some of the things she really told herself when no one was around. The things that rang in her head like the roar of a car engine that just eventually becomes comfortable background noise. Never fully going away. Never completely shutting up. Just blending in with the rest of the rattles bouncing around in her head. Her throat stung as she tried to hold back the flood of tears that wanted to consume her. But she was not going to cry. Not in front of them at least.

"What if I messed up?" April shook her head as her mind started to speed up again, like the acceleration of a needle on a car dashboard, the numbers climbing higher and higher with each passing second. "Maybe I did overreact. Maybe if I hadn't been so insecure like he said— maybe he would have changed once he saw how much he realized—"

"April," her mother interrupted. April gulped, catching her words in the back of her throat as her mom continued to speak in a hushed tone. "You know that's not true."

April hung her head. Her hands felt sweaty. Her chest weighed heavy. The same way she felt after waking up from her dream earlier that morning. How she felt every time she thought too much about Preston.

"You made the right choice. It wasn't your fault," her mother scanned April with sympathetic eyes. Worry scribbled on the wrinkles on her forehead like the wrinkles of a silk sheet.

Everyone kept telling April the same things. Probably the right things. That she needed to move forward. Stop clinging to the past. But April didn't want to move on. She didn't want the memories to fade and the songs to lose their meaning. She didn't want to forget Preston's voice or all the empty promises he made her. She dreaded the idea that she might never hear his voice again. April only wanted to lie in bed all day, letting the heavy weight of the pain and loss sink into her bones. She didn't want to move on.

What April really wanted was a new ending to this sadness of her reality. A happy ending. One where she and Preston were perfect for each other. One where they proved to everyone that they weren't crazy for feeling the things they did at such a young age. She wanted an ending where she wasn't crying over him for months to the point where her stomach was ready to throw up.

But most importantly, April longed for what wasn't even possible in either of her two worlds. She wanted Preston to stop being the reason her heart was in constant agony. She wanted that thing inside her chest to stop feeling like it was being shredded. But April knew the truth; her heart hurt because of Preston whether she was with him, or gone. In either scenario, her heart lost. And that was April's most disappointing reality of all.

2019

Michael

Chapter 1

He ran his hands through his blond, wavy hair in the reflection of his rearview mirror. He wasn't ready to go out into the cold, early March air that awaited him. The black Jeep sat in the mini parking lot of BitterSweet: Coffee and Ice Cream shop. It was local in Atlanta only. Not one of those plastic-looking Starbucks places all the other seniors went to. No acoustic versions of cheesy pop songs you hear on the radio. BitterSweet was the most underrated spot in town. Ice cream on one side of the room, coffee on the other, all connected by one long industrial wooden counter. It was just about the best place for any boujee mom to spend $7 on a reusable steel straw to go along with their animal cruelty-free, all organic caffeinated drink. Michael could care less about all that silliness, though. That wasn't why he enjoyed coming into the shop.

The blonde boy got out of his car and pulled open the heavy glass door to the cozy building. The sound of a bell chime went off as it always did when someone entered or exited the modern little shop. The walls were rustic brick. Cold, silver metal furniture was scattered around the majority of the room, more for the aesthetically pleasing look than for actual comfort. The only people in the room at the time clustered around a tall circular table. Four teens gathered underneath the trendy bare bulbs that hung from black wires, dangling from the sleek, black ceiling. Three girls sat halfway on the silver bar stools along with one guy standing next to a seat but refusing to be seated. They were always complaining about the odd arrangement of furniture.

"Like, why can't they just put a cute sofa on this side?" Michael heard Jenni's raspy voice from the other side of the room.

"Um, Jenni," another voice interrupted. "I think I've already seen that show."

The tan girl who spoke was leaning across the table, chin propped in the palm of her hand. Head tilted slightly to the side. She smiled at Jenni. Her chocolate brown eyes beamed with light. "The one where all those friends sit around on a sofa talking in a coffee shop? You're not fooling anyone, Capri." Capri. Short for Jenni's last name, Caprio. Also, an ongoing joke referencing to her shortness in height.

Michael quietly made his way over to his friends, knowing he was the last one to show up. He had stopped at The Blu gas station by his house to get gas on the way. It also didn't help that he seemed to hit every red light on his route to Bitter-Sweet. The sweet smell of sugar almost gave Michael a headache. But he would never admit that to his friends, of course. He bet to himself if one let the room get cold enough, the giant windows would start to crystallize with sugar rather than ice on the edges because of the amount of sweetness in the air. As obnoxious as the smell was, he put up with the overwhelming scent anyway.

April's ombre purple ponytail swished behind her as she turned her head to see Michael. Her eyes met his for a brief moment, an excitement in them maybe. They darted away just as quickly as they had been found.

"There's a reason that show was very successful!" Jenni continued. "Mikey! Hey, you made it! Back me up, will you?"

Jenni was the only one allowed to call him that nickname. Mikey. He hated it. But Jenni had grown up with him since preschool. She had earned the right to annoy him with it for the rest of his life. Michael didn't reply, he just smiled shyly as he glanced at April.

The purple-haired girl peeked up at him through her dark lashes and smirked. Her eyes quickly redirected back to her black braided bracelet around her wrist. It had a few turquoise charms on it. Of what? Michael wasn't sure. He had never paid enough attention to notice. But she was always fiddling with it. In a cute, nervous way.

"What took you so long to get here, Michael? We were all waiting for you." Nick threw an arm around Michael. He was always so loud. His shaggy, dark hair looked like he just rolled out of bed. His pitch-black eyes forced intense eye contact at all times. He leaned closer before mumbling, "*Someone* has been waiting for you."

"Stop," Michael shook his head, embarrassed, desperately hoping no one heard his overly-enthusiastic friend's comment.

Hoping *she* hadn't heard the comment.

"Look at this girl!" Nick continued to instigate as he moved toward April. "While the rest of us are drinking coffee at 10 am on a Saturday, this chick is drinking a milkshake. *Ice cream. For breakfast.*" Nick had no volume control. Everything he said was either loud or louder.

April rolled her eyes playfully. She had a slight obsession with ice cream. Everyone knew that about her. Or at least anyone who paid even the slightest bit of attention to her. Anne threw her hands up in surrender.

"Okay, so when I drink ice cream for breakfast, it's fine. But the second April does it, y'all have to jump on her back about it?" She took another sip of her almost gone strawberry milkshake. Her messy blonde bun sat happily on top of her bobbing head as she danced to the chill lo-fi music playing through the shop speakers.

"Exactly," April shook her head playfully. "You guys always pick on *me*."

The bathroom door in the corner suddenly swung open. A solidly built guy suddenly emerged from the bathroom behind Jenni, still wiping his damp hands on the back of his blue jeans. His dark hair was clean cut and his brown eyes were ready to antagonize.

"Hey, Michael. What took you so long?" Ethan was tall and sturdy. Easily over six feet with freckles scattered across his face. He always carried himself with confidence. "Oh, by the way, April. Hand dryer in there is broken."

April nodded her head taking a mental note.

"Hey, I think Michael wants to order a drink." Nick gave Michael a nice slap on the back. The sound startled Anne who was trying to balance her stool on just one of the legs. The sudden smack almost made her collapse backward into the wall. Michael chuckled at Anne's attempt to save herself before jumping down from her barstool.

April's whole attitude seemed to change as she switched back into 'work mode.' She was still on the clock, but so was her coworker with colorful dreads scrolling through her phone in the corner behind the coffee section. Both employees seemed to be on the same page. Michael followed his friend as they approached the front counter. He could still feel the sting in the shape of a hand on his back even after Nick had walked away.

On the side facing Michael, two shelves displayed souvenir coffee mugs and ice cream bowls. A few spoons that cost a whopping $4 each. But some trendy moms liked to spend that kind of money. It made a good prop for their Instagram photoshoots they were always forcing their children into. Millennials were so strange.

April had already been wearing her black work t-shirt and light blue jeans, but once she stood behind the register, she pulled a black cap from under the counter and laced her ponytail through the back. The word "BitterSweet" was embroidered in white across the face of the hat. Her silver name tag that was pinned near her left shoulder looked faded, the letters all mushing together to make one squiggle of a word.

April.

She wouldn't look at Michael at first, keeping her eyes focused on the register as she adjusted and pulled on the hat to make sure it was secured on just right. He peeked back at his friends all piled up in a group as they observed from afar. Their muffled giggles and pointing was the opposite of 'acting natural.' Nick gave a nod of approval and two thumbs up. My gosh, how badly Michael wanted to punch him in the arm.

"Hi."

Michael quickly turned back around to face the brown-eyed girl. Her skin was clear, her body lean, plump lips naturally pink and never chapped.

"Hi," Michael grinned shyly.

Hi. Like always. Not, 'hey.' Not 'sup.' *Hi.* As if they were being introduced for the first time, every time. A lingering excitement to the word. An unspoken understanding. Michael could hear whispering behind him, which meant April could not only hear it but probably also see the look on their obnoxious friends' faces all watching the encounter like it was entertainment.

Michael took in a deep breath as he looked up at the chalkboard on the wall behind the girl. Lists of oddly named drinks were all carefully written in different colors. Whoever was in charge of writing these down weekly had to have a lot of focus and incredibly neat handwriting. He wondered for a second if April had been the artist responsible for the board. He noticed her forearm was stained with scattered specks of blue and white. But was that from chalk or paint?

April waited. "Do you know what you want?"

Michael's eyes darted between the board and the pretty girl. He didn't know which one of them had the answer he was scrambling for.

"I guess the same thing as last time," he shrugged.

"Wow. So unoriginal," April sighed. "Always copying me. I see how it is."

The truth was that Michael really wasn't interested in coffee or ice cream at the moment. But she had already put on the hat. He was just trying to do what he thought would have been polite. April turned her back to Michael as she pulled a pair of plastic gloves out of a cardboard box.

"Um, I don't know what you mean. Everyone knows Rocky Road was my favorite flavor ice cream way before you," he teased shyly.

The tan girl looked over her shoulder and flashed a white smile. Teasing and picking on each other was basically the only way the two of them knew how to communicate with each other at this point.

"You know, I heard a rumor..." She picked up a metal scoop and swirled it in the clear bucket of water beside her. Michael panicked just the slightest bit.

"Oh," he tried to act casual. The girl just stared. A playful smile on her lips.

"I heard your favorite ice cream wasn't always Rocky Road."

That had not been what he was expecting. However, he couldn't say he wasn't relieved. Michael shook his head at the floor.

"I don't know what you're talking about. That's not true," he obviously lied. "Who told you that? Was it Ethan? I bet it was Ethan, wasn't it?"

"I'm not going to say who it was," April giggled as she began scooping the spheres of brown ice cream into the clear, plastic blender. "But apparently you used to only eat vanilla ice cream up until you were like, seven or something."

"It was Jenni. Jenni told you this lie, didn't she?" Michael pinched his lips together smiling. April chuckled loudly, peeking over at the table of weirdos as if she was debating whether or not she was going to snitch on their friends.

"It was Ethan," she smirked. Michael's eyes went wide as he took in a deep breath.

"I knew it," he hissed, pretending to get fired up over the silly detail. April just giggled as she turned around to finish making the rest of the drink. Michael checked his phone that had been vibrating an unusual amount the past minute.

13 notifications. All text messages. All from Anne. Although Michael suspected there were at least three other potential culprits behind the harassment. His phone kept buzzing. The messages just kept coming in. Most of them just kissy face emojis. Hearts. Drooling faces. A few random "My man" messages thrown into the mix. Michael shoved his phone back into his pocket and glared at the table behind him.

"Are you going tonight?" April set the full plastic cup in front of him as she snapped on a lid to fit. "To the movies? It's one of the superhero ones. Seventh Saber or something? Everyone's going." She nodded in the direction of the hooligans still giggling around Anne's phone.

Michael pulled out his wallet as he thought of a response. The movies sounded boring, especially today of all days. It was still chilly outside and rainy. Not to mention he had already seen that particular movie last week with his dad and younger brother. He really wasn't in the mood to be out. Granted, he also told himself that this morning when he first woke up, and yet, here he was. At BitterSweet. Paying for a milkshake that he didn't even want at 10:30 am.

"Are you going?" He swiped his card on the electronic tablet in front of him.

"Depends," she shrugged her shoulders as she patiently watched the boy make his best attempt at his signature on the screen. After a messy scribble and a swipe, April peeked back up at him with curious eyes. "So, you going tonight?"

The sound of the little bell rang.

"Jimmy!" The group yelled harmoniously. A short, lanky Italian dude casually strolled over to the only group of people in the shop.

"Who invited Jimmy?" Michael whispered to no one in particular, sounding more annoyed than probably necessary.

"He always shows up here on Saturday mornings," April chuckled. "Every Saturday at 10:30 on the dot. He comes in, asks me about my week. Never buys anything. I usually give him a generic response to his never-ending list of questions and then he proceeds to tell me all about his week in detail. Monday through Friday. You know, not including Sunday because of course, he uses Sunday evening at youth group to catch me up on all the things he did on Saturday and Sunday. Which by the way, is nothing. Ever."

"Is he going to the movies tonight?" Michael was feeling slightly irritated already. April giggled at his sudden mood change.

"I'm not sure yet... Should I ask him?" She lifted a hand. "Hey, Jimmy!"

"No, no! Shhh!" If there was anything that would make Michael want to go to the theaters any less at the moment, it was the thought of having Jimmy there, too.

"Hey, April. How are you? What's up?" Jimmy's small, skinny figure strutted its way across the shop over to the counter. Michael scooted off to the side, trying to put a little more distance between him and the freshman's overpowering cologne. The ad on TV claimed the scent was a 'babe magnet' but Michael had seen mosquitos drop dead just by coming five feet within range of that scent.

"Nothing much," April had that look in her eyes. The same look she got whenever she was about to antagonize. "Michael was actually just talking about you right before you walked in. I believe his exact words were, 'I kinda miss Jimmy.'"

There it was. That flash of pride across her face. She really thought she was some genius at times. She loved to entertain herself by harmlessly teasing others.

"Awe, man! I missed you too, buddy!" Jimmy gripped Michael's hand and forced him into an awkward bro-hug with an aggressive pat on the back. His sweaty smelling, oversized synthetic leather jacket stuck to Michael's shirt.

"I did not say that," Michael said dryly as he shot April a look of annoyance. But she just gleamed with amusement.

"I can't believe you guys graduate in three months. I'm gonna miss you, dude." As if Michael couldn't get any more irritated with Jimmy. He always had to say stupid stuff like that, pretending they were friends when they were most definitely not friends.

"Awe, look at you two besties," April's voice was thick with mockery. Michael wanted to get back at her. She had a much higher tolerance for Jimmy than Michael did. But he needed revenge for his extremely uncomfortable bro-hug he had been cornered into.

"Hey, Jimmy?" Michael pulled away from the awkward embrace. "How are the Jayhawks doing?" He glanced at April for a second. "You know, I heard that April thinks the Shockers are the best team in basketball."

April's eyebrows furrowed in confusion for a second. She glanced at Jimmy before realizing what Michael was actually doing. The confusion melted away and her face beamed with anticipation. If there was anything April loved more than teasing someone, it was teaming up to tease someone. Jimmy slowly turned his head back to Michael.

"Wait, what did you just say?" The little freshman tried to stay calm.

"Yeah, and honestly I mean, she's not wrong," Michael said matter-of-factly.

April leaned forward. "It's true! Michael's the one who

taught me all about basketball. I give him all the credit."

Jimmy's eyes went wide. "Wait. Hold up. This guy clearly doesn't know what he's talking about." Jimmy was panicking only a little.

Michael leaned on the counter with one elbow as he continued his improv banter with his friend. "So the Jayhawks, right?" April nodded along with Michael's basketball lesson. He tried to keep a straight face as best as he could. "Worst team in the league. Without a doubt."

April nodded once. "Jayhawks. Worst record. Got it."

Jimmy's face shot red with anger. "Wait! Are you *stupid?*" He yelled. "The Shockers are absolute *garbage!* Jayhawks are the best! Dwayne Cannon is the king of threes. Klay Vicks! One of the best shooters in the league. Chandler Green— cheats like crazy, but—"

"Jimmy, hush," April hissed. "Michael's trying to teach me about basketball."

"You can't listen to this guy!" His hands were now flying through the air with each word that flew out of his mouth, like a true Italian. "He just said the Shockers were better than the Jayhawks!"

"Jimmy, seriously. Pipe down," Michael squinted his eyes at the kid. He figured allowing himself to smirk might just set the little dude off even worse than before. Sure enough, it did. Jimmy was too easy.

"You think this is funny?" The freshman slammed his keys on the counter. April covered her mouth with her hands to keep from laughing. No one ever knew why Jimmy walked around with a set of mix-match keys considering he didn't even have a car. Ethan had a theory that Jimmy actually collected random keys he found in the street, not knowing what any of them belonged to. "How stupid are you?"

Michael just smirked, waiting to see how much longer it would be before he decided to back down. Knowing Jimmy, this could go on for a couple of minutes. Five tops. But after realizing he had just called a group of seniors 'stupid,' he then started to realize yelling wasn't the way to finally be 'part of the squad.' Not that Michael's squad was the coolest group around, but they were the only seniors who tolerated Jimmy as much as they did. And Jimmy desperately needed that.

Picking up his keys that he had slammed on the counter, Jimmy took a breath. He shook his head and rolled his eyes dramatically.

"Whatever," he snapped. Game over.

That was more fun than Michael had expected. Probably because he had the proper audience. April seemed to be enjoying herself. Well, until the moment was suddenly ruined by Jimmy's next words.

"Anyway, how has your week been, April?" Jimmy said in a caring tone. That was Michael's cue to sneak off before it was too late. Out of the corner of his eye, he saw April reach out to grab his sleeve, trying to hold him hostage while she had to endure the upcoming ten-minute conversation with the chatterbox. But Michael had moved just in time. She missed the white sleeve of his white sweatshirt by an inch.

Michael turned and mouthed the word 'sorry.' April knew

he didn't mean it, which only made him want to laugh even more. She deserved it for making Jimmy hug him earlier with his sticky hands. She shot him a look of disdain. Her lips were pouty, but still cute.

"Wait, where are you going?" Anne exclaimed to Michael as he almost walked out the front door.

"I have to drop Isaac off at a soccer tryout." His brother seemed to have more of a social life than Michael sometimes.

"Awe, tell him I say hello." Anne waved her hand aggressively, still swaying to the background music. Michael pushed the front door open with one hand. The high-pitched bell chimed through the entire store as the boy turned around to face the counter. He raised his chocolate milkshake in the direction of the cash register towards April and Jimmy, who was still chatting away.

"I'll go tonight," Michael tried to talk across the room without yelling.

April looked up from her dreadfully boring conversation. It took a second for her to figure out what Michael was talking about. After a brief moment of coming back to reality, excitement gleamed in her eyes. She pursed her full lips, trying to hold back a smile.

"Okay. I'll go too," she spoke softly. Michael smiled. A genuine smile. She beamed back at him.

"Bye, Chad," she blinked cheerfully. Michael smirked back before backing out the door.

"See ya, Bandkid." Michael could still faintly hear Jimmy's voice as the door closed behind him in slow motion.

"Wait, where are y'all going tonight? You know, if I asked my mom to drive me, I could probably come too," Jimmy spoke at a million miles an hour.

Michael looked over his shoulder just in time to see April rolling her big brown eyes one last time. Man, she was beautiful.

April

Chapter 2

The graffiti-painted tunnel was April's favorite part of the campus. It didn't even look like typical graffiti. Instead, every inch of the concrete surface was decorated with vibrant swirls of yellow and pink and blue, creating lively beauty and art rather than slang words. Abstract patterns sparkled wherever bright rays of sun hit. The array of colors spilled out of sight as the long tunnel curved around the corner. She couldn't yet see the end of the art from where she stood.

"Plenty of our students walk through here on their way to classes in the mornings," the young woman smiled. Her skin was a rich, red-brown. Thick, black hair hung past her waist in air-dried curls. Her eyes were big like a cartoon. Black-brown and full of intriguing mystery. April could understand why this spot was such a hidden wonder. The 12-foot tall walls were impressive, to say the least. She couldn't even imagine being given a canvas this big. She imagined every shade of blue rolling into each other. A roaring ocean. A sea of secrets you could walk through without drowning. An artwork life-like enough to still make you want to hold your breath.

But at a college like this, April figured any art major had the same fantasy. And they probably had much more creative ideas for such a space than something as basic as ocean waves. In a sea full of artists, April didn't feel like she would stand out so much at Savannah College of Art and Design.

"If you all will follow me this way, we can continue the rest of the tour." The beautiful Indian woman extended her arm to lead the handful of parents and high school students through the other side of the tunnel. They crept deeper and deeper into the concrete structure. April noticed gages the size of nickels through the young Indian woman's ear lobes. She wore a flowy, short sleeved red shirt with black ripped jeans. April didn't know how the girl wasn't freezing in this chilly weather. But what really stood out to her was the tattoo on the girl's forearm. The permanent ink still looked fresh and clean.

"A lot of photographers here in Savannah love to shoot at this location," the woman continued. April felt the energy of a person sneaking up behind her shoulder. The mysterious figure whispered in her ear with excitement.

"Just think about it. This time next year, you could be starting college here!" Mrs. Lyndon squeezed her daughter's arm as they approached the tunnel to walk through it to the other side. "You know, people say if you hold your breath the entire way through, you're supposed to make a wish."

A wish.

April didn't believe in wishes. And neither did her mom. But still, it was sometimes fun to wish for things. Even if she knew they wouldn't come true. She took a step into the square tunnel. The light from behind began to fade as they ventured deeper into the tunnel and brightened as she exited again. She wanted to touch the walls. Feel how the paint felt after it had spent years drying against the cold surface. But she had no idea what had been on those walls, so she didn't bother risking the germs that might cling to her fingers if she allowed her curiosity to get the best of her.

"I love your hair." The colorful college student had been waiting for April on the other end of the tunnel, catching April slightly off guard. "I know a lot of people with colored hair. None of them pull it off like you do."

"Oh, thanks," April released her breath as she stepped out into the light once again. The tour guide smiled. She was pleasant and seemed confident. An artistic vibe seemed to radiate off of her. April didn't know how to explain it, she could just feel it.

"I know purple is such an unnatural hair color, but somehow you make it look... natural. Does that make sense?"

"Yes, actually," April politely laughed as she peeked back at her mother who was slowly trailing behind. "You'd be surprised how many people tell me that."

April's eyes were drawn to the woman's body art again. The pointy petals all arched into make a semi-circle. Two thick leaf petals were supporting the bottom half. She wondered what it would look like to add color to the black outline. A rich turquoise color sprinkling the edges and bleeding away toward the center. Art without color could seem so naked sometimes.

"My name is April, by the way."

"Fatima," she extended her left arm to shake the girl's hand with her forearm turned upward to let the girl have a better look at her tattoo. "I noticed you keep looking at it. It's a lotus flower. The Hindu symbol for purity."

"I thought all flowers were symbolic of purity," April shrugged. "But it's beautiful."

Fatima squinted her eyes, trying to read April's sudden change in mood. "Sure, flowers, in general, symbolize purity. But each flower has its own poetic meaning." She adjusted her shoulders to face April, trying to engage deeper in the conversation. "A lotus is unique because it is rooted in muddy water. Closing within itself at night. But each day it emerges to the surface clean, muddy water easily sliding off its slick petals. Rebirth."

April just nodded her head. Pretending to follow along.

How much longer is this boring conversation going to go on? Isn't this girl supposed to be focused on the group as a whole? Why is she singling me out?

"My sister has a small gladiolus inked behind her right ear." Fatima refused to change the subject. "A symbol of strength."

"Ha, that's kind of ironic," April chuckled. The dark-haired girl seemed to be prying more than necessary.

"Why would that be ironic?" Fatima squinted.

April sighed heavily, her eyes looking for any escape from the meaningless conversation. Where was her sister to save her from awkward moments like these when she needed her? They even had their own signal, the way most siblings did. There wasn't a specific moment it was invented or a conversation where it was agreed upon, but they knew. Scarlet would know too.

"You know. A flower," April explained. "Which is like, fragile and weak and ridiculously delicate. It's just funny to think someone would try to use it as a symbol of strength. Something so vulnerable and weak. That's all."

Fatima's eyes lit up. April was so done with this conversation. She desperately wanted to leave already. She ran her fingers through the roots of her hair trying to distract herself.

"Well, in some ways, yes. But it takes so much strength for that delicate flower to bloom into something beautiful." Fatima spoke slowly, and carefully. "Do you believe it's possible for something to be both vulnerable and strong at the same time?"

"Honey!" April's mother came shuffling behind the two girls unaware of the fact that she was interrupting the uncomfortable conversation.

Thank goodness.

"Look, I found a great extra-credit program you could go to next summer. And guess where it is?"

Fatima smiled politely. Taking her cue to leave. "I'll be at the front of the group if you need anything."

April watched the swish of the girl's long, dark hair as she floated away. Finally. She was gone.

What's wrong with that chick?

"April, are you looking? I found a booth with extra-credit programs so you can add more college credits to your dual enrollment hours."

"Oh, right," April turned back to her mom. She felt another annoying headache starting to make itself comfortable above her right eyebrow. "That sounds good."

"It's at Clanton University in Alabama, only a few hours away from us."

Ew. Alabama? When would I ever want to go to some crusty school in Alabama?

"Now, I know it's kind of expensive," April's mom continued scrolling on her phone looking for more information. "But if you keep saving the money you're making at BitterSweet, I think it would be a great experience for you."

"Yeah, Mom. I'll look into it."

Her mother's Hispanic eyes looked up from her phone, watching April as she slowly realized her daughter was acting off. "Was it something I said?"

"Nope," April shrugged but looked away trying to avoid eye contact. She wasn't the best liar. Mrs. Lyndon's shoulders sunk. She pinched her lips as she studied her clone's face.

"Is this because of all the college stuff with you and Preston?" April shook her head as she readjusted the purse on her shoulder.

She turned away from her mom trying to find the tour group again. "No, Mom. I told you. That was forever ago. I'm not sad about that stuff anymore. He has a girlfriend now."

Why does she always have to blame everything on Preston? This whole family always acts like I'm never going to be able to live that phase of my life down. I can be upset for other things besides that stupid boy.

"Okay," her mom replied, sounding unconvinced. The two

of them followed the rest of the group that was now ahead of them up the concrete stairs. They walked through the heavy glass doors and back inside the heated building that contrasted the chilly air outside.

Clanton, Alabama. Summer Honors program. Getting extra college hours before the school year even started? That sounded incredibly boring to April.

Why Alabama? Why not somewhere exciting like New York or LA?

Gosh, April loved New York City. It would be a dream come true to study art there. But getting her dual-enrollment credits to transfer was already becoming such a hassle. If she knew these 6 credits from some little college in Alabama were guaranteed to transfer, why shouldn't she take the opportunity? In less than three months, April would be graduating.

What's the likely hood I would even be able to make it into that summer program, anyway? What is the likely hood of saving up enough money from my part-time job in time? What's the likely hood that Preston would have ever actually followed through with moving down to Georgia this summer after all?

April sighed to herself as she tried to get a grip on her thoughts again. She knew better than to let them slip away to Preston anymore. Some days were easier than others. But asking herself the same questions over and over for the past almost two years was not what April wanted to continue to do. She really wanted to let go of all her lingering questions she held onto when it came to her ex-boyfriend. But more honestly, she wanted answers.

"When do you think he realized he didn't love me anymore?" The words slipped through April's mouth before she could seal her lips shut. She felt awkward at first for the sudden question but decided to continue anyway. Her mother was always ready to listen. "You know, like, before he met... her." April's mother peeked at her suddenly quiet daughter, waiting to see what else she might add.

"I'm genuinely asking," April confirmed. "Like, what was that moment like for him? How did he know for sure that he loved her? And that he could no longer love me the way he said he used to?"

April wasn't sad. She knew what it was like to be deeply sad for months at a time. Her heart didn't feel that empty anymore. But she did feel confused. Curious. Slightly insecure about her not-so-recent replacement in his life. Her eyes wandered to the three plastic horse head figures sticking out of the walls ahead of her. One red, one blue, one yellow each positioned in the center of three empty rectangle frames. A 3-D piece of art that demanded attention. An odd choice of art. But art, nonetheless.

"Do you still love him?" Mrs. Lyndon asked. April kept her gaze fixed on the plastic red horse in front of her. It looked so life-like. It made her feel the slightest bit uneasy.

"Sometimes I think if I stopped loving him, it would mean I never loved him in the first place." She shrugged painfully. Her chest felt slightly tighter than usual. "And maybe that would mean I admit defeat. I surrender and accept that it was all just a lie since the beginning."

Her mother stepped up to the blue horse beside April, also

examining its extreme detail and precision. There was a long, drawn-out silence between them.

"I believe you loved him," she nodded softly. April turned to look her mother in the eyes. A deep, sympathetic look stared back at her. "He just didn't know how to love you the same way."

That was the first time April's mom had admitted she believed April. Like a punch to the gut, it left her rib cage with a faint soreness.

Why would you admit that now? After years of telling me that I was too young to understand what love was. After years of making me feel like I was overexaggerating my feelings for him. You picked now to be the moment you give my heart the validation it had been craving all those years? Now?

"I can't believe I was going to let him come to college here with me," April looked blankly back at the horse head in front of her. Whether she really loved him or not, the truth was in what was real. April would be here this fall, and Preston would not.

"Come on," her mom half-smiled. "Deep down you knew he wouldn't have followed through with that plan. I think that's part of why you said no. You really dodged a bullet there."

Dodged a bullet.

Everyone was always telling her that. But if she really did dodge a bullet, why did it feel like she was still walking around with a scar?

"He seems happy," April sighed. Her mom watched her

daughter for a second, studying her like one of the horse heads in front of them.

"Are you happy, April?"

April turned to face her mom again, surprised she asked such a question.

"Yeah," she nodded. "I'm not sad anymore."

Her mom gave a half-smile as she shook her head slowly.

"But not being sad doesn't always equal being happy."

April thought about that idea for a moment. She was sure she wasn't sad anymore. Thank goodness for that. But maybe her mom was right. Maybe she had just found a comfortable place in-between happy and sad.

What would that space be called?

"I'll be okay, Mom," she smiled. "I promise."

Michael

Chapter 3

The stale smell of butter popcorn clung to the red carpet like velcro, permanently saturated with sticky oil and soda stains. If you stood in one spot for too long, the carpet started to hold the shape of the shoes on top of it, which was exactly what was happening to Michael at that moment. He leaned against the wall lined with movie posters. One romance. Another thriller. Two superhero movies and of course, a second romance film. Michael checked his Apple watch.

9:43

He had been waiting for almost 7 minutes. Had April snuck past him at some point when he had been looking down at his phone? She technically didn't know he was waiting. Maybe she had walked past him without a clue. He did feel like she had kind of been avoiding him all night.

She had shown up late for the movie, barely making it into the theater during the last trailer. He knew she had gone straight to the theater from her college tour in Savannah, hence the reason the group agreed to push back the showtime. Still, she was late. There had been an extra seat next to Michael, but April had sat on the opposite end of the row next to Anne. Maybe she hadn't wanted Michael to come to the movies so she could hang out with him, after all. Maybe she just didn't want him to be left out of the group. The only reason Michael was still hanging around was because of a text Jenni had sent him. She was the first one out of the movie theater. He pulled out his phone again to check the message again.

A picture of April's little green car and Michael's black Jeep Wrangler parked side by side. Jenni had circled the two with one giant heart and wrote "Now's your chance!!" with a winky face emoji. Even though April had shown up late, she still made it a point to park right next to Michael's car. It was a subtle thing she had started doing a few weeks ago. Now it had become a regular thing. They always parked next to each other. No matter where they went. Without ever making a single comment about it.

Michael leaned his head back on the wall and shoved his hands in the side pockets of his khaki pants. He decided if April didn't come out within the next two minutes, he would go home. Maybe she really was avoiding him.

Right then, April's purple hair whipped around the corner. Black t-shirt with an open grey jacket and ripped mom-jeans. She always wore her tri-colored Air Force 1's with every outfit. Unless she was in a dress of course, which she would wear on occasion. She looked really pretty in dresses. She jingled her keys in her hand as she walked towards the glass exit doors. Michael quickly stood up straight and adjusted the hem of his white sweatshirt as the girl's eyes skimmed passed him before doing a double-take.

"Oh," April froze. Her eyes looked surprised. As if she were embarrassed or something. "I didn't know you guys were still here."

Michael shyly looked down at the dirty floor. Smashed bits of popcorn were scattered around his feet. "No. Well, I mean, they already left."

April didn't say anything. She just continued to stand there awkwardly. Michael wasn't sure what to do or say. He just stood there for a long moment, waiting for a response or something.

"I'm sorry," April forced an awkward laugh. "If I had known you were waiting on me I wouldn't have let my mom go on for so long on the phone. I should have just told her to tell me her story about their waitress when I got home.

"You're fine," Michael smiled lightly as he started inching in the direction of the door.

April followed him out of the movie theater and into the dimly lit parking lot. The air was slightly crisp but felt nice after coming out of the stuffy building. The black asphalt glistened under the streetlights, still glossy from the rain earlier that evening.

"Dang, look at the moon," April crossed her arms as she walked alongside him. The slight heat from her breath danced under the parking lot lights around them.

The sky was impressive. The full moon was glowing with specks of stars scattered above them. It was quiet besides the only sound of a distant plane zooming somewhere unseen above them. It was gorgeous. Perfect really. April passed the Jeep and approached the green car but didn't get inside. Instead, she just stood there in front of the driver's door staring up at the moon, glowing in the sky like a newly lit streetlamp.

Michael checked his watch. Several new notifications from Jenni.

"You've got this!"

Michael quickly swiped the notifications away from his watch and stuffed his hands in the pockets of his pants again. He took only a few steps to stand right next to April, their backs to her car door. The two teenagers stood there in silence staring at the moon. It felt like a whole minute went by before April sighed.

"Okay, well, I'll see you at youth group tomorrow night." She abruptly turned to her car door and opened it. She paused. "Did you like the movie?"

Michael didn't bother mentioning it had been his second time watching Seventh Saber in theaters. The first watch was better. He only came this time because of April. He still wasn't totally sure if it had been worth the two and a half hours of screen time this time around.

"Yeah," he smiled.

April nodded her head and looked at the seat of her car. She paused for a moment as if she was debating something with herself, her hand was still on the edge of the door frame.

"Goodnight," She suddenly blurted out and swung herself into the driver's seat.

Michael panicked. She was about to leave and he hadn't said a word. Anything to her. Well, basically. He already knew how much crap he was going to get from Jenni later that night. He could already hear her impatient voice over the phone, chattering away about how he totally missed a great opportunity.

"Your car is tiny," he blurted out.

Silence.

April hesitated before peeking over her shoulder at him.

"Did you just... insult my car?" She looked confused but couldn't hide her smile.

Michael poked the green back door with his index finger. "It only takes up half the parking space."

"Don't talk about Holly like that!" Holly. Short for 'jalapeño.' April enjoyed naming inanimate objects. And animate ones. It was slightly odd at times. But one of her quirks. "She's tiny and she's perfect."

"I bet people get really mad when they think a parking spot is open only to realize your car is hiding there."

April rolled her eyes and turned so her feet were hanging out of the still-open door. She laughed in her defense. "I mean, the gas costs practically nothing."

"And look at this," Michael walked around to the back of her vehicle where she could no longer see him.

"What?"

Michael searched for a handle to open the trunk door but couldn't find one.

"What are you doing?" April climbed out of her car as Michael found the button to pop the door. It made a sort of spaceship sound as it zipped up over his head. "Michael!"

"Look at this tiny trunk!" Michael felt April's hands grip his left arm as she laughed. "What the heck is all this?"

The most random items were arranged all across the bed of the miniature trunk. A black purse. A first aid kit. A pair of flip flops. A blue, wrapped gift box. A grey sweatshirt.

"Will you stop?" She playfully pushed him away. "It's almost 10. I have to be home soon."

"What is this?" Michael pulled the grey sweatshirt out. Indiana State University was spelled out across the front in blue letters. The numbers 1865 were stitched in the center. "Are you planning on going to Indiana State?"

"No," April snatched the shirt out of his hands and threw it back into the car.

"Flip flops? For what?"

"Oh my gosh," she dragged out the '*gosssssh*' and reached up to grab the trunk door.

"What's in the gift box?" He smiled.

"Stop being so nosey!" She laughed.

Michael smiled teasingly. "Awe, what did you get me?"

"It's not for you."

"Then let me see it. Why can't I see what's in it?"

April giggled and pushed him away with her free hand. "Michael," she rolled her eyes.

"Why can't I see? I just want to see it—" Michael stepped forward towards the trunk right as April jerked it down, the edge of the door collided with his skull. The loud thud sound seemed to echo through the whole parking lot.

"Oh my gosh!" April released the trunk door from her grip and rushed over to Michael, grabbing his shirt sleeve with both hands. Michael's head throbbed in pain. He felt dizzy for a second, and then even dizzier the next. Could anyone else hear that weird ringing out in the distance?

"Oh my gosh, oh my gosh, oh my gosh! I'm so sorry!" April's face was ablaze with panic. She sounded like a bad record stuck on repeat. "Are you okay? Oh my gosh."

Michael reached up with his free hand and gripped the top of his skull. It burned. It throbbed. It felt like it was on fire while the rest of his body tensed up in pain.

"Now might be a good time to use that first aid kit of yours." Michael didn't even bother looking at April. If she was even still there. It was dark, and his vision felt kind of blurry. But he could still feel her hands clenching his bicep, her short nails almost digging through the thin cotton fabric of his sleeve.

"It was an accident! I swear!" From her reaction, any stranger walking by might have assumed Michael had just been shot. Although it did kind of feel like it. Like hitting your elbow on the corner of a wall except worse. A lot worse. "Oh my gosh, are you okay?"

Michael pulled away from her grasp and walked a couple of steps from the car still holding his head. Man, did it hurt. Michael felt like he might even cry. But there was no way he was going to cry right now. Not in front of April. What the heck had this night turned into?

"Gaaah-ouch!" Michael squinted his eyes and yelled up at the sky. He purposely made a funny voice when he did it and heard April try to suppress a laugh.

"Are you gonna cry?" She hunched over and crossed her arms, staying in her spot next to the car. She rubbed her face with one hand and tried not to laugh again. "Because it's okay if you cry. I won't judge you. I would definitely be crying right now."

"I'm not gonna cry." Michael was going to cry. Every part of his body wanted to use tears as a way to release the pain and tension built up in his body. But there was no way he was going to let that happen. He would have rather gotten hit in the head three more times than cry at this moment.

April carefully made her way over to the victim, trying not to startle him. "I'm so so so sorry. It really was an accident."

"Sure it was," Michael teased as he continued to rub his wound. April tiptoed her way next to him, her arms still crossed.

She watched him, her face still grave with concern. "It's not bleeding, is it?"

"Probably just a bump... or a concussion," Michael peeked through one eye to see her panicked expression.

"What— Are you serious?" She practically yelled.

Michael chuckled again, allowing her to realize he was just teasing her. She hit his arm with the back of her hand and rolled her eyes at his joke, but Michael still thought it was pretty entertaining. Her reactions were always so dramatic.

"Don't scare me like that," she scolded him before sighing. She stared at Michael's head for a moment, frowning. Her eyes looked heavy with regret. The pain had already gone down some, but his head still burned with heat. The chances Michael actually had a concussion were slim. He knew that. But he wouldn't have been completely shocked if a doctor had confirmed the diagnosis.

After everything that had happened so far, maybe he really should have just gone home when everyone else had. If he had just stopped teasing about the mysterious present in the back of April's car he could've avoided this uncomfortable moment. There were a lot of things Michael would have given to go back in time just 30 seconds to avoid this pain. This was definitely one of the worst nights of his year so far.

Suddenly, Michael felt two arms slide around his torso. April's arms gently made it around his rib cage and squeezed carefully. The side of her face barely pressed against the space between his arm and chest, her body small and warm.

All at once, Michael forgot about his throbbing head. What was that sweet scent? Maybe her perfume. Or was it the shampoo she used? Either way, she smelled like lavender. He hadn't noticed that until now.

"I'm really sorry," she mumbled into his side. "Like, I wish saying sorry would actually make it better. But I know it doesn't."

Michael carefully wrapped his arms around her. Barely even holding her. He didn't want this really sweet moment to be ruined.

"Really, it's fine, April," he chuckled.

"But I feel really bad!" She whined. "I hate seeing people

hurt. And now I'm the one who caused it... to you, of all people!"

Michael smiled to himself. 'Of all people.'

April pulled away from his side and looked up at him. "I'm sorry."

Michael didn't even know what he was supposed to say anymore. This back and forth of the phrase 'I'm sorry' and 'it's fine' was becoming less meaningful each time.

"What's your favorite candy?" April squinted her eyes.

"Why?" Michael tried not to smile. He could already guess why.

"Just tell me. Please." It didn't sound like a question. Michael started walking away from April towards his car, hoping she would follow him. She didn't.

"M&M's... Or snickers."

"Okay," she still looked worried.

"I'm fine," Michael reassured her. "I'll see you tomorrow."

April nodded her head and walked over to close her car's trunk that was still open. Michael climbed into his Jeep and waited for April to start her engine.

Michael wasn't even entirely sure what the original plan had even been. Jenni had just said it was his 'chance.' He had been kinda making it up as he went. What was even supposed to happen before? Was he supposed to ask her out? Tell her he liked her? If the moment was right, maybe even kissed her? Michael had no idea. But in any of the scenarios he tried to come up with, none of them included getting physically assaulted by her car 'Holly.' Michael rubbed the top of his scalp with his hand again. There would definitely be a bump in the morning.

The black Jeep followed the little green car out of the parking lot and onto the freeway. April gave a little wave before she took her exit, something she always did when they drove the same direction home. Michael arrived at the cul-de-sac of his little yellow suburban house on the corner ten minutes later. The neighborhood was still surprisingly quiet for 10:15 on a Saturday night.

He walked through the front door to see his dad in the kitchen. His greying blonde hair messy. His reading glasses rested on the edge of his nose. He was going through papers that were most likely phone bills or water bills, annoying money stuff adults have to take care of. He tried to sneak upstairs before he could be stopped to chat.

"Hey, son," his raspy voice boomed.

Michael halted only halfway up the staircase. He pinched his lips together.

"Hey, dad…" He didn't move, hoping he would let him just go straight upstairs to his room without turning this into a long conversation.

"How was the movie?" He heard the swish of pages. "Was it just as good the second time?"

Michael considered the question honestly as he ran through the night in his head. The empty seat next to him, waiting in the hallway for almost ten minutes, April almost abruptly driving off, the teasing, the head injury, the really great moment after that. Michael leaned over the railing so he could see his dad. He was scribbling something down on a yellow notepad.

"Yeah," he nodded. "It was kinda better."

Chapter 4

Bloomington, Indiana was an eight-hour drive from Atlanta. A two and a half hour flight. But sometimes it felt like home could have been all the way in California and it still wouldn't have made a real difference in location. Distance wasn't always about numbers, a lot of times it was just about space; a gap between hearts.

It had been two years of April trying to detach from her old home and settle down in her new one. It wasn't terribly difficult for her. She had kind of gotten the hang of moving by now after a long childhood of moving from house to house. The difference between now and back then was her age. The older she got, the more awkward she felt trying to blend into her new environments. Although she was good at pretending to adapt with confidence, the truth was that she often felt like she didn't belong. A swan in a flock of ducks.

April anxiously sat in her little green car waiting in the long line of cars outside of Terminal A of the Hartsfield-Jackson Atlanta International Airport. Scarlet's flight had landed late which ended up working out in April's favor since she happened to arrive late herself. After a few more minutes of barely moving through the congested traffic of vehicles, a gorgeous, green-eyed girl dragged her black suitcase out the automatic doors across the way. Her cheeks and little nose were lightly sprinkled with freckles and a thick, brown braid hung down her back just past her shoulder blades. She wore a comfy, oversized grey "Indiana State" sweatshirt and tight black leggings with her bright blue tennis shoes.

"Hey, hobo. Need a ride?" April ran over to take the suitcase from her friend. "If you get in my car, I'll give you candy."

"Okay!" Scarlet released her luggage handle from her grasp and sprinted towards the green car. April had been expecting a hug, but instead Scarlet bolted right past her to the driver's seat of the car.

"Wait, Scar! What the crap?" April chased after the girls swinging braid. The suitcase practically flew behind her. It wasn't heavy. Scarlet never had to pack much clothing when she came to visit. She just wore whatever she wanted from April's closet. Why waste the time packing if April had more than enough clothes for April to fit into at the house?

Scarlet slammed the driver door shut and clicked the lock button. She reached over to the stereo and turned the knob a few twists to the right so that the bass pounded in the speakers, rattling the petite vehicle as Scarlet whipped her braid side to side. Her eyes squinted shut as she screamed the lyrics to whatever new Ariana Grande song was blasting.

"Scarlet!" April banged on the window. She jiggled the handle of the passenger door. "Okay, stop playing, Scar. Unlock my car."

"What?" The girl's voice was almost completely drowned out by the muffled music. "Sorry! Can't hear you!" She turned the knob a few more notches and went back to dancing like she was having a seizure.

What in the world is happening? I know Scarlet's wild. Of course, she is. But I wasn't ready for this. Okay, April. Calm down. Just... don't totally freak out.

April looked around at the strangers now pausing to watch the odd scene. An old Asian lady shook her head at the girl's with disapproval and disgust at their obnoxious bit. April twirled her index finger by her right temple while mouthing the words 'she's crazy' and pointed inside the car with her other hand, unsure of how to explain.

"I can see you!" Scarlet howled. She put her hands on the stick shift and started backing out of the line.

"Scarlet!" April squealed nervously. She jiggled the handle aggressively. The car braked, then started to drive forward. The blaring of a horn honking made April jump in her skin.

The green car abruptly halted. A red truck zoomed around and passed Scarlet, giving another long honk just for good measure. Scarlet hopped out of the car holding her stomach. She was laughing so hard she looked like she might pass out.

"You craz-o!" April marched over to the trunk and threw the suitcase in the back. She was trying to hold back her laughter that couldn't seem to shut up within her. April was a sucker for exciting moments like these. But the little 'mom' side of her knew better than to let things get too out of control. "Get in the back! You've lost your rights to sit shotgun."

Scarlet put her hands on her knees as she continued to laugh. Or at least what April assumed to be Scarlet laughing. No sound came out of Scarlet's mouth, her shoulders just shook up and down like someone had put a taser to them. With one heavy squawk, Scarlet picked her head up to see the little old lady watching her judgmentally.

"Heyyyy!" Scarlet waved. The poor stranger probably thought this minor was under the influence of something. She wasn't. This was just April's best friend whenever she was in a good mood.

"Oh my gosh, will you please just get in the car, you weirdo?"

"Nice meeting you!" Scarlet waved a final goodbye at the old woman. She almost lost her balance as she stumbled her way over and into the passenger seat, ready for April to drive her to her second home.

The Blu gas station near April's house was as close to the version they used to go to back in Bloomington. Blue and white building, basic gas station chips and snacks, but the Blu Blastz; that was the most important part. 32 ounce Blu Blastz, that looked more purple than blue colored.

It had become a summer tradition for Harper, Scarlet, and April since middle school. Twice a week, during summer break, they would all go walking down the scorching hot

sidewalk up to the little ratchet gas station on the corner behind April's old house. They'd each fill their plastic cups to
the brim, slurping the edges and refilling them a few times
until the cashier would glare, shooting them daggers with her
eyes telling them it was time to pay or get out.

Harper always grabbed Taki's. April squirted the unnatu-
rally yellow nacho cheese into the plastic container. Scarlet
would claim she didn't want any food but would always end
up eating from the two sisters stash the second they walked
out the doors. That had been their routine since middle
school. April wanted so badly to reconnect with those memories. It was the reason she had driven her sister and best friend
to The Blu on a Sunday evening. But deep down she knew it
wasn't the same.

The drive was short. The weather was still chilly out. The
building was empty of any real memories or life. Life was just
different. April was different. What she really wished for was
to go back in time. Back to when she was home. When her
heart was bursting with curiosity and excitement and all the
exciting things that come with being a teenager. But things
were different now. This was different.

"I'm cold!" Harper hunched her shoulders as she slurped her
icy drink. Her curly blonde hair was up in a bun. The sleeves
of her red sweatshirt hung over her black-painted fingernails.
"But that's not going to keep me from drinking this."

April paid for the snacks at the cash register with the
rough grey-haired woman who looked like she had a mouth
full of shattered seashells for teeth.

"Blast the heat!" Harper screamed from the back seat the second she closed the car door.

"Where's the freaking seat warmer button?" Scarlet frantically poked her finger at random red buttons around the radio until she accidentally hit one that blasted a male radio host voice through the speakers at full volume.

"TRAFFIC UPDATE FOR MARCH 21ST WITH AMANDA. THERE WAS AN ACCIDENT TODAY ON POWERS FERRY—"

All three girls screamed in unison. April violently hit the mute button with the palm of her hand as hard as she could. Silence. April stared straight at her dashboard. Her heart was pounding. A shot of adrenaline made its way through her veins and melted away. She felt like her body had gone into a mini shock from the startling moment.

Scarlet burst out in hysterical laughter. Harper followed. And after catching her breath, April cupped her hands around her face and giggled with them as well.

"What the heck was that?" She massaged her forehead with her fingers.

"I was just looking for the seat warmer button. My butt was cold!" Scarlet tucked the heels of her feet under her butt while sipping more of her purple frozen drink.

Harper flung herself forward in the space between the two front seats. "I don't even have seat warmers back here. My cheeks are freezing!"

Scarlet and April exchanged a glance with wide eyes. "*My cheeks!*"

"What else do you want me to call them?" Harper giggled. "My buns?"

April snorted. "Hey, guys. My buns are frozen."

"I've got some nice, frozen buns right here," Scarlet started messing with the radio again. This time it didn't attack them.

"Speaking of which," Harper sat back in her middle seat. "Scarlet, have you seen where April works yet?"

"What did that have to do with frozen cheeks?" April asked.

"Frozen. Ice cream. BitterSweet. That's how I got there. And there's coffee and ice cream. It's super cute. It's where all the cool kids hang out."

April rolled her eyes at Harper's 'cool kids' comment. "No cool kids. Only people who try too hard to be hipster when secretly they're just as boring as everyone else on the planet."

"Oh stop, complaining." Harper propped her dirty black tennis shoes on the counsel in front of her. "Your boyfriend comes in like twice a week just to see you."

"Boyfriend?" Scarlet practically choked on her straw. "Wait, are you two actually official now?"

"He's not my boyfriend," April's face flushed pink. "We're just friends."

Crap.

"They're a thing. Definitely a thing," Harper nodded her head, excited.

Okay, maybe. Kind of. I think. Or not. Probably not.

"He probably doesn't even want to actually date me," April rolled her eyes and sighed as she leaned her head back against the grey headrest. "We like, talk and have been flirting some, I guess. But I think he just likes the attention. It's never going to be anything serious."

"That is the dumbest thing I've heard all day," Harper gave her sister a serious glance. "Any guy would be straight up dumb to not want to date you."

No. Any guy would be straight up dumb to make the mistake of getting trapped in a relationship with someone like me. Get your facts straight, Harper.

Harper popped a few more Taki's in her mouth as she continued to talk with her mouth full. "Well the real question is, do you want to date him?"

April took a deep breath through her nose. She didn't know what she wanted. Michael was great. She loved spending time with him and hanging with him in their friend group. He constantly teased her about everything and made her laugh. Not to mention the fact that he was pretty attractive. She had a secret obsession with his bright blue eyes—

Or are they green? It depends on the day.

She spent a lot of time debating the color of his ever changing eyes for someone who claimed to not be interested like that.

"I don't know. He's like, one of my best friends," April sighed again.

"Okay, but honestly, Harper has a point." Scarlet unbuckled her seat belt and sat up. "You clearly like this guy—"

April interrupted. "Woah, what makes you think I like him like that?"

Scarlet looked back at Harper, who exchanged a silent glance with the girl. "Um, probably the fact that your face is so red right now."

April pinched her lips together as she tried not to laugh. Okay, so what if she did kind of like Michael? Right now was not the time to be getting into a relationship. College was coming up faster than she could keep track of and being tied to someone would only cause problems. April needed to focus on graduating and going to her summer honors program at Clanton University, and soon, going off to college in Savannah by the fall. There was no need to get into a relationship right now. Michael was just a crush. It didn't matter. It would go away soon enough.

Right?

"Look, guys. The timing is so off," April shook her head doubtfully. "It's just, it's not like that. Okay?"

April looked up at the black ceiling of her car and stared. She didn't say anything at all. She just blinked slowly a few times and took deep breaths in and out her nose. She glanced down as she fiddled with her black bracelet on her left wrist, waiting as the tension in her body continued to grow as the seconds of quiet passed. Harper and Scarlet looked at each other sending telepathic signals, quickly changing their playful mood to a more sympathetic one.

"Well, I think you should give him a chance," Harper smiled.

"Yeah, April. I mean, you haven't dated anyone in— what? Almost two years?" Scarlet shrugged her shoulders casually. "I just think you shouldn't close yourself off so soon. Just... see what happens."

April sighed knowing full well she was not going to take their advice. She knew they were looking out for her. They just wanted what was best for her. "I'm just... I don't know."

Harper leaned back, studying her conflicted sister's expression. "What do you want, April?"

That is a good question. What do I want?

For so long she thought she knew what she wanted. She wanted passion and excitement. Over-the-top feelings and romantic gestures. Crazy loud love that made her body ache and her heart beat like the crashing of waves. She used to want Preston. But she didn't want that anymore. She couldn't want it. He was just a ghost. A faded memory that she would never get to relive again.

"I don't even know what I want anymore," April sighed. "I don't even know what to look for at this point."

"I know," Harper smiled sympathetically. "But maybe you'll find it. When you least expect it. But you'll never know unless you—" Harper gasped. "Duck!"

"Duck?" April had been expecting the word 'try.' But this seemed just as disappointing of an answer.

"Get down!" Harper threw her body flat, taking up all three seats in the back of the little car. "Jimmy is walking out! Get down! Now!"

April squealed as her head snapped in the direction of the door. Sure enough, a skinny boy figure with brown gelled hair pushed the front door of the gas station open and stepped outside.

"Hide!" April sunk as far down into her seat as she could. She gripped the sleeve of Scarlet's grey sweatshirt and jerked it along with her.

"What's happening?" Scarlet yelled, wild-eyed. She started to peek her eyes over the dashboard. "Who's Jimmy?"

"Stay down!" April hissed and jerked her friend by the sleeve again. "Jimmy. The kid I told you about. We're always picking on him. I told you. You know. Jimmy?"

"Does he wear a brown, oversized cheap fake-leather jacket?" April could see Scarlet was holding back a laugh.

"Yeah... usually," April whispered, slightly confused.

"And does he wear a blue, basketball t-shirt under it? With plastic glossy hair and olive skin?" Scarlet's face looked like she was about to burst with laughter.

"Wait, how did you—" April jumped when she heard a tapping at her window.

"Hey! April!" He had a faint Bronx accent. Some people in the group claimed it was fake. Some people being Michael, who started the joke.

Are you kidding me?

April stayed frozen staring at Scarlet. She didn't sit up. She didn't even roll down her window to be polite.

"Oh! Hey, Jimmy," she continued to stare at Scarlet.

"I had no idea you guys were here! Is this your friend?" He shouted so April could hear his muffled voice better through the glass.

"Heyyy," Scarlet waved while laughing.

"Oh, shoot! You know what?" April sat up and started her engine. Harper and Scarlet were still giggling like five-year-olds. "I forgot I actually had to head to the bank before it closes! Sorry! See you later, Jimmy!"

He blinked. "Wait, but—"

The car jerked back and sped out of the parking lot as fast as possible. April felt bad. For a second. Then she remembered all the times she had been especially nice to Jimmy before. All the times she had made her friends stop teasing him when they took it too far. Yeah. She deserved a few quick escapes.

Michael

Chapter 5

It had probably been a full three hours of sitting in front of his flatscreen TV in the family living room watching episode after episode of New Girl. April always accused Michael of having an addiction to the show. He enjoyed resting during his free hours. Laughing at a screen usually seemed like a good way to spend his evenings after school. Pre-calc homework could wait for one more episode. School was almost over. Most of the pressure was gone by now.

Except for when it came to college. Michael, unlike many of his peers, still felt like he had no idea what his plan was. Most of his friends were excited about going away. Jenni was headed out to Auburn, Nick to South Eastern down in Florida and Ethan had been planning on UGA since sophomore year. Fortunately, Anne was only a junior and still had time to figure out her plan after high school. Maybe that was something both Michael and Anne had in common. Not knowing what to do with their future yet. Except what Anne had was time, and Michael was running out.

He had his handful of in-state options in front of him, including UGA, Georgia State, and Georgia Southern. College felt like a lot of pressure. Like this massive semi-truck approaching at full speed out in the distance, and no one could make it stop or slow down. His parents were constantly on his back about it.

"Make a decision," they kept beating him over the head with the phrase. But why was anyone his age supposed to make such a drastic life decision so soon? Everyone kept saying it would "change the course of his life" but how was he supposed to know if he was making the right choice? It all felt like such a mess to Michael.

"I hate this show!" Michael's little brother, Isaac stomped into the room. His hair also blonde and wavy, but instead of sharing Michael's green eyes, Isaac's were dark brown, puppy dog eyes.

Isaac practically threw himself on the cushion next to his brother, his arms flailing through the air like wet spaghetti noodles. He reached over Michael to steal the remote that was propped up next to him, but his little frail hand was blocked by his brother's large arm.

"Hey, no. You had the TV yesterday." Michael took another handful of M&M's from the family size bag resting in his lap and shoved it in his mouth. "You can't just snatch the remote and change the show."

"But you've been watching for so long!" Isaac whined. He was way too old to still be whining like this. "It's not fair!"

Michael furrowed his eyebrows. He defensively held his

palms facing up in front of him. "It's totally fair!"

"Mom!" Isaac shouted in the direction of the dining room around the corner.

"Michael," her voice called back, calm and collected. "Be nice to your brother."

Michael hated that phrase. It seemed there wasn't a day that went by where his mom didn't say that to him. And why was Michael always supposed to be the nice one? Why wasn't Isaac ever supposed to stop being such a pain?

"Ha," Isaac pursed his red lips together, expecting his brother to actually hand over the remote. But Michael wasn't going to let the kid's attitude win again. Isaac always won. And this was just about a stupid show. Isaac shouldn't always have to win. That couldn't be healthy for his self-esteem.

When Isaac realized Michael wasn't going to back down, his expression completely changed. He went from looking like a smug, proud little man to a now very aggravated and impatient young boy.

"Give me the remote," Isaac snapped.

"No," Michael whispered, afraid his mom might hear. Isaac gave his brother a bone-chilling glare. He may have been only 12, but the look in his eyes could scare even the grim reaper.

"Fine," he hissed and reached out to snatch the remote from Michael's hand.

It was probably a comical sight really, as the two of them tried to wrestle silently so their mom wouldn't hear from the other room. Isaac dug his nails into the side of Michael's hand that was gripping the remote. He then propped his foot on the kid's chest as he tried to create more distance between the attacker and himself.

"Let go!" Michael grunted. But Isaac didn't back down. He dug his nails deeper, sending a sharp stinging sensation throughout his whole hand. Michael still refused to loosen his grip. He pushed his leg out further instead, creating even more distance between them. Isaac noticed the foot on his chest and used his other hand to shove away. But what Isaac seemed to have forgotten was that all his weight had been leaning on that foot. The moment it was removed, he flung face-forward, his head smashing into his brother's shoulder.

"Ow!" Isaac screamed in his awkward alto voice. "Ouuuch!" He screamed even louder, sounding like someone had just stabbed him.

"Michael, what did you do?" Mrs. West came storming into the room, her face red with anger.

"He attacked *me*!" Michael shouted defensively.

Isaac rubbed his eyes, like he was about to cry but trying not to. A classic little brother move. "Michael kicked me in the eye."

Michael's eyes practically popped out of his skull. "That's not what happened!"

"Did your *foot* touch him?" Her voice was stern. She wasn't panicking. She seemed more annoyed than anything. Isaac slowly limped over to the tired lady so she could examine his face. Why was he pretending to limp? There was nothing wrong with his legs!

"Well, yeah but he tried to take the remote from me!" The blonde woman now looked shocked.

"Seriously, Michael? All of this over the stupid TV remote?"

"Ouch," Isaac rubbed under his right eye.

"It was my turn to have the TV!"

After studying Isaac's 'wound' for a moment, she sighed heavily. "You'll be fine. It will probably just swell up a little bit. But it's not that bad." She patted his other cheek. "Now both of you. Outside."

"Wait, what?" Isaac suddenly looked panicked. "Why outside?"

"I can't deal with you two right now! You're both grounded from TV. Now go outside and learn to get along."

Michael threw his head back, annoyed. "Mom, can't I just go to my room?" Basically anything would have sounded better than hanging out in the driveway.

"No," She marched out of the room, still shouting as she made her way to the dining room. "You boys are staying out there *together* until your dad comes home from work. Go. *Now*."

Perfect. Just what Michael needed on his one extra day to relax. Spending quality time outside with his annoying little brother. Michael shot Isaac a dirty look as he threw his blue fuzzy blanket to another seat and followed him out the front door.

"Great. Now look at what you did," he hissed at his younger brother.

The two boys stepped out onto the small driveway. The weather wasn't too bad. The sun had already passed the trees down the street. The air was sticky with a gentle breeze to balance it. Even the sky looked nice. An in-between orange and blue stage as the day melted away. The beginning of March was unusually warm for Georgia weather this time of year.

Isaac squinted. "Well, if you hadn't kicked me—"

"I didn't even kick you and you know that!"

Michael was tired of this. He didn't even want to argue anymore. Instead, he sat down in the grass patch near the curb of the street. His hand still stung. Sure enough, three little red crescents were indented into the space between his index finger and thumb on his left hand. What a punk.

"Do you want to play basketball?" Isaac sounded shy. Michael looked over his shoulder at him for a second.

"No," he returned to examining his hand.

"Fine. Whatever. I'll play by myself." Isaac ran back inside the house. Michael assumed he was grabbing a basketball. He rubbed his hand again. Still salty about the whole encounter.

Why was it that every time something happened between them, it had to be Michael's fault? Isaac got everything. Was it really fair that his mom expected Michael not to be bothered?

'Where does Isaac want to eat?' 'What does Isaac want to watch?' 'Michael, move so your brother can sit.' It was ridiculous.

Isaac walked back outside with an orange ball and a handful of something else. What was that? Colorful little candy?

M&M's.

Michael stood to his feet. "Did you just go back inside and eat my M&M's?"

"It's a family-size bag," he tossed the rest of the treats into his mouth like he was taking some medicated prescription. "Share with your *family*."

"Those aren't yours," Michael snapped, but it was too late. They were already being chewed to brown mush. What was Michael supposed to do? Make him spit it out?

"Spit that out," he barked before realizing how dumb it sounded. Spit that out? What for? How was that going to make the situation any better?

Isaac laughed, opening his mouth to reveal the chocolate mess sticking to his teeth. "You're just jealous because this is the candy April gave you. Because she likes you."

Michael's face heated up. "Shut up. She just felt bad for hitting me with the trunk of her car."

"Yeah? And what were you guys doing at her car? Smooching?" Isaac proceeded to taunt his brother with obnoxious kissing noises, squeaking and slurping.

"Knock it off," Michael walked over and slapped the basketball out of Isaac's arm. He dribbled it out into the cul-de-sac where the hoop sat on the curb as he stepped back to what he imagined to be the equivalent of a three-point line. The ball swished through the net.

"Michael and April. Mwah. Mwah." The little pest continued.

Michael threw a hard chest pass. Isaac barely caught it. "Why don't you focus on working on your jump shot?"

"Why work on jump shots, when I can hit every three?" Isaac followed his question by hitting two three-pointers in a row. Nothing but net. The crisp sound of the ball racing through the net was almost musical. Michael went back to his spot in the grass and pulled out his phone.

Michael: Hi

The day was almost over and they hadn't had any interaction at all yet. Michael's phone almost immediately vibrated.

April: Hey! Whatcha up to?
Michael: Playing basketball with my brother.

Well, it wasn't a lie. He shot the ball a few seconds earlier.

April: Awe, that's so sweet haha. He's adorable.

Geez, Isaac always got all the attention. Why did he have to be so adorable?

April: Who's winning? I bet Isaac is kicking your butt.

Okay, so maybe Michael didn't play on a team. But messing around with friends, Michael could hit 80% of his shots on a good day. He was still much better than his younger brother by no surprise. April was just teasing for fun.

Michael: I would say we should play sometime... but I wouldn't want to embarrass you.

Michael watched the typing bubble bounce for a few seconds.

April: Oh, wow. I see how it is. Bring it on, Chad. I can take you.

He smiled at his phone.

Chad: April's nickname for the blonde boy to tease him over his stereotypical white-guy look. Plain sweatshirts, Patagonia hats, khaki shorts, he even drove a Jeep. The private school preppy look. Any stereotypical VSCO girl with her scrunchies and hydroflask would have been thrilled to score such a basic white guy as Michael.

Bandkid: Michael's nickname for the purple-haired girl to tease her over her stereotypical artsy-chick look. She had done one year of playing the clarinet in band during sophomore year, however, when Michael found out about her past hobby, he wouldn't let the nickname go. She was the opposite of basic or preppy. Colored hair, black t-shirts with some quote or deep meaning, off-brand mom jeans. Any guy with rounded, trendy glasses and a black scarf hanging around his leather jacket would have killed to score such an artsy girl as April.

Truthfully, April was no real e-girl and Michael was no true frat boy. They both hated when the other teased them about such extremes. The two teenagers were opposites on the outside. No one could deny it. But ultimately, they were rooted with the same kind heart and antagonist sense of humor. They were almost best friends.

Michael: Nah, I'm good. You'll probably just hit me in the head again.

The typing bubble appeared. Then left. Then appeared again. And left a second time. Finally, it appeared a third time a buzzed.

April: Soooo I guess the candy, balloon and apology poem wasn't enough?

Michael: What candy? I never got any candy.

He could already imagine what her response would be. Sure enough, it was a full paragraph.

April: Michael! I literally put the bag of M&M's in your hand! I watched Ethan suck the helium out of the balloon and read the card. It's been two weeks and you won't let me live it down! How much longer am I going to have to keep apologizing?

The poem in the card had been ridiculously cheesy on purpose. It was total garbage but listening to Ethan read the humorous poem in a high-pitch girl voice only made it even more hysterical.

Michael: I'll just let you feel guilty for a while longer.

"Michael's smiling at his phone!" Isaac chucked a hook shot at the basket. It hit the backboard and barely made it inside the rim. "He's texting his girlfriend. 'Oh, April. I love you so much!'"

Michael didn't even bother telling the kid to shut his mouth this time. He didn't even bother denying that April was his girlfriend, even though she wasn't. Yet. His phone buzzed again with a message from April.

April: We could settle this on the court.

Michael felt jittery.

Michael: Okay. One of these weeks I'm gonna come over and you better bring your A-game, Bandkid... cuz I don't give out pity points.

An immediate buzz.

April: Bring it on, Chad.

April

Chapter 6

The clean, crisp sound of a swish echoed through the driveway. April hit another shot. She was secretly a good shooter. Usually, the one who scored the most points during a family game on a Saturday morning at the gym. Christopher was good with his ball-handling skills, but even his shots weren't as accurate as April's. Yet. Maybe by next year if he kept practicing.

"You gonna play like that when Michael gets here?" He said as he stepped out the side door of the house. Their concrete driveway was large, and Chris had invested a decent amount of money into the hoop to practice on in order to make the JV team next year. Being outside around the early month of April was one of the best in terms of cool weather. "Because we better not lose because you're dumbing yourself down in front of a boy. It's okay to score on a guy."

April hit another outside shot. "I don't want to mess with his self-esteem," she winked jokingly.

"Wait," Chris stopped dead in his tracks. "Do you like him?"

Crap. April, why would you say that?

She panicked and chucked the ball. It hit the backboard and bounced off into the grass. "What? No. We're just friends."

The two siblings stared at each other for a moment. April was a terrible actress. "Chris, don't you dare make it awkward."

The kid was still a freshman in high school. He loved getting a kick out of finding little ways to embarrass his sisters any chance he got. He resembled so much of April, taking after their Puerto Rican side of their family. Tan skin, dark hair, dark lashes, and surprisingly fit for his age.

"Oh my—" He rolled his eyes. "April you're blushing. You're the worst liar." Chris ran over and picked up the orange ball. He did some sort of fancy behind-the-back-spin-around-layup move to the basket. So many unnecessary steps. "Okay, so how about this? If he beats me at a one-on-one game, he can date you. But if I win..."

"Will you stop that?" April rolled her eyes as she watched him show off with more extravagant, made-up basketball moves. He looked more like he was doing the choreography from a scene in high school musical than playing an actual sport. "First of all, we're not going to date. Second of all, even if we were, I don't need you to approve of any guys for me. You're like, a child still."

"Yeah, well, I might be five-years-old to you, but I'm actually old enough now to keep you from screwing up."

She gulped. "What is that supposed to mean?"

Chris dribbled the ball between his legs a few times. Three-point shot. Backboard. Net. "Well, I mean, back when you met

Preston, I was like eight or nine."

April blinked when she heard her ex-boyfriends name. She was caught off guard. "You were nine," she corrected.

"Right. Back then, I was too young to pay attention to any of that. Even when..." he hesitated. "Everything happened, I was only twelve-ish."

April blinked her eyes rapidly and shook her head. The whole conversation was making her very uncomfortable. "What's your point?"

The ball flew into the air and hit the orange rim, bouncing out into the grass again. Chris turned to April, hands on his hips as he tried to catch his breath. Apparently talking while shooting was exhausting.

"Well, back then, I wasn't old enough to protect you from him. And we all know what a disaster that turned out to be." April pinched her lips feeling slightly insulted and yet still confused. Chris continued. "But I'm older, now. And I know if a guy is good for you or not. I can actually look out for you now. Trust me. If I could go back in time and stop the whole Preston thing from happening, I would." Chris ran away with his back to April.

I'm sure you would have tried, bro.

So many of her friends back home used to say that to April. 'If I could go back in time, I would have stopped you from making that mistake.' She knew they were just looking out for her. Her close friends and family wished they could have guarded her young heart from all the toxicity Preston contained. But if April could go back in time, she wasn't sure she would do the same. Erase him from her history? She couldn't even imagine what that might've looked like. There were a lot of things she wished she could have changed. But meeting him wasn't one of them.

So, if I don't want to erase him from my history, what am I supposed to do with all these randomly shattered pieces?

A matte black Jeep Wrangler suddenly pulled up in front of the beige brick house. Its giant wheels rolled to a complete stop in front of the glossy mailbox. The rumble of the engine cut off, and the sound of the driver's door opening echoed down the street. April felt faint butterflies in her stomach.

"Okay, don't embarrass me." She tried to shake off the previous conversation. "Also— don't bring up..."

He rolled his eyes as he passed her the ball. "Well, obviously."

The sound of the car door slamming shut made April's head snap in its direction. A handsome blue-eyed boy walked around the back of the car.

"Hi," April tried to act casual.

"Hi," Michael smirked as he walked over to the hoop.

"Alright, so we're playing 21?" Chris chuckled the ball at Michael who caught it before it hit him hard in the chest. "How good are you?"

Michael casually dribbled the ball in place a few times. He bent his knees and extended his arm up and out as the orange ball was sent spinning through the air making a crisp sound as it cut through the net. His face lit up just the tiniest bit as he peeked over at April.

"Yeah, he's better than you'd expect for a white boy," she teased. Her blonde friend turned to face her.

"Yeah. Especially for a white boy still suffering from a concussion."

April scrunched her nose and pinched her lips together. "Stop it. That was like a month ago."

"Abuser," Michael whispered at the ground.

She gasped. "I'm not abusive!"

"Okay, enough flirting, you two." Chris missed a three. April and Michael didn't even look at each other. She wondered if his face was getting just as red as hers from Chris' comment. That was exactly the kind of stuff she didn't want her stupid brother saying. "Let's just play some basketball alright?"

April had never actually played a game of '21' before. The rules never made sense to her. It was basically a game of two on one? But the teams kept changing. It was like every man for himself, but also not at the same time? Basically, a made-up match for a group of three people. What other options did they have besides Horse?

Michael made a shot. Christopher made a layup. Michael missed a shot but later stole the ball from Christopher, which really ticked him off. After about ten minutes of playing under the warm sun, the boys were getting a little worn out.

"April, why aren't you playing?" Chris sighed, already knowing the answer.

"I am playing," she forced a smile.

Chris and Michael stopped moving for a second. They both

stood in front of the hoop as they caught their breath.

"You haven't done anything since the match started," Michael put his hands on his knees. April rested her hands on her hips.

"Um, I blocked one of Chris's shots earlier."

Michael tilted his head to the side, trying not to laugh. "You screamed because you accidentally got in his way and he crashed into you."

"Did he miss the shot or not?" April sassed back. Michael rolled his eyes and took the ball from Christopher's grasp.

"Okay, let's play." He threw a bounce pass to April who caught it awkwardly. She held the ball for a second.

You'll look dumb. Don't do it.

"Wait, why is it my ball?" She stalled.

"Just go," Michael stood in front of her like he was going to play defense. He didn't look totally on guard though.

"No, seriously," April put one hand on her hip. "It wasn't my ball. Why did you just give me the ball?"

Michael sighed at the ground. He peeked back up at her. "Just play."

"No," April casually threw the ball back to him. "I don't want your pity."

"Pity points?" Michael chuckled.

"Yeah, sure. Whatever that is." April was getting annoyed. "I don't want your 'pity points.'"

"Fine," Michael shook his head and passed the ball to Christopher. "Keep playing."

A few more minutes went by. The air was sticky and

warm. The salty smell of sweat reeked off all three teenagers. The ball bounced off the rim and into April's hands. Neither of the guys moved.

"Pity points!" Christopher mocked. April didn't think that term was near as funny as they did.

"Whatever. It's really hot out here," April threw the ball back at Chris, who went back to performing his dribbling dance choreography. She had given up on the game a long time ago. She needed to find something to do that wasn't this terrible game anymore. "Do you guys want to get ice cream?"

"Yeah, okay. If you want to." Michael wiped his sweaty forehead with his hand.

"Okay, I'll go get my keys." April went back inside her house and found her mom still working in the kitchen. She popped up on her toes next to her, using the cold granite counter to help keep her balance.

"Hey mom?" She spoke sweetly. "So, Michael and I are gonna go get ice cream but I need Chris to stay here."

April's mom looked at her suspiciously. "You want me to tell Chris he can't go with you guys?"

"Mom," April pleaded. "He'll just embarrass me and make things awkward. Seriously. It's better for everyone if he just says home."

Her mom just raised her eyebrows, as if she wasn't even going to bother arguing. She didn't agree to go along with the plan. But she also didn't disagree. If this was going to work, April knew she had to move quickly. She casually jogged back outside and she swung her car keys around her finger.

"Chris, mom needs you to stay home." She didn't enjoy lying, but she also didn't enjoy the idea of her brother third-wheeling any more than he already had. "She needs your help putting up something. I don't know."

Christopher looked incredibly suspicious. "Mom needs help with what?"

April approached her little green car parked in the open garage, pretending she couldn't hear her brother.

"We can go in my car," Michael volunteered to drive.

April peeked at Chris who was still trying to decipher what was actually going on. "Okay. We'll be back."

She followed Michael to his Jeep without Chris, picking up her pace as she reached the passenger door. It was heavier than she anticipated, sturdy and strong. She had to hop a bit to make it up to the leather seat. The heat stung her thighs as she held back a hiss.

"You want to go to BitterSweet?" Michael hopped up into the driver's seat and started the engine. He blasted the air that was hot like a blow dryer in their faces. It took a few seconds before it cooled.

"Sure," April shrugged. Michael hesitated as he pulled his door shut. He noticed April's door was still wide open, trying to release the trapped hot air that still lingered. They could see Chris sprint into the house to ask his mom if he could go with the two older teens. "I'll give you directions as we go."

Michael looked at April, then down at the phone she was holding. "You don't just want to put it in my GSP?"

"No. It's more fun this way." She gleamed with pride. "But

we better go now before my brother finds out there's not actually any work for him to do inside."

Michael smiled shyly as he put the pieces together. He ducked his head and buckled his seatbelt. "Okay. You lead the way."

Michael

Chapter 7

April claimed she had no idea it was free ice cream day at the shop, but it actually ended up working out in their favor. Michael wasn't sure if he was supposed to pay for their spontaneous outing. Was it a date? Did April want it to be a date? It didn't matter anymore. Free ice cream. Once the pressure of who was paying was gone, the two studied the array of flavors that were displayed behind the glass wall that separated them from the frigid air. Michael wasn't sure why they were even looking when they both knew what they were going to get: Rocky Road.

April frowned at Michael. He wasn't sure why. She looked really cute when she pouted. A tall, college-aged dude stood behind the counter and looked over April in her black shorts and red tee shirt. He seemed very interested in the way her hair bled from its dark brown roots to deep purple the rest of the way.

"When's your next shift?" The employee asked. He had messy brown hair and a sharp jawline. A certain rugged look to him. He smiled flirtatiously at April, who acted disinterested.

"Um, I don't know," she said.

Even Michael vaguely knew her weekly work schedule at this point. The fact that she just told 'Jericho' (that's what his name tag said at least) meant she was lying.

"Rocky Road?" April watched Michael, waiting for a reaction. But the blonde boy just kept looking at the board on the wall in front of them, trying not to show how uncomfortable the worker was making him.

"Yeah," Michael nodded. The messy guy peeked at Michael, trying to figure out if these two were 'together.' Michael thought he saw the black edge of a tattoo peeking out from under the guy's black short sleeve.

"Cool. I can get you an extra half-scoop for no extra charge," Jericho smirked.

April looked at Michael again. A soft smile. Big puppy eyes.

"Cool," she shrugged.

The two went back to the Jeep with their cups of dessert. It felt like instead of the weather getting cooler as the day went by, it only got stickier and warmer. The sound of the busy street beside them occupied the silence. The swish of cars that raced by replaced the regular chirping of birds in the area.

Once both teenagers were in the car, Michael rolled down their windows and hooked up his phone to the aux cord. His playlist acted as background music for the whole street. The two of them ate their ice cream in silence for a little while without saying a word. Finally, April broke the silence.

"Are you okay?" She pried. "You're acting different."

"I'm fine," Michael shrugged, pretending he had no idea what she was talking about. But still, April studied his face as if the answer were written somewhere on his skin and she just had to find it. She finally gave up and went back to eating her frozen treat, barely swaying to Stevie Wonder. Another minute passed. And then another. Neither of them had said a word.

Again, she cut through the awkwardness with more awkward questions. "Is it because of that guy?"

No response.

Michael watched his spoon twirl through his ice cream. He was the kind of person to turn it all into one thick, ice cream soup. April was silent for a moment. She looked as if she didn't know if she should continue to address the elephant in the room, or back away slowly before it got even more unpredictable. But this was April. Her curiosity always got the best of her. She leaned back in her seat, calm and careful, fiddling with her spoon in her paper cup.

"You know," she sighed. "A lot of people like to tell me what I should want in life. What I should do with my talents. Why I shouldn't make the choices I do. People enjoy pretending they 'know me.' Like, they take pride in 'knowing things about me' without ever asking." She scooped more ice cream into her mouth, letting it melt as she stared out the open window for a long second.

"I don't know," she shrugged. "I sometimes think they do it because I'm not completely average. Like, because I have purple hair or can paint that I must be so different than everyone else. But the truth is, I'm not as different as everyone likes to pretend. Or even as different as I like to pretend." She looked back at Michael and smiled as she shook her head. "Many people think they know 'my type' but they really have no idea."

Michael was quiet as he mixed around his ice cream some more, trying to follow her long thought process. "So, what is your type?"

College-age guy. The messy, carefree vibe. The tattoo. Slightly edgy. Mysterious. It's true. April seemed like the kind of girl to be totally into that vibe. Her purple hair almost demanded a just as artistic guy to go along with it.

A smile crept on the corners of her mouth. Her cheeks started to flush pink. She ducked her head and scraped the bottom of her cup with her spoon. She hesitated as if she was picking her words very carefully.

"I kind of got a thing for blondes," she raised her eyebrows innocently. As if she were completely clueless. But her pursed lips that were holding back a smile said otherwise.

Michael couldn't help it. He ducked his head as his face heated up. The original awkward tension was released and instead replaced by a new one. A good awkward. The best kind of awkward. Exciting awkward. April giggled and redirected her attention to the quiet music. She reached out and turned up the volume, swaying to whatever Jackson 5 song was playing through the speakers.

"Is this your playlist?" She scooped a clump of brown ice cream into her mouth, completely changing the subject. Her cup was finally almost empty.

"Yep. Oldies Goldies, baby." Michael licked the side of his red paper cup.

April smiled, still beaming. "I feel like I should already know most of these. They're all classics. But I only know, like, one line of each song."

Michael turned up his radio a few more notches. "Well then, time for me to educate you on good music."

"Hey," April giggled. "I have good taste in music. I'm more diverse than you'd think." Michael reached over to his phone and skipped to the next song in his Spotify queue.

"Do you know this one?"

April listened for a moment. "I think this is the one where they sing 'Dancing in the moonlight... buh dum dun dun hmmm.'"

"That's not the words," Michael smiled.

"Whatever," April chuckled. "I told you, I know, like, one line. Next song."

A weird banjo sounding instrument plucked slowly. A raspy tenor voice sang.

"My Girl!" April closed her eyes and obnoxiously sang into her red spoon, pretending it was a microphone. The song abruptly stopped and was replaced by a choir of upbeat trumpets.

April's eyes got wide with excitement. "Sweet Caroline!"

The song changed again. This time April was stumped.

"What the heck is this?" She scooped more ice cream into her mouth. "It sounds like they're playing glass cups with chopsticks."

Michael almost choked on his ice cream. "Like what?" He

leaned forward, his smile bright with curiosity.

"Yeah!" April laughed. "I just imagined a dude with a bunch of glasses all around a table and he's drumming on them with two little chopsticks like—" April proceeded to elaborate on her description by air drumming the dashboard in front of her. Her cup was in her lap and plastic spoon was in her other hand. She bopped her head to the music and swayed side to side as her wrists flicked at tempo.

"This is the Copacabana," Michael smiled. "This is one of the greatest songs ever. You can't just insult quality artistry like that."

April danced as she continued to listen to the new song. Pieces of her braid had loosened since their basketball game and hung lightly around her tan face. Even with no makeup, she was beautiful. Her lashes were still dark, her skin still looked fresh. She had an effortless vibe to her look.

Michael shook his head as he pulled the car out of the almost empty parking lot and drove back down the slightly busy street to April's neighborhood. Any time Michael had to ask for directions, April would just point her finger to the left or right. Which was way more confusing than one might imagine. She never made it clear which way she was actually pointing. To Michael, it all looked the same: forward.

The goofy boy took the falsetto harmony of every song to crack April up. He drummed on the steering wheel with his fists as April cracked up. She had a loud laugh. One that boomed and echoed through the entire car. She threw her head back and squinted her eyes shut. Her nose scrunched up whenever she laughed.

"No, no, no! You were supposed to turn left here!" April sat up in her seat. Michael's face burst with a mixture of playful shock and frustration.

"You didn't say that you just went—" He pointed his finger straight ahead.

"No, I pointed it this way!" April wrapped her fingers around his wrist and gently shifted it slightly to the left. Only slightly. Michael's eyes were still bright. His smile was even wider now.

"How was I supposed to know?" Michael shouted as she leaned back cracking up again. He teased her relentlessly. "All you do is point like this and this—" Michael reached his arm out and playfully bumped her with it as he pointed randomly out the window. "Like, you could just say, 'Michael, turn left!' But no. You'd rather confuse me and make me figure it out."

April held her stomach with one hand as she continued to spill with laughter. She playfully pushed his arm away.

"Ouch, my stomach hurts," she giggled and looked out her window. "I don't even know where we are anymore."

Michael looked around at the rows and rows of fluorescent green trees. All these streets looked the same. Rich black asphalt roads were painted with fresh white lines. Brand new stop signs and fancy new business buildings were scattered about. And trees. Lots and lots of freshly bloomed trees all around.

Michael turned on his blinker to make a U-turn at the upcoming stop sign. They could probably backtrack their way to her house if they just turned around.

"It's okay," April wiped under her eyes as if she was check-ing for traces of liquid laughter. "You'll get used to this area. Next time, I'm not helping you."

Michael smiled to himself. 'Next time.'

Chapter 8

Thick bristles danced across the canvas saturated in deep indigo blue. Up and arching. Down and swirling. The brush tip followed whatever choreography her wrist made up to the piano track playing in the background. The melody was sweet and slow. Not following any specific time measure or tempo. Just flowing. The same way April's paintbrush was just flowing.

An ocean seemed like a very basic portrait. A go-to for many artists whenever they have run out of creative ideas. April had created dozens of ocean paintings over the past two years. Her friends and family used to be interested in her recurring theme of art. They started offering to buy the pieces from her to display in their own homes. April wasn't as flattered by the idea as her parents' friends had anticipated. But she figured selling them made sense. It was better than letting them all collect dust together on the opposite side of her room.

One day, her dad's coworker, Mr. Franklin, had approached April. His coarse, bushy brown mustache looked like the end of a beat-up broom. His sagging chin swayed whichever way his mouth dropped.

"Miss April," his voice was gruff but welcoming. "My wife has shown me some of your artwork on your social media pages. Not only are you lovely on the outside, but I now see you are also immensely talented as well."

She felt it was probably unreasonable to get so internally angry whenever a man commented on her looks. She knew he was just being polite, and that Mr. Franklin meant no harm. But still, she didn't enjoy accepting the compliment. She would have preferred that her looks didn't come up at all.

Still, she followed the polite routine she had been taught since she was young. She smiled and thanked the familiar man, slightly peeking over to find someone else in the room to save her from the awkwardness. Sure, he was just being polite. But if she let him go on with the compliments, he would only get more detailed and slightly creeper with each passing phrase. It was wise to accept it and move on as quickly as possible.

"I do have one question for you, though," he scratched the side of his round tummy, digging his fingers in like he was trying to kill a spider. "I noticed that further back in your collection of albums, you used to post a lot of sketches. Grey lead and white paper. Beautiful pictures of detailed trees. Close up, realistic impressions of a human eye. The lashes are so precise." He smiled kindly for a moment before continuing. "And now, you only paint the ocean. Over and over. And it seems it's been that way for a long time now."

He squinted his eyes as if he were Sherlock Holmes trying to crack an innocent case. "Why is that? Don't get me wrong, your acrylic work is stunning, there's no doubt about that. But doesn't that ever get boring? Painting the same picture over and over?"

April had asked herself that same question many times before. Why the same painting over and over? She guessed there was something special about never being able to create the exact same picture twice. Sure, all of her paintings were oceans. But they were each different variations. Some bluer. Some more white. Some with fewer waves. Others with lots of massive ones. The same. But each unique. However, April often wished she could find something else beautiful to paint.

Why was it that every time she sat down on the color stained wooden floor of her room, all she wanted to create was the same blue ocean? A blank white canvas in a completely different size than the ones previously. Fresh new paints. Every color of the rainbow imaginable possible at the tips of her fingers. But still, the only colors her hands were drawn towards were the blues. The only shapes her fingers wanted to spell were the curves and dips of crashing waves.

She wondered sometimes if she had lost her creativity somewhere along the way. Chasing her dreams of pursuing an art degree at SCAD used to seem so exciting. Now, she felt like her creativity to keep making new things had died out. In the same way you can lose your voice. Slowly. As it fades away. Disappearing out of reach until finally, it's gone.

April reached to her right and dipped her brush in a smear of white. She dabbed some water from a nearby cup that sat on the floor and began mixing small beads of green into the mixture, creating a new shade of teal to add to her work. The fresh color followed over the previous waves. A new level of depth and mystery was bringing the picture to life. She added white foam where the water collided with each other, creating a soft fizzle that bled out.

Waves. In motion.

That was one of April's favorite things about her paintings. It was like by just looking at it, she could see the way the sea breathed through the restless dance of intense splashes. She could almost smell the salty sting of saltwater. Her nostrils stung just the slightest bit remembering how unpleasant it used to feel as a child to accidentally swallow a gulp of that sour pool.

April could hear the melodic crashing of water in the back of her mind as she added more shades of teal and green. The roar of shattering waves that never seemed to quiet down. The aggressive and chaotic water that stopped for no man. So intense and loud it could drown out all sounds. Suffocating and exhausting. Always in motion. Never still.

April often felt that her heart was like these oceans. Loud. Intense. Restless. Always in motion. Never still. Splashing in her face over and over. Her little body coughing up salty water that tried to overtake her lungs. Trying to waterboard her. Most days, she felt so tired. Tired from trying to swim in a storm that felt like it was out to get her. A storm that she couldn't escape because it was inside her.

How do you escape a storm when you are the storm?

April knew she had gotten a lot better since her last storm. The destructive hurricane that had occurred two years ago and left her stranded in a colossal mess. Her biggest storm. The age of 16 was supposed to be magical according to all the movies she had watched growing up. But life wasn't a movie.

The week of her 16th birthday, she felt like her life was crumbling apart. One thing after another. The punches life had thrown at her came from every corner of her life. She was trapped.

But now? April couldn't complain. She lived with her family. She had learned how to fall asleep at night again. There was food on the table and a fancy roof over her head and a Creator who looked out for her. April was fine. She was going to be just fine. She had chosen boring over passionate and that was the way she lived life now. It kept her heart out of trouble.

Passionate.

That was also how April viewed the ocean. Beautiful and passionate. She sometimes wished her heart still felt like that bit of the ocean again. The small sliver of the storm. The piece that made her feel alive.

Alive and unstoppable. The waves pushing their way through every obstacle. The way Preston made her feel. Like an ocean. As if she, herself, were beautiful and blue. Mesmerizing and worth something. Something special. Most of the time.

The purple-haired girl was thirteen when she was hit by her first wave. The first kind of wave she actually liked. Passionate and mesmerizing. From the moment she laid eyes on Preston. Completely out of nowhere. Totally unexpected.

He had walked into the room and her heart was thrown back against her chest. It felt like a semi-truck colliding with a two-story brick house, blaring its horn as it crashed through the walls at full speed. Or a waitress carrying a tall stack of glass plates suddenly slipping in a puddle of water. Fumbling and falling. The dishes all crashing onto the glossy tile floor. Shattering into a million tiny pieces.

But it wasn't her fault. She didn't see the "Caution" sign. The truck couldn't brake in time. Even if she had tried, she couldn't have stopped it from happening. It just... happened.

The track playing through April's speaker switched. One of the only songs in her playlist that wasn't instrumental. It was a song that pulled emotion out of April. So deep and gorgeous. It made her body feel like it was somehow sinking into the music with her.

Sinking.

That was how April felt when she left Preston two years ago. Like she had been sinking into this wild ocean that tried to consume her. Her heart fractured. So deep and painful. She wished someone could pull her up. Drowning. No one could save her.

Her mind began to recite the words she had scribbled down on a dirty old piece of paper she found on her desk that morning. Her random bits of unofficial poetry were only for herself. It was the only part of her art that she didn't have to worry about other people validating.

April 18, 2019:
This feeling often goes away,
just like the steady tide of waves.
But like the tides, they always rush
back without my mind's permission,
drowning heart in submission.

I wish I could control the tides,
but the moon won't seem to listen
despite how much I beg or cry.
So the waves will keep retreating
and running back to shore.
Slowly accepting defeat in
my internal war.

-April Lyndon, My Mind Does Not Belong To Me

April's wrist stopped moving. Paintbrush still in hand. Bristles still against the canvas.

There was silence. The music had stopped. Maybe her phone had lost signal. Or maybe her speaker had died. April watched her hand. It was vibrating. Ever so slightly. Shaking. Unsteady. For no reason at all.

She felt a heated feeling of hatred creeping up in her chest. Slowly. The way the darkness takes over the horizon after the beautiful sunset melts away. Bleeding evenly all over. Spilling everywhere until it takes up the whole sky. Hatred towards herself. Why couldn't she just be normal?

April wished she had explanations for a lot of things. Like why her hands would shake. Or why some nights she couldn't fall asleep and would just lie in bed staring at the ceiling until the sun came up. Her head so loud, impossible to shut up. She wished she had an explanation for why she was so drawn to Preston. She had no tangible reason. She loved him before he even spoke to her. She cared so deeply for him without him ever giving her a reason to. Why did she want him? After all he put her through. Why did she still miss him?

April continued to stare at her unsteady hands with disgust. Hatred towards her body. Hatred towards her restless heart. She dropped her paintbrush in her cup of water and brushed her damp hands on her grey paint-stained t-shirt. The same one she wore every time she painted, adding a new mark every time she completed another day of art.

She would finish this painting some other day. Right now, her head had become too loud with distractions again. Bouncing off the walls of her skull. Chattering and obnoxious. She needed to take a break. Painting her ocean had started to bleed in more places than just her canvas.

Michael

Chapter 9

The cool water sent a tingling sensation across his warm face, shocking his nerves for just a second. The hot sun beat down on them, reflecting brightly off the plaster of the pool deck. So bright. Almost blinding.

The private pool neighboring April's house practically looked like it was part of the Lyndon family's property. You could see the big glass stairway window from behind the trees. All they had to do was walk out the back gate and they were practically in April's green backyard, making it the perfect summer hangout spot for the seven teenagers. The noisy group splashed around in the water next to Michael, shouting and screaming inaudible chatter at the top of their lungs.

"April, get in the pool!" Jenni called. Her brown hair hung in a soaking wet bun, her black bikini was blurry underneath the blue-tinted water. April stood on the edge of the surround smiling nervously with her eyebrows scrunched. Her purple hair was tied back out of her face, her fists clenched beside her long, tan legs.

She squeezed her eyes shut and squealed. "It's so cold!"

"Get in the water!" Michael shouted with his hands cupped around his mouth. "Jump already!"

April peeked at him through one eye, taking in a deep breath. Her shoulders scrunched up toward her chin. She shut both eyes tight again and bent her knees like she was going to do it. But nothing happened.

"April!" Nick aggressively started swimming toward the deep end of the pool where she stood. His arms hit the water hard, making small waves as he approached the edge. "Get in the pool!"

"No!" April screamed. Her body looked so tense. "Don't you dare touch me, Nick!"

She wrapped her arms around her waist. Her white halter one-piece covered her up and she wore black sport shorts over her swimsuit.

"It's not that cold!" Anne popped back up from trying to do a handstand underwater. Harper and Ethan were trying to do the same beside her. "The sooner you get in the sooner we can play basketball."

"I literally can't bring myself to do it!" April beamed anxiously.

"That's it." Michael quickly made his way to the steps and started to climb out of the pool. Water poured out from the bottom of his navy-blue swim trunks as if they had been collecting gallons of the chlorine infected water.

April's eyes went wide. "Wait, no. What are you doing?"

Her body looked even stiffer than before. Panic sparkled in

her eyes as she tried to process what was happening. Michael shook out his soaking wet hair as he started to jog his way over to April, leaving a track of sloppy wet footprints on the hot deck behind him.

"Michael, don't you dare!" April suddenly began to back away from the edge as he approached her. "Oh my gosh! Running around a pool is dangerous! Michael!"

"Get her, Michael!" Jenni screamed with amusement. He had his eyes targeted at her waist. A teasing smile already played on his face as his feet carefully sped up to chase her down.

"Michael!" April screamed when she realized he wasn't going to back down. She sprinted away from him, running around the edge of the pool squealing. Her steps were careful as she tried not to trip over Ethan's flip flops that he had left sprawled across the deck or slip on the half-deflated pineapple floaty lying in their path.

"This is how people get hurt!" She screamed nervously as she carefully hopped over each obstacle. Michael sped up even more as he aimed for the water. He swiftly made his way around each small hurdle. His footsteps pounded louder and louder as he came up right behind the girl.

"Look out!" He wrapped his arms around her waist and threw his body backward, yanking her sideways into the water with him. Her yell was ear-piercing as gravity took control.

April's scream cut out right as they collided with the water. But Michael could still hear the muffled sound of her laughter as they floated beneath the surface for a moment. He could feel her body chuckling in his arms. Under the water, away from the obnoxious chanting of their ridiculous friends, everything looked different. The world tinted blue. Sparkling and smooth. Everything moved in slow motion. It was so much quieter down here. As if the two of them had just jumped through a different dimension away from the madness of their friends and were now peaceful under the blanket of the water.

April didn't try to squirm out of Michael's arms. Instead, the two just floated for a long moment. He thought he felt her squeeze his arms around her tighter for a second. It was one of those moments. The ones that remind you that you are alive and present. One of those moments he wished he didn't have to leave.

Michael couldn't hold his breath for much longer, though. His feet finally found the floor of the pool and launched the two of them upward. With April still in his grasp, they emerged back into the real world as they simultaneously took a deep breath of oxygen again, refilling their lungs with fresh air.

They were back to reality. Loud and crazy. Their friends were splashing and crashing around. Someone was obnoxiously shouting the lyrics to Don't Stop Me Now. Probably Anne.

"Wow, you guys," April's sister smirked playfully. "You were gone for so long we thought you might have drowned."

Michael naturally released his grip around the pretty girl and wiped the water away from his eyes. April didn't acknowledge Harper's comment. Instead, she smiled shyly at Michael and shook her head.

"You're such a punk," she giggled, playfully. Michael threw his arms up defensively, intentionally splashing her some more while doing so.

"You should be thanking me," he teased. "I just saved you."

"No thank you," April flicked some water at him, still beaming with excitement. "I don't need saving."

Nick had gotten out of the pool at some point during all the commotion when Michael wasn't paying attention. His American flag swim trunks clung to his muscular but pasty white legs. He was now frantically searching around the generic private pool chairs for the miniature blue basketball.

"Okay guys, split teams!" Nick shouted as he tossed the ball in the direction of the hoop.

"I've got it!" Michael dove forward and caught the ball in the air with both hands. He turned and dunked it into the short, plastic hoop beside him.

"Touchdown!" April cheered jokingly. Michael slowly turned to April, who looked highly amused.

"Goal!" She pumped her hands up in the hair, having a blast all on her own. Totally dorky. Kind of adorable, actually. "Yeah, home run! Woohoo!"

Michael slowly shook his head at her with his lips pinched, like he was judging her so hard. He was trying really hard not to smile. She was such a goof sometimes. Michael said his next words so fast they seemed to all merge into one.

"Three-two-one—go!" He splashed Ethan as he swam in front of April to play defense on her.

The group played several rounds in the pool. Michael

stopped keeping track of how many times his ever-changing team won. He didn't care who was on his team as long as he got to play defense on April. Even during the rounds where she was on his team. He would poke at her and crash into her. She screamed and squealed every time he held her back from the ball by gripping both her arms. She beamed with laughter the entire time. A great laugh. Pure and real.

The clear sky wasn't completely dark by the time everyone left. A light purple color bled over the skyscraper evergreen trees. The sunlight dimmed as the minutes ticked by. The muggy air smelled sweet with dew and the sound of crickets singing in the bushes and lightning bugs dancing in the grass was music to Michael's ears. Southern nights were special in Georgia.

April was dancing around the empty pool parking lot. She held her cup of ice cream in one hand and a red plastic spoon in the other. She sang Copacabana loudly into the utensil like it was a microphone, the way she always did when she was in a goofy mood.

Michael had the top of his Jeep down, playing the song through the speakers just quiet enough that the neighbors across the street wouldn't complain. He leaned against the vehicle as he watched her perform. Her chlorine-poisoned hair hung in a tangled messy ponytail. Her short black dress she had thrown over her swimsuit was swaying back and forth as she walked barefoot on her tiptoes.

She looked comfortable. Unapologetic. Completely unconcerned by anything the old couple walking their dog thought of her. The woman with short grey hair chuckled at the teen-age girl from the brick sidewalk as she watched her sway around the small, empty lot they walked by. April's voice was silly and carefree. Just beaming with joy.

Finally, the stranger spoke up. "That's one of my favorite songs, right there!"

April swung around to meet eyes with the stranger. She looked startled at first and then pleased that the woman seemed so amused by her performance.

She beamed back in her best southern accent for fun. "Nothin' like a sweet summer night in Georgia, ma'am!"

"Ain't that right," the woman nodded and continued on. She linked her arm through her husband's as they continued their evening walk. Still smiling, the older woman peeked back at Michael and April one last time. Her eyes lingered on April for just a moment until they were out of sight.

"Ain't that right?" April repeated to Michael. Her face was still playful and excited. "Y'all oughta behave *yer-selves.*"

"That's slightly offensive," Michael teased. "And your fake southern accent sucks."

April giggled as she walked back over to Michael with a slight skip in each step. She closed her eyes and took in a deep breath through her nostrils.

"I really do love Georgia. There's something homey feeling about the south. Sweet Tea and grits and people who say 'y'all.'" She grinned at Michael and giggled. "And I don't even drink sweet tea. I don't even *like* grits. And 'y'all' only recently started to seep into my vocabulary as of a few months ago and

I'm still not sure how I feel about that."

Michael smiled and looked at the tall trees surrounding them. The sky was getting darker. He could barely see the stars starting to appear above them now. Faded, but growing brighter with time. The half-moon glowed up in the sky.

"Georgia is nice," April followed Michael's gaze up to the trees around them. "Those things aren't even part of me, and yet they make me feel like I'm at my second home. I think this month is the first time Georgia has kind of felt like a home to me. I didn't think it would be the month I was leaving high school that my heart would finally let itself fit here."

"Do you miss it?" Michael asked. "I mean, Indiana."

April glanced down at her empty ice cream cup before setting it on the ground temporarily. Her voice rang softer now than before. "Sometimes. For a long time, I just wanted to move back there. I kept thinking, 'as soon as I turn 18, I'm going back home.'" She was silent for a moment. Her eyes lingered on the cup she had just placed on the ground in front of her. "But eventually, I realized I had to move on. And now I have people like Jenni and Ethan and you and Anne who became my friends here. I only still miss a few people from back home."

April sighed again, watching the exterior lights of houses flicker on as it got darker. Michael remembered meeting her best friend Scarlet a few times. But he mostly saw her on April's Instagram. From the few encounters he had had with her in the past, he remembered her as a fun person, always dancing, even when there was no music playing. April and Scarlet seemed similar in that way.

"It's weird leaving pieces of your heart in faraway places," April continued. "When you're a kid you just kind of assume everyone is going to be in your life forever. You give love to lots of people, expecting them to keep it safe and give love back in return. But, as you get older, you start to realize that people mess up. They make mistakes and didn't intend on keeping your heart safe after all. And, one day, you wake up and look at all the people that walk around with pieces of your heart and remember all the places you left a bit of who you are and think to yourself, 'I wonder if anyone else notices a part of me is still there.'" She barely shook her head at the sky before finishing her thought. "Moving out of a house is a weird thing. But trying to move out of a heart? That's a whole other detachment process. You never know how long it's truly going to take until it's over."

Michael didn't say anything. He just listened. He wasn't entirely sure what he was supposed to say to all she had expressed. But April didn't seem like she was expecting any specific answer anyway.

She was just standing there. Peacefully. Staring up at the stars. Admiring the way they sparkled and twinkled and gleamed from afar. Michael silently wondered if the stars were secretly watching April back. But instead of admiring her, what if they were burning with jealousy? Envious of the sparkle in her eyes. Even the stars had to know their radiance was incomparable to hers.

April turned and glanced at Michael. Her arms were crossed, head slanted. She blinked slowly. Michael glanced down at her lips for only a second, but April noticed. It was too late to take back the glance. He watched her bat her eyes and awkwardly shift her body away. Michael tried to think of something to say to take the focus off the sudden awkwardness of the moment. Anything would have been fine at this point.

"We graduate in two weeks," Michael finally broke the silence, as if he were saying it to no one in particular. Just stating a friendly reminder. A realization.

"Yeah," April thought to herself for a long minute before replying. "It all happened so fast."

Maybe for April it felt like her high school years went by quickly. Moving around a lot seemed to keep her on her toes. But for Michael, the past four years had felt like the longest years of his life. His entire life had just been one, never-ending year of the same routine from as long as he could remember. To Michael, it felt like graduation had finally come. He had been waiting for so long.

His ceremony was scheduled for Saturday morning at almost the exact same time as April's. It was disappointing for both of them. They wouldn't get to see each other walk across the stage in their cap and gown. He could already imagine a big grin across his face as his diploma would be handed to him. He could imagine waving down to his proud parents that would be shuffled somewhere in the crowd below. Michael and April wouldn't get to experience that with each other. They would only share the moment later through blurry, shaky videos taken by parents.

"I'm just gonna take my paper and run," April joked.

"Watch me kick my heels into the crowd and sprint off that stage with the diploma under my arm like I just robbed a bank and the police are out to arrest me. Just— *zoom!*"

"So, you'll be running barefoot all the way home? Yes, that sounds like a *great* plan right there," Michael laughed.

"Oh no, I'm not running home. I'm running straight to Alabama so I can get my two weeks of college credits out of the way and over with." She rolled her eyes as if she were annoyed just thinking about it. "Stupid honors program."

Stupid honors program was right. If April and Ethan weren't going to Clanton University for two weeks after graduation, she could come be a camp counselor with Michael and Harper and all their church friends. But apparently college credits were more important than chasing around a bunch of crazy middle schoolers in the hot sun.

"Maybe you should just wear a pair of shoes with wheels on the bottom to the ceremony in that case," Michael teased. "Take one of those little red scooters? It'll help get you there faster and you won't have to deal with blistered feet."

"Shut up," April scrunched her nose and crossed her arms. "I was obviously exaggerating."

"Oh, wait, you were?" Michael grinned. "Well, now I'm offended that you saw my brilliant idea as a joke. Clearly, I was being 100% serious about the Heely's."

"Stop it," April laughed as she threw her head back up at the sky, but Michael kept going.

"In fact, I think Isaac has a pair in his closet that I'll wear to *my* ceremony just to show you what a great idea this is. I'm going to start a trend and you're going to regret not being a part of this monumental moment. Class of 2019. Taking your phrase 'zooming off the stage' to a whole other level."

April was holding her stomach now as her booming laugh echoed around the parking lot. She attempted to catch her breath as she shook her head at the witty boy. She grinned brightly.

"You know, I laugh a lot when I'm with you," she said. Michael looked at her squinted eyes, her pinched lips. She seemed so happy.

"Yeah, me too," he looked down at his shoes. "I'm always really happy whenever I'm with you."

April innocently peeked up at the sky, a few more giggles slipped out from between her lips. She looked back at Michael. Her smile kept growing like she was ready to laugh happily again.

"Me too," she sighed.

Chapter 10

"Samantha Grace Larson," the gruff male voice boomed around the crowded football field. The morning sun was radiating a golden glow across the puzzle of perfectly aligned emerald green caps. Each pointy, satin square was precisely organized in rows of fifteen. The air was crisp, but not cold against April's foundation painted face.

Her purple hair curled in big waves that hung in front of her shoulders, sparkling gold-colored earrings dangled by her cheeks. They had been a gift from her sweet Abuelo for her 16th birthday two summers ago. April tried to stand still, proper, the way a lady would as she lined up behind five other seniors leading up to the creaking stage.

The crowd crackled with polite applause. There were a few 'whoops' and 'yeah's' from across the way where all the mix-match colors of family and friends sat in rows to enjoy the graduation ceremony. The blend of colorful faces each read similar expressions. Ones that said, 'Yay! Okay, can we go eat now?'

"Trey Anthony Lewis."

More monotoned applause. More 'whoops' and 'yeah's from across the way. Three steps closer to the podium. April could feel in the air that the weather was starting to shift. The beautiful morning glow wouldn't last much longer.

It's okay. You're getting closer.

"Sarah Kate Lin."

April's thumb tapped her opposite wrist in rhythm with the tempo she kept in her head. Her white painted nails clicked loudly against the turquoise charms of her thin, woven bracelet attached to her left wrist. There was no song playing. No recognizable beat. But she could hear herself rapidly counting to 12 over and over again in the back of her mind.

1, 2, 3, 4, 5, 6, 7, 8, 9, 10, 11, 12—

"Kailah Maria Lopez."

Another green cap and gown crossed the stage. April watched the dark-haired young woman receive her hard-earned diploma with a firm handshake. She paused for a picture with Principle Gilmore and then continued off to the other side of the stage with ease.

1, 2, 3, 4, 5, 6, 7, 8, 9, 10, 11, 12—

"Babatunde Loza."

More applause. More 'whoops' and 'yeah's. Two steps closer to the podium. The atmosphere smelled like rain.

1, 2, 3, 4, 5, 6, 7, 8—

"Jackson Marcus Lutes."

April's tapping thumb came to a halt as she felt the slightest twinge of panic in her chest.

You only got to 8. How did you only get to 8? It's always been 12 taps. How did you not reach 12?

Her eyes glanced ahead to find her parents and two siblings sitting in the middle row of the crowd. Their cell phones were already being held up to record the moment. She already could imagine how obnoxious their cheers would be. Her family was so extra sometimes.

April's vision took in the large gap between herself and her principal in the time waiting to be called. The path looked to be a mile long now that no one was standing in front of her. She felt her stomach start to tighten as if she were looking at walking across a tightrope over the width of the grand canyon. Exciting and intriguing, and yet completely terrifying. But walking across this slick stage wasn't near as dangerous as her imaginary tight rope. So why was she so afraid?

"Victoria April Lyndon," her name echoed from the surrounding speakers the way a screeching tire echoes through a lonely parking garage.

"Let's go, April!" Harper jumped up to her feet screaming. "Whoop, whoop!"

The crowd clapping sounded more like a roll of bubble wrap being crushed under the weight of a tire. April smiled at her sister as she took long strides towards the podium.

"I love you, April!" Jenni squealed from the group of soon-to-be graduates from the Cambridge class of 2019. A few other encouraging cheers rang from the group of students, although April couldn't quite place whose voice belonged to who from so far away. Lots of people knew April. More people knew of her than she knew of them.

The purple haired girl tried to relax into an excited smile as her heels clicked against the hollow sound of the stage. Approaching Principle Gilmore, she held out her always cold hand for him to shake. His grip was firm, eyes bright with joy. He handed off the green diploma and turned to the photographer for a quick photo.

Stop shaking. Stop shaking.

Her hands didn't listen. It was so much more aggressive than usual. She wondered if her parents would be able to notice from the floor. Probably not. Hopefully not. The flash of the camera left white spots in April's vision for a few seconds. Her eyelids rapidly blinked away the distraction.

"Yeah, April!" She heard her brother call. His voice barely cracked on the 'yeah.'

Puberty.

"Congratulations," Principle Gilmore nodded. His clean-cut, white stubble across his round face looked prickly and precise. The wrinkles in his forehead were more prominent than anything else on his face, like the uneven creases of worn-out leather.

The old man smiled politely, then quickly redirected his attention to his next upcoming graduate in line. There had only been one more left behind April. Thank goodness she hadn't been the last student in the 'L' category. Not that it would have really mattered to anyone else. But it did to April. At least there was a buffer between her and the next group to come up.

The young girl carefully but confidently made her way off

the stage and down the stairs into the grass. Her heels sunk into the damp dirt as a fork sinks into a slice of cake. Her parents and siblings were still standing, taking pictures of her tassel hanging on the opposite side. April playfully stuck out her tongue and held up the 'rock on' sign with her free hand, posing for any last minutes shots before heading back to her seat.

The scary part was finally over. She had made it across the stage. She was now holding her diploma. Gold lettering read 'Cambridge High School' across the front. April let her index finger glide along the surface, tracing the shape of each letter. This is what she had been waiting for. The years of hard work had finally paid off. She was finally done.

Now what?

"Psst, April," she heard a whisper in the distance behind her. She peeked over her shoulder to see Jenni in the same green cap and gown a few rows back holding two thumbs up.

"So freaking close!" April whispered back with glee. "You've got it!"

She held her left hand up and crossed her fingers. Jenni smiled and did the same. It was a thing between them. Fingers crossed. 'It's all going to work out.'

The thin, grey clouds were building out in the distance, coming together to make one massive pillow for the sun to rest behind. But those clouds were still somewhat far away. They wouldn't be overhead for probably another twenty minutes. Thirty if they were lucky.

Eventually, after what felt like an eternity, Jenni went up to walk. April screamed extra loud from her seat to make up for all their other friends who couldn't be at their ceremony. Finally, Principal Gilmore gave his closing speech. The clouds had made their journey to the football field faster than April had expected. The event was still in the clear though. For now.

"And now, with open minds and ready spirits, it is time for you young people to take on the world." Even he had to have known how cliché he sounded. Did they really use the same speech at every graduation? And more importantly, was anyone ever actually moved by this garbage?

"There will be life challenges ahead that will mold you into the person you are becoming. It will not be easy to overcome, but it will be worth it. With determination and perseverance, you will learn to conquer life's undoubtedly difficult obstacles. You will do amazing things, as long as you set not only your mind to it... but your heart as well."

Blah, blah, blah. More stupid empty words that mean absolutely nothing. Get on with it already. I'm hungry. I need food.

"And with that being said," all the students had anxiously been awaiting this final moment. The only thing they had all been waiting to do since dressing up in the traditional cap and gown ensemble. It was time.

The distant sound of thunder rolled its way over the sky. April could smell the sweet fragrance of rain so prominently all around her now. She looked up to see the clouds floating in closer above them. It would be sprinkling any minute now.

"Congratulations, newest graduates of Cambridge High School. Let us count down as we prepare to throw our caps in celebration."

The crowd roared in unison."Three—"

This is it. This is the end.

"Two—"

Goodbye, high school. Wasn't nice knowing ya.

"One—"

"Let's go!" Babatunde yelled with excitement.

The entire group erupted in hollers and happy shouts as they flung their dark green caps up at the sky, like popcorn exploding out of a kettle with no lid. It was beautiful to April. They almost seemed to float in slow motion above their heads for a brief second before each one came shooting back down to their heads like pointy cardboard ninja stars.

April smiled to herself as she made her way through the chaotic crowd to go find her family. She already knew they would be waiting with open arms to give her squeeze hugs and encouraging words of affirmation about how proud they were of her. She couldn't wait for all the love she was about to receive.

"April!" She turned around to see Jenni who was having to stand on her chair in order to be seen over the crowd of hectic teenagers.

"Hold on!" April cupped her hands around her mouth to better communicate with her friend. "I'm going to find my family first!"

"Huh?" Jenni tapped her ear. Her face scrunched with confusion. Her eyes scanned the crowd with caution, making sure no idiot boy was going to bump the chair she was standing on and make her lose balance.

"Family!" April shouted again, this time pointing in the direction of where they might be. Jenni finally nodded and held a thumbs up. Hopefully they would find each other later when the crowd had calmed down. The friend's small self sunk back into the crazy group, disappearing in the sea of green gowns.

April spun back around in her original path to search for her parents. They had to be around here somewhere. If she could just manage to break her way through the crowd.

A figure in a black shirt crossed April's line of vision, causing her heart to jolt in shock. Her chest tightened. Her stomach sunk to the floor.

April's eyes locked on the back of his head. His hair was dark brown and short. Shoulders broad. Posture strong. She noticed the way he moved with such confidence, the sight causing the veins in her wrist to strain.

"Preston?" April whispered to herself.

A shoulder jabbed into her lower backside, the sudden collision making her jump with surprise. A shot of pain raced and bled through her body like a cup of spilled hot coffee.

"Ouch!" April whipped around to find out which reckless punk had just been so careless. She lifted her face to see Babatunde's dark skin and bright smile staring back at her.

"Oh, I'm sorry, April! I didn't mean to!" He didn't look fearful. But he did look genuinely apologetic. Baba readjusted his square glasses on his face. "Are you okay?"

April placed her hand on her lower back, wincing a bit at the now sore area. "Yeah, I'm fine." The spot of impact still stung, but she really believed it happened by accident. "Don't worry about it."

April tried to brush the distracting moment aside as she went back to looking for the mysterious figure in the crowd. Where had he disappeared to? He couldn't have gone far in this traffic jam.

"Congratulations!" An excited Puerto Rican woman wrapped her arms around the disorganized girl and squeezed to an uncomfortable tightness. "I'm so proud!"

"Thanks, Mom," April tried to breathe between her arms while her rib cage was being jabbed by the chunky bracelets on her mother's wrists. "Too tight, lady! Too tight!"

Mrs. Lyndon released her grip. "Sorry, mami!"

April smiled forgivingly and kissed her mom on the cheek before turning to her sister.

"Congratulations," Harper smiled with high cheekbones and embraced her sister. "You're the first one out."

"Heck yeah, I am!" April shouted at the sky nonchalantly. She did not seem near as excited as her siblings and parents.

A broad man with dark hair and strong jawline held his phone camera right up to April's face as he pushed his way past Harper. "Hey, look who it is! Our first baby is done with high school." He kissed her forehead. "Proud of you."

"Thanks, Dad," April smiled back at her father. A playful punch hit the side of her arm as she turned around once more to face her younger brother.

"Good job not dropping out," Chris teased. "Also, you look terrible in green."

"Thank you!" She jabbed her finger playfully in his side to make him jump uncomfortably before being engulfed by his brotherly bear hug.

"Hey," their mother interrupted. April assumed she and her brother were about to get nagged for picking on each other again, even though it was just playful. But instead of commenting on Christopher's teasing, Mrs. Lyndon scanned the area around her with worried eyes. She leaned in towards April and spoke in a hushed voice. "Is Preston here?"

Her mind lit up again. She wasn't crazy after all.

"Did you see him, too?" She quickly gripped her mother's forearm as her head spun to follow her gaze. "I swear I just saw him a few seconds ago, but I couldn't tell if it was really him."

The crowd was too big now. All the parents and family friends had mixed with the students. It would be nearly impossible to find the black shirt again with this many people moving around.

"I thought Janet said they couldn't come," Harper was now also scanning the field with her eyes.

"Yeah, his mom told me they were going to be at a wedding or something this weekend," April said.

She remembered not being bothered when she received the text from the Schuyler family declining the invitation to her ceremony. Janet had been so nice and apologetic, explaining with 'sincere apologies' as to why they couldn't make it to the event. At first, April assumed Janet was just being nice, but after the Schyler mother had randomly apologized three more times over the past month, April started to wonder if they really would have come if their plans hadn't been already scheduled.

April wasn't offended. She had sent the graduation card more as a gesture than an actual invite. She surprisingly had felt a lot of relief when finding out they wouldn't be taking the Lyndon family up on their offer to join the celebration. But now, the idea that Preston may have actually shown up today was too much for April to handle. He would have totally done something like this. Showing up unexpectedly to catch her off guard? Preston loved shocking turns of events.

"Oh, I see him!" Harper pointed to her left. She called out over the crowd. "Preston!"

"No!" April slapped her sister's arm with the back of her hand and ducked.

What is wrong with you April? What if that's really him? Why would you invite him? Why would you try to sabotage yourself like this?

Harper looked back at her sister, her lightly freckled face saturated with sass. "Well then he's probably looking for us, isn't he?" She turned back to her original direction. "Preston! Preston Schuyler!"

"Harper!" April reached out to stop her sister again but froze when she felt her phone buzzing in the pocket of her black jumpsuit hidden underneath her green gown.

Shoot.

What if that was Preston calling her? Looking around the field right now trying to figure out where she was? This couldn't be happening. There was no way this was happening.

April dug her phone out from under her gown and checked the caller ID.

Chad.

A picture of April being given a piggyback ride from Michael on a green football field took up the screen. Their vibes looked playful, faces bright with laughter.

Crap. Not now, not now, not now, Michael.

"April!" Her head shot up to see her sister standing directly in front of her. "I've got good news. And bad news."

What the heck is happening right now? This is no time for games, Harper.

"The good news: that guy we saw? Yeah, that's not Preston after all."

April felt her tense body starting to unwind somewhat again. It wasn't him. It was probably stupid for her to even get so worked up over it in the first place. Everything was fine. False alarm.

"Bad news is," Harper continued. "Now I look like a crazy person for calling a stranger 'Preston Schuyler' over and over until he turned around. He looked more like Jack. It was very awkward."

April's phone continued buzzing in her hand. "Hold on," she apologized to Harper. "I have to take this really quick."

April's thumb pressed the green button as she maneuvered her way out of the chaotic crowd to a less populated section of the field. The empty end zone looked like a quieter place to escape to for a brief moment.

"Hello?" April held her device up to one ear while her free hand covered her other ear. Despite her new location, she felt like she was still having to shout into the mic in order to be heard.

"We did it!" Michael cheered enthusiastically. "Congrats, Bandkid!"

"Oh!" April laughed nervously. She wasn't exactly sure what she had been expecting the conversation to be about until now. But this made sense. "Yeah, congrats, Chad."

"You know, the combination of the Heely's with the gown? Not such a good idea after all." He sounded like he was in a really good mood. April should have been too. She rolled her eyes playfully.

"You're ridiculous," she chuckled. She knew he was just making fun of her.

April looked back over her shoulder. She just wanted to see the face of whoever that stranger was. Even though she knew it wasn't Preston, she just had to know what he looked like. She has to be 100% certain to put her mind at ease.

"I'm still picking you up to celebrate tonight, right?" Michael also seemed to be surrounded by lots of noise. It was difficult to understand him. "Unless you don't want to see me."

April smiled big. The air was getting cooler against the exposed skin on her ankles, causing goosebumps to decorate the surface of her skin.

"Are you kidding me? Of course, I want to see you. I can't wait," she smiled to herself.

There was a long pause over the call, but April knew the signal hadn't dropped. She could still hear all the commotion in the background on his end.

"Wait..." Michael hesitated. "Did you just say...? No, never mind. You probably said 'are you kidding me.' Sorry. It's really hard to hear you with all the noise."

"Wait, what? What's happening? What did you hear?" April said.

"Nothing," he was obviously toying with her. "Forget I said anything."

"Michael!" April stepped further away from all the craziness to hopefully hear him better. "What the heck did you hear?"

"It's dumb," he hesitated. Both of them just waited. He was going to tell her. April could tell he wanted to.

"I heard you say, 'Are you kissing me' and *then I realized* you said 'kidding' which made way more sense."

April felt her face get hot. "Oh wow."

She wasn't sure what she was supposed to say. Her mind was going blank.

"And you know what I thought when I heard you say 'are you kissing me?'" Michael kept going. April gulped nervously. She felt mini butterflies dancing in her stomach.

"What?" she said.

"I thought," Michael chuckled. "'I mean, if you want me to.'"

April felt a terrible punch to her gut. As if all the butterflies swirling around in her stomach had just dropped dead and weighed her insides down to her feet.

She had been avoiding this subject for so long. She knew it

would come up eventually with Michael. It was almost expected at this point for it to be mentioned. They weren't officially boyfriend and girlfriend. Still, April wasn't ready for this topic. She hadn't prepared herself for how she was supposed to explain herself to Michael.

Now standing in front of an emotional door, she felt terrified. A door that she had been avoiding for years, fearful of opening, so nervous about going back to those uncomfortable memories. Even if she could find a way to put her feelings into words for Michael, now was not the time. Not here at graduation. Not now.

"Wow," April forced an awkward laugh. "Well, we'll definitely have to talk about that later."

'Talk' about that? Why would you say that? Now he's going to think he's in trouble or something. What if you just scared him away? Seriously, April? Why can't you just be normal?

"Alright," Michael laughed with excitement. "Well then, I'll let you go. I'll see you in a few hours."

"Okay, bye."

Before the phone call, April couldn't wait to be with Michael again. It was an exciting day for both of them. But now, she was feeling nervous about their next encounter. She wasn't sure she was ready for that confrontation. Maybe she could find the words before tonight. Maybe she could push herself to get over her stupid fears.

Why can't you just be normal?

April sighed heavily as she stared out into the not-so-impressive view of green trees ahead of her. They lined the rest of the field to create a boundary between the school property and neighboring houses planted on the other side. April wondered what that small strip of woods looked like from the inside under the canopy of dewy leaves and flimsy branches, all laced together to create a possible shelter from the upcoming storm sitting above her.

The sky had already lost its radiant glow, still fading darker as each cloud slowly merged with its neighbor.

"Scarlet," April pinched her lips together, fingers gripping the sides of her gown. "I wish you lived here. That would help me so much right now."

A gentle breeze brushed April's big, wavy curls over her shoulders. She could hear the patter of rain falling on the aluminum bleachers surrounding her. A few drops carefully hit her exposed hands and toes. That was her cue.

Time to go.

Michael

Chapter 11

Sweaty palms and nervous jitters. Michael tried to summon up the courage to make his move. Just a simple, stupid move. He had been waiting for the first hour and a half of the boring, new Space City movie to get up the nerve to hold April's hand. Why was it so difficult for him to just go for it? It wasn't like he wasn't sure if he was 'supposed' to or not. Michael had held her hand before.

For example, he had just last week during one of the many nights that the two of them had been goofing around in the dark, miniature parking lot in front of April's neighborhood pool. She had been trying to teach Michael how to dance bachata with nothing but his Jeep headlights on and the thin stream of a few distant street lamps to provide any sort of illumination for their straining eyes.

Michael remembered trying to focus on April's bare feet as he attempted to follow her lead. But instead, he had found himself stumbling, overthinking every little instruction. He felt silly and had tried to give up more than once. But April pulled him back each time and chuckled, telling him he was doing just fine.

"You just have to stop taking it so seriously," she has shaken her head with sympathy. "Loosen up and just have fun."

Michael couldn't help but smile anytime she teased him. It was one of his love languages; teasing and sarcasm. He had already been coming up with a witty comeback for the sassy girl before a pair of voices so rudely interrupted his train of thought. The obnoxious chatter had seemed to be making its way from the other side of the trees surrounding the parking lot.

"Who's that?" April had whispered. She turned in the direction of the voices, her curiosity about what might be always seemed to be distracting her from whatever was right in front of her. Before she had the chance to process the whole moment, Michael spontaneously reached for April's elbow, and gracefully slid his hand down to her wrist.

"Come on, let's go this way," he spoke softly and hastily tugged April towards his massive Jeep. The bright-eyed girl followed him willingly, the patter of their feet against the asphalt was almost as noisy as the uncontainable laughter they tried to suppress. He led her around the vehicle to the driver's side of the car where he crouched low and tried to see through both layers of glass windows.

April giggled with excitement. She was always ready to make any dull moment fun. "What are we doing?"

Michael had lifted an index finger to his lips and leaned towards April. "Shhh," he smiled.

April peeked down at her hand. Her fingers were still tightly locked with his. She hesitated before looking back up at him with a surprised, but pleased grin. With a charming shrug, Michael gave her hand a gentle squeeze and crouched lower as he leaned against the cold surface of the car door. April did the same, her eyes scanning his like she was still waiting to figure out what was supposed to happen next.

Michael smiled at the pretty girl with his lips sealed tight, the suspense growing stronger and stronger with each passing second. His heart rate sped up as he considered going for it. It was the perfect moment.

Right before Michael had made his move, April's face melted from excited and playful, to a blank stare. She took a quick glance at Michael's lips. She knew it was coming. Just as Michael had started to lean in, April swerved and planted a quick kiss on his cheek before running off. He had felt his heart skip a beat. Partly confused. Partly still excited. It wasn't what he had been expecting, but he wasn't exactly complaining either.

Maybe Michael had just caught April off guard last time. Maybe the timing hadn't been as perfect as he originally thought. But this time, before tonight was over, he was going to do it the right way. But first, he just needed to hold her hand.

Coming back to the present, Michael took a side glance at the divider between him and April. Their arms rested side by side, hands only a few inches away from each other. He took in a deep breath as his eyes focused on the movie screen in front of him.

As his pinky slowly searched for her fingers, he felt the cold skin of her knuckles brush his for a second. His pulse jumped the slightest bit when he felt her pinky extend out to greet his hand back with slight hesitation. Their fingers awkwardly danced for a second to the rumble of the starship in the background. Each finger slowly searched for their matching dance partner, stumbling and slipping as they locked into place like the internal gears of a clock. Their hands fit into each others' like a matching puzzle piece.

Michael relaxed, breathing out in unison with April as their hands sunk comfortably together. He hadn't realized he had been holding his breath up until now. His hand gave hers a gentle squeeze of affirmation as his thumb carefully grazed her skin with subtle affection. Man, he was so happy to be finally holding her hand right now. It made this never-ending movie a whole lot easier to watch.

Michael thought he heard a sniffle in the crowd. So faint, it had to have been made from way back in the rows of seating. It didn't matter. A minute later, he heard the sound again.

Did someone have a cold in the beginning of June? What person gets a cold in the middle of summer? The movie only played for several more seconds before Michael heard the soft noise for a third time, this one seemed to be right next to him.

With furrowed eyebrows, Michael peeked at the silent girl sitting to his right to make a comment about the noise just as her free thumb was quickly brushing the surface of her cheek. Michael felt a warm splash of confusion flood his head. Was she crying?

Maybe he should just watch the movie and pretend he hadn't noticed the single tear. But then again, that wouldn't solve anything.

Michael inhaled deeply as he gently squeezed her small hand. Her cold fingertips pressed against the back of his hand like cool raindrops dissolving on the surface of his skin. His thumb stroked the back of April's hand, carefully and calmly. Out of the corner of his eye, he could see her wiping her face with the tips of her other hand. Her sadness was silent.

Eventually, the screen faded black and the wave of credits began to roll. The dimmed lights illuminated the aisles and the slow flood of moviegoers rose to their feet, carefully tiptoeing their way out of the massive room. Without saying a word, Michael squeezed April's hand and led her out and around the heavy building.

She didn't say anything. Michael didn't say anything. The unofficially-agreed-upon silence followed them all the way to the grey, empty parking deck. Silence made himself comfortable in the backseat of Michael's Jeep and stayed the entire ride back to his house. Silence's presence changed the air in the car, impossible to ignore, never once being considerate enough to say 'This is my stop, you can drop me off here.' Silence stayed the whole car ride and then some. He invited himself all the way into Michael's house like an intrusive guest. He made himself right at home in the thin space between April and Michael on the living room sofa, keeping the two separated for a whole 30 minutes of their first episode of New Girl for that night.

Michael didn't like the sudden third-wheel April had invited along to their date. It was messing up his plans. It was throwing off the whole night. Michael wasn't getting to spend his last night with April the way he intended. He wasn't even getting to talk to her. Silence had interrupted the entire night, and April had seemed to slip away behind it.

Michael wanted to know why April had clicked like a light switch. What happened during the movie that caused her to want to hide? How was he supposed to bring her back without losing the last hour they had of the night before he took her back home? This was not how Michael wanted them to remember their last night together before they both left for two weeks. He didn't want *this* to be their first final night.

Michael reached through the space between them and broke April's fidgeting hands from each other. Through his peripherals, he could see April's chest rise as she inhaled deeply and fall as she accepted his hand in return. She scooched closer to Michael on the sofa, bumping Silence out of his seat. April made herself comfortable leaning on the side of Michael's arm, but he readjusted so he could wrap his arm around her. His thumb stroked her shoulder as she leaned her head on his chest. They breathed in sync with each other, now able to watch their show together in peace.

Michael's mother was just a few feet away in the dining room folding laundry. He wasn't completely sure how his mom might react to seeing her son and his girlfriend getting so close on the sofa. In fact, Michael realized while he was sitting there that this was the first time he had brought a girl to his house. He hadn't realized until then how natural it felt to have April in his home. Two more episodes went by before the screen froze with a notification.

Are you still watching?

Neither of the two kids moved. They just continued to stare blankly at the screen with no motivation to get up and look for the remote. It was another unofficially-agreed-upon silence. Only this time, it didn't keep them separated.

April's soft voice finally chimed in. "I guess I should go home now."

Michael didn't respond. He just sat there stroking her arm with no motivation to leave the moment.

"Sure," he whispered. But neither of them flinched. A minute went by. And then another. Still, no one moved first. Michael started to wonder for a second if April might have fallen asleep.

"You awake?" He whispered again.

"Yeah," she sighed softly. "Just thinking."

Michael gulped before asking the question that had been bothering him the whole night. "About what?"

Michael was left with no response. There were no indications that she had even heard him. Just empty space.

"I'm sorry," April finally murmured under her breath. "About... I just— sometimes— like today—" She held her breath for a long moment before releasing a sigh of defeat as if she had given up on trying to fish for words.

"You make me feel safe. And… I've never really felt that before." Michael felt her body freeze up as if she had just said something terrible. "Sorry," she sighed gently as the tension in her body now melted away. She sat up. "I just… yeah."

The girl looked over her shoulder at Michael. Her big, brown eyes seemed to sparkle from the glossiness of her emotions. She smiled gently as her eyes drifted away from his to her hands.

"You can take me back home now. For real this time," she said.

The car ride back to April's house was much less awkward than the car ride before. The conversations were just as absent, but this time the quiet was shared between them. They both hummed to Oldies Goldies. He had even rolled down the windows all the way to let the cool breeze of the dark night rush over their faces.

The backroads to April's house were always the best at night time. No traffic. No obnoxious Atlanta drivers. Just a stoplight every five minutes to break up the pace of things. Although there was a new sort of tension growing between them as they neared April's house. One that they both seemed to share.

"Michael?" April randomly spat out when they pulled up to the last stoplight on their route to her house.

"Yeah," he turned to her nonchalantly, but when he saw her eyes fixed on the road in front of her, confusion started to creep up on him again. April gulped. Her hands were fidgeting again as she squinted off into the distance.

Finally, as if it took everything inside of her to force the sentence out, she confessed. "I've never been kissed before."

Michael puffed up his cheeks with air as he held his breath in surprise. Not even necessarily at the content of the message, but more at the shock of yet another awkward moment. Man, April had a natch for that.

"But didn't you date a guy—"

"For a year and a half, yeah," April nodded before turning her head to Michael again.

The red illumination of the light reflected off the right side of her face like the glow of a heated ruby. Her glance fell back to her nervous hands. "I don't know how to explain it. We had a lot of opportunities. And he wanted to, I just..." her eyebrows furrowed in confusion as she processed some more.

April brushed her hair behind her right ear as she looked back up at the red light in front of them. Worry was painted vividly all across her face. It was a long light and she had known that coming in. She must had planned it out this way. It seemed as if she was timing out the light in her head as she continued to think of her next words.

"I know. It's weird. I can't even explain it myself. It's not normal, I know—"

"April," Michael finally interrupted. He wanted to be sensitive toward her emotions. "Do you not want me to kiss you?" Her eyes went wide as she tried to interject, but Michael continued over her. "Because if not, it's okay. I don't want you to say something you don't mean—"

"Michael, wait—" April reached out and rested her hand on

his bicep as if she stopped time itself. The two teenagers looked at each other for a long moment in the glow of the stoplight.

As Michael stared into April's dark eyes, the previous stress that consumed the car started to evaporate away. The thin breeze that slid its way through the windows tickled Michael's face.

April pinched her lips before shaking her head. "That's the thing. I want you to kiss me. I just… needed you to know."

Michael could feel his heart beating slowly, but strong inside his chest. His focus was completely consumed by April's eyes. Her eyes that glowed even when she wasn't smiling. Even when it was pitch black at 10 at night and the only light was the glimmer of a red, bright traffic light, her eyes still glowed.

Michael glanced at April's mouth for only a second, but when his eyes found hers he saw she had glanced at his mouth too. The streetlight flashed green across both their faces. Michael hesitated before stepping on the gas pedal of his car. He stared at her for a split second longer before they drove away into her quiet neighborhood.

The black Jeep pulled up in front of the Lyndon's beige brick house.

"Wait here," Michael said before hopping out of the driver seat. He opened the heavy trunk and reached to grab a surprise gift he wanted to give her before she left for two weeks. He really wished she didn't have to go tomorrow. He so badly wanted her to just come to summer camp with him and all their church friends in a few days. But this would be good. He knew she was making the right choice.

Without saying anything, Michael opened the passenger door to proudly present his gift. A two-foot stuffed elephant was sitting on his shoulders with more of the body structure of a teddy bear than an elephant. Michael's smirk split into an uncontrollable smile when he saw April's jaw drop.

"Is that for me?" Her expression was priceless.

"Yeah," he said. He couldn't get himself to stop smiling even if he tried. "You like it?"

April's eyes lit up as they flew from the elephant to his. "Are you freaking kidding me? You… how did…?"

She shook her head as Michael watched her shocked face grow into one of uncontainable excitement. She covered her face and laughed into her hands for a moment, as if she were embarrassed. Michael tried to pinch his lips together to tone down his smile as he stepped up to her. He carefully swung the stuffed animal off his shoulders and placed it in her lap as she looked up again. Her brown eyes searched his for a long second as she continued to shake her head in disbelief.

"You know, for a Chad, I never expected you to be such a sweet-heart," she laughed.

Michael could feel himself blushing as he took her left hand in his. "Whatever you say, Bandkid. This doesn't mean I'm going to stop antagonizing you, though."

"Okay, good," she gulped. She looked nervous. "Because I wouldn't want this to change anything."

Michael smiled as he glanced at her mouth. He started to barely lean closer.

Her eyes fell to his lips. "I think the elephant is super cute.

Honestly…I love elephants. They're… adorable."

Michael smiled even bigger at her nervous banter as the space between them became smaller. He watched her eyes, waiting for her to finish whatever she was saying before he went for it. April stayed frozen as her blank face stared back at him. She looked like she was holding her breath. Finally, he started to lean in.

"Are you about to kiss me?" April blurted out. Michael froze.

"Yeah," he nodded slowly. "Is that okay?"

April pinched her lips as she thought for a second. Finally, she shut her eyes and nodded. "Yes."

Michael smiled softly. He watched her for just a second to see if she might change her mind, then he leaned in and slowly pressed his lips against hers. He breathed in for a second taking in the warmth of her mouth, feeling a wave of happiness flood his brain. It felt comforting, the way it feels to sit next to a fireplace after a chilly night outside. It was one of the best feelings. Before Michael could even think of pulling away, he felt her mouth suddenly detach from his.

"I'm sorry— I'm sorry," she sniffled in a panicked state. She had tears bottled up in her eyes as she ripped her hand away from his. "I'm sorry— I'm fine. I didn't mean to—"

Michael looked down at her hands that were suddenly shaking. He felt a heavy wave of concern rush over him.

"April, what's wrong?" he stared at her unsteady fingers. The sudden turn of events was startling, and her hyper-sensitive reaction was slightly frightening.

"I'm sorry—" she wiped her cheeks quickly. "I'm sorry. It's not your fault. I'm sorry. It's me. I don't know why I'm acting like this. I'm sorry—"

"Stop saying sorry," Michael spoke gently. He tried to stay calm when really, he was nervous. "It's okay, April. You're okay."

He reached out to take her shaking hand in his, but she flinched and pulled away. April shook her head and squeezed her eyes shut tight, refusing to look at him.

"I'm so sorry. I'm so sorry," she ducked her head and cried. "I didn't know."

Chapter 12

The miniature apartment was dull, lacking in any color or vibrancy. The poor lighting partly helped hide the blandness of the room as the little bit of natural light spilled through the paper-thin blinds. It painted stripes of dark and light across the room of off-white walls and an old crusty carpet that looked like it hadn't been washed in years. No furniture except a random, uncovered mattress made itself comfortable against the wall. This was the 'living room,' but the space didn't seem much bigger than the kitchen that took up the other half. April only took a quick glance at the electric stove before deciding she would worry about the kitchen situation another day. Right now, all that really mattered was the sleeping situation.

Two open doors stood mysteriously on either side of April leading to what she assumed were the two bedrooms she and her future suite-mates would be staying in. From the looks of it, April seemed to be the last one to show up to the lonely suite. She dragged her turquoise suitcase into the room to her left as she looked for any signs that this was the right place.

The square room wasn't as cramped as she had originally anticipated. To the right, both corners of the quiet room fit two extra-long twin size beds perfectly along either blank wall. The ends of the wooden posts of the bed barely touched the reddish-brown desks that were already beaten up with scratch marks, permanent marker lines and dented edges from previous users.

The room was perfectly symmetrical, which seemed to put April's mind at ease in the smallest of ways. The only thing really keeping the room unbalanced was the fact that the bed and desk against the wall closest to her were already completely put together with a full, navy blue comforter, a massive load of matching pink and blue pillows, and a desk stacked with pens, pencils, folders, and books. Nia came prepared.

Two similar doors rested on the left side of the suite. A single bathroom with a sink, toilet, and bathtub. The other door led to a decently sized walk-in closet, already filled to the max on one side with what April could only assume were her soon-to-be-roommate's clothing. April didn't think she was that late showing up to check into her room, but clearly, these other girls were much more eager to settle in.

April took in a deep breath through her nostrils as she tried to make peace with her new environment. She plopped herself on the bare bed across the room as she heard the squeak of rusty springs underneath her legs. Clanton University. Alabama would be her temporary home for the next two weeks.

No, not 'home.' Not even 'temporary home.' The word 'home' has no right to this little place. I'll be out of here soon. No need to get too attached with words like that.

A plump, silver-grey stuffed elephant rested on top of the suitcase April had pulled in with her stuff. His satin pink bow was pinned to his chest right under his fluffy trunk. His body was more the shape of a squishy teddy bear than an elephant, but his giant floppy ears were the cutest part of his soft figure.

"Hey, Leo." Leo. Short for Leopard. An elephant named after a wild cat. April made herself laugh. Her hand reached out to take her new friend onto her lap. She gently stroked the face of her stuffed animal as she noticed the faintest hint of glitter blended into his fur.

An elephant with fur. How realistic.

"See, this isn't that scary," she continued to talk to her stuffed animal the way a little girl might when she's alone in her room. "We're going to be fine."

April checked her phone to see if she had any new notifications from Michael. There were none. It wasn't surprising. He had left for summer camp that morning and would not have signal until he got back at the end of the week. It was weird thinking the two of them would be only communicating sporadically over the next two weeks.

Michael and April were used to talking to each other every day for a while now. They were in the habit of hanging out together at least once a week, sometimes even twice. And even though none of that had been called an official date until last night, April couldn't help the fact that she felt like they were together.

When Michael smiled at her, it made her heart warm. When he hugged her, the smell of his shirt was the same smell as his car, and it brought her comfort. Last night, when he held her hand in the theater, she felt her heart slow down and sink. When he wrapped his arm around her on his sofa, she had leaned her head on his chest and could hear his heartbeat against her ear. What a weird feeling that was to listen to someone's heartbeat and think about how that steady rhythm was the thing keeping that person alive. Never in her whole life had April felt that feeling she did last night.

Kissing. That's what people who like each other do, right? They kiss each other. That's normal.

For three years with Preston, she had been trying to convince herself of that idea. It was probably normal to feel anxious when holding someone's hand. She blamed it on all the jitters she felt around him. It was probably normal for her to feel awkward whenever he would hug her. She blamed it on the fact that he was so much taller than her. And it was probably normal for April to hold off on kissing Preston. She blamed it on the fact that she was waiting for the right moment... for three years. How could she not find one single moment in three years? What was her excuse for that?

April had known from the moment she met Preston that he would be her first kiss. From the moment he told her he liked her, to the day he told her he was in love with her, she knew this was the boy of her dreams. Every Cinderella story, every romance movie, all of them pointed to Preston.

Their first kiss was supposed to be life changing. It was supposed to be magical and beautiful; something she imagined to be like fireworks going off. And even though she never did convince herself to give that moment to him, she had believed nothing was ever going to be able to live up to the moment they were meant to have together.

You gave your first kiss away. You held on to it for so many years, and it didn't even go to Preston. And when you finally had that moment with someone else, you couldn't handle it.

Why did April cry? Michael did nothing wrong. Actually, Michael did everything right. He had an open conversation about it beforehand, he even told her in the car that he would be okay if she wasn't ready. He was so sweet, and patient, and understanding. She wasn't scared when Michael touched her arm. She really did think she could kiss him.

When Michael had kissed her, her eyebrows had scrunched tight as she tried to hold back the flood of tears that wanted to consume her. Her head had felt light and fuzzy, like the most happy feeling. His mouth sent a warmth all the way from her lips to her chest. But as soon as that warmth collided with her beating heart, it sent a panic signal through her whole body. One that she wished she could stop. She wished she could control her body that she often felt like she was prisoner to.

Why did you cry? How were you supposed to know that would happen?

April believed only Preston could make a kiss feel like fire-works. But Michael was different. It felt like drinking a cup of hot tea on a chilly night. The way her lips soaked in the sweet-ness from the very first touch, the way the warmth made its way from her mouth down to her heart and spread throughout her whole body. It felt secure, safe even. Which was exactly why her heart needed to run.

The elephant on April's lap brought her back to the present moment sitting in her college dorm. She felt her throat sting at the memory of the night before. She felt hot tears rushing to her eyes again.

"It's okay, Leo." She hugged the elephant tightly to her chest in her room. "It's going to be okay."

The sound of the main door opening from the other room startled April. She quickly brushed her eyes with the tips of her fingers before heading out to the living room to meet her new roomies. She would just smile and push away the bad feelings.

Three girls made their way through the front door into the living room each with paper packets in hand.

"Hey," April waved before stuffing both hands into the back pockets of her jeans. "I'm April."

A dark-skinned girl with blonde braids waved back. She was absolutely stunning. Her green eyes glowed with energy and her dark lashes curled to touch the skin underneath her eyebrow. Her spaghetti-strap top was a bright yellow color that contrasted beautifully with her chocolate brown skin. Light blue jean shorts and basic white Air-Force 1's completed the cute-but-casual look.

"Hi, I'm Nia. Your new roommate," her glossy, plum-colored lips smiled. "I love your hair by the way."

The other two girls stared at April like she was a zombie. Both a ghostly white skin color. Both with ghostly blonde frizzy hair that reached halfway down their back. Both wild-eyed. Both scrawny and timid. Actually, April was having a hard time finding any differences between the two girls.

"I've never seen purple hair like yours," the first girl in a baby blue t-shirt dress sounded shy.

"Yeah, most people's colored hair doesn't look like yours," the second girl in plain overalls sounded just as timid.

"Are you two twins?" April stepped forward to get a closer look at the spooked girls. It was almost scary how identical they looked.

"No," both girls replied at the same time, in the same mono-tone voice.

April stared blankly, unsure of how to save herself from the awkward situation. She bit her tongue as she tried to think of something to say to break the uneasy silence in the room. The girl on the left in the plain dress grinned shyly.

"We're kidding," she blinked more times in a minute than anyone April had met in her entire life.

"We like to say that as a joke," the sister on the right in over-alls didn't seem to blink at all now that April noticed.

April forced out an uncomfortable laugh. "Oh, wow!"

She glanced wide-eyed at Nia who was now standing by April's side. The roommate nodded her head slowly back at April, her eyes just as wide, seeming to share the same message April was secretly trying to say.

"They did the same thing to me just half an hour ago," Nia forced a smile. "They are some very *funny* girls," she made sure to emphasize the word 'funny' hinting there might have been a different word she would have rather used to describe the duo that giggled innocently at their own humor.

"You know, actually I do something similar when people ask me, 'What are you?'" April tried to lighten the mood. "I say 'human.'" A silence even more awkward than before seemed to suck all the air out of the room. "I mean, I know they're actually trying to ask 'what's your ethnicity?'... Because of my skin tone? I'm Puerto Rican, but I say 'human' 'cause they ask, 'What are you?' Get it?"

More awkward silence. The twins glanced at each other as if April was now the odd one in the room. Even Nia didn't seem to know how to salvage the moment. Suddenly, April just wanted to jump out the window to escape.

"I'm Lynn," the blinker introduced herself, as if the past ten seconds hadn't just happened. But the awkwardness was still thick.

"I'm Lauren," the non-blinker added without breaking eye contact.

More silence.

"Nice to meet you guys!" April sighed heavily. More silence. "Cool, so, um... I'm just gonna go start unpacking and stuff... in my room."

"Oh, yeah, no you're all good," Nia encouraged warmly. "Totally. Go ahead and unpack, make yourself comfortable. All that stuff. We're headed to dinner in twenty minutes at the caf if you want to come with us."

"Yeah, that would be great," April forced a smile as she slowly backed her way to the door. The twins still didn't shift at all, like two porcelain dolls with a bad taste in fashion. "I'll be out in a few."

April backed into the door to close it behind her and looked up at the ceiling. She closed her eyes as she tried to let the tension from her body melt away from the previous two minutes. She hadn't realized she had been holding her breath before. Her lungs expanded and collapsed as she tried to breathe again. Where was Ethan on campus right now? She wasn't sure how much help he would be, but even a friendly hug would have meant a lot at that point.

13 more days, April. Then you can leave this awful place.

Michael

Chapter 13

"Go! Go! Go!" Jenni screamed over the chaotic chants of competitive middle schoolers. The large crowd of 200 campers rioted as they cheered on their color team from every section of the crowd. Waist-high boards of wood enclosed the competitors in a large octagon-shaped space just big enough to be a gaga-ball pit. The obnoxious air-horn blew as seven middle schoolers darted at full speed towards the center of the arena. All at once, they collided into one massive inflatable tire like it was life or death. They struggled to wrap at least one arm around the object and fight to drag it to their side of the arena. Tug-of-war on steroids.

"Let's go, Abigail! Use your legs!" Jenni's face was exploding with passion from the outside of the arena. The humid heat and intensity of the game had caused her petite face to flood a dark shade of pink. The beads of sweat that had collected all across her nose were causing the black dots of face paint to drip like tears down her cheeks. Her green bandanna was moist around the front of her head. The black and green stripes around her biceps were also beginning to smear down to her elbows and transferred onto the rolled-up sleeves of her green t-shirt.

Michael smiled as he took note of the messiness of her braid. Jenni was competitive. She didn't care about what she looked like at that moment. All she wanted was for the Green team to win by the end of the week. And that was why Michael picked her to be his other team captain. For exactly what he was looking at right here. Passion.

"What are you doing just standing there?" Jenni snapped at Michael, her big, brown eyes were wild with adrenaline. "Get our team to cheer! Come on Green! Scream!"

Michael smiled once more as he hollered and hooted as loud as he could from his side of the mess of green attire. The cheering bounced from every side of the octagon whichever way the tire leaned more towards. The grunts and squawks of the contests echoed around as the strawberry-blonde girl jerked the tire two steps closer to the green side.

"Let's go, Abigail!" Michael's throat was already sore by the second day of camp. He wondered for a split second if he would even make it to the end of this week before completely losing his voice. "You got it! Keep going!"

The strong girl yelled as she planted her feet and jerked the tire with all her force yet again. This time, her move caused a boy and a girl to fall to the ground, completely losing their grip on the tire: eliminated from the game.

"Yeah!" Michael felt the excitement rising to his chest. "Let's go! You've got it! You've got it! Pull!"

Abigail took another step, only a few feet away from her side. She seemed to move in slow motion as she dragged the tire closer. Another student hit the ground. Only three remained to hold onto the piece. Jenni screamed like a madwoman, her face now bright red. The girl jerked the tire over and over. Her shoes ground into the dirt. Michael could see the determination on her face as she gave one final pull.

"Let's go!" Michael screamed.

The girl threw her entire body forward with everything inside her. The tube ripped from the grasp of the other two players' arms and flew over the green line in front of her team. The enthusiastic crowd erupted in triumph. Cowbells clanked and toy horns boomed across the field. Jenni's voice cracked as she jumped up and down with her fist punching up into the sky.

"Another win for the green team!" A deep voice crackled through the megaphone. A skinny, bearded man walked out into the center of the toy arena. "Students, please find your counselors and head back over to the dining hall. Lunch is being served."

Without following proper instructions, the mass of kids swarmed the dirt path through the trees heading back in the direction of the camp. The weather outside was excruciating. None of the leaders exactly blamed the middle schoolers for being so desperate to get back indoors. A small hand aggressively slapped Michael's shoulder. Jenni's smile beamed with pride as her tiny self practically skipped her way beside her friend.

"Another win for Green Lightning," the messy girl threw her head back. "Second day and we're already crushing the competition."

"I knew we would," Michael chuckled. "The only team we have to look out for is Harper and Chris. They're doing better than I expected."

As the slow-moving crowd funneled through the forest, Michael and his co-captain followed the tail end of the group into the shaded woods. The entire day felt like it was taking so long to get through. It was only noon and Michael felt like he had lived through three whole days already. The rowdy group of boys he and his junior leaders were in charge of seemed to have way more energy than previous years. Every five minutes one of them was either hanging off of Michael or screaming just because their parent wasn't there to scold them. Putting them to bed tonight was not going to be a fun task.

Michael held the door open to the cool cafeteria as Jenni walked in front of him. The icy breeze of AC hit Michael like a wave, fresh and heavy. Michael felt relieved to be indoors again where he belonged. However, the screaming of children and chairs being dragged across the floors was not near as welcoming to walk in to.

"Hey, way to go on the win today, Green Team."

Michael's head snapped to his right to find the face associated with the mysterious voice. A blonde, freckle-faced girl stood behind a table full of female students all decked out in purple gear. Purple glitter in their hair, purple wrist bands and body paint decorated the young children's arms.

"I just want to let you know right now though... by the end of this week, my team will be taking the trophy home," Harper teased.

"Oh really?" Michael smirked. "Because I bet if you asked your sister, she'd disagree with that statement."

Harper cocked an eyebrow back at her antagonist. "Um, excuse me, but I think you forgot the most important detail about my sister." Harper leaned across the table to get a closer look at Michael's vivid green t-shirt. "My team is Purple."

Michael's face lit up at the mention of April. He so badly wished she were here. At this camp. In this room. She was overly competitive, just like Jenni, always coming up with chants for her team, decking her kids all out in purple gear. She led the purple team for the past two camps. How could she not?

"Don't worry about it," Harper chuckled, going back to twisting one of her seventh-grade girl's hair into a French braid. "April would pick any team that wasn't yours anyway. She's way too competitive. She'd have more fun competing against you rather than with you."

"Yeah, I know," Michael grinned lightly.

A female leader called for all the students to get in line for food. Most likely some bland tasting burger with sad lettuce and soggy tomato. Camp food was the worst but was all part of the experience.

The group of girls at Harper's table all stood up and rushed over to the opposite end of the room. The entire population of the space seemed to wash over in one uniformed sweep as their growling stomachs led the way to the assembly line. Michael debated going to stand in line or wait at the table with Harper. The idea of being able to talk about April sounded like it could partially make up for not having phone signal to contact her himself.

Michael lingered by the table. He awkwardly gazed around the room, poking the plastic chair in front of him with one finger to distract himself.

Finally, Harper interrupted the awkward silence. "You going to get in line or...?"

Michael's head quickly turned to face the blonde girl again as he processed what was just said. Although he had been waiting for her to talk, her sudden question still caught him off guard.

"Yeah, well no— um... well I was just going to wait till the line went down some," he said.

Michael wasn't sure why he was getting so nervous all of a sudden. The two teens had had more than a few interactions before. Always civil. Rarely anything interesting. Now that April wasn't around to break the ice though, he felt a new sort of pressure to not look dumb in front of the sister. An unnecessary pressure that didn't seem to be doing much in his favor.

Harper nodded her head, smiling to herself as if she wanted to laugh at the awkwardness of the conversation.

"So, um," Harper added out of nowhere. "April really loved that stuffed elephant you gave her the other night."

Thank goodness the conversation had circled back around to April. At that moment, it felt like the only thing the two of them had in common.

"Oh, yeah!" He laughed to himself as he went on. "She named it Leo."

"Yeah, Leo. Short for Leopard?" Harper chuckled as she rolled her eyes. "She loves to name things. And always the weirdest names, something she thinks is 'quirky' but really it's just random."

"Yeah, I know," Michael smiled at the ceiling. The light-hearted excitement of the humorous conversation faded as both teenagers stood at the table. The clatter of campers on the other side was becoming more muffled background noise than anything. Michael could feel the tension in his chest as he tried to muster the courage to ask Harper the question that had been on his mind for the past 48 hours. It felt too awkward. Too intrusive to even be asking about. April was her sister, though. If he were to ask anyone, it would be Harper.

"Did, um..." Michael gulped. He really didn't want to make things more awkward if Harper didn't know what was going on. "Did she tell you? About... the other night?"

Harper watched Michael, trying carefully to understand what he was really saying. There was a long pause before she replied. "That you guys kissed?"

"Yeah. Well— kinda," Michael shifted uncomfortably. "I mean, like, what happened... after..."

Harper stood steady. She took slow, deep breaths as she patiently thought her responses through.

"April is... a complicated girl... with a complicated past." Harper spoke slowly and softly, as if she were trying to explain to a child why it's dangerous to go swimming in the deep end of a pool. Michael listened but didn't make eye contact. Instead, he kept his eyes on the purple, glittery tablecloth in between the two of them. "I hope you know you didn't do anything wrong, Michael. You actually did everything right from what it sounded like."

"Yeah, that's what she told me," Michael shook his head, feeling slightly frustrated. "I just— I don't know. I just felt awful. Like, weird. And she said I was fine but... I just feel bad about the whole thing."

"If anyone feels bad about the whole thing, it's April," Harper huffed lightly. "She felt... humiliated."

"I mean, it was weird for sure," Michael took a deep breath and exhaled slowly. He stared back at the line of kids that had cut down more than half of the way by now. Right then would have been a good time to get in line, but still, Michael stayed. "Why did she cry?"

Harper pinched her lips, still watching Michael. She pulled out the chair in front of her and sat to make herself comfortable. Michael followed her lead but still didn't face her directly.

"Listen, Michael," Harper smiled politely. "That's really a conversation you should be having with April."

"What does that mean?" He shook his head.

Harper scratched the back of her neck. She tucked a strand of curly hair behind her ear as she leaned a little further into the table. "Has April told you anything about Preston?"

Michael felt his arms grow tense. "Um... I don't know." He squirmed a bit in his seat. "I know she mentioned a guy before that she dated a while ago. I think they were together for a long time if that's the guy you're talking about. But she never told me his name."

Harper nodded her head. "Yeah, they were on and off for about three years."

Michael's face twitched just the slightest bit. Confusion flooded his brain as he tried to put the pieces together. April never said three years.

"Wait, I thought she said it was a year and a half?"

"Listen, Michael," Harper lowered her voice. "April and Preston went through... a lot together. That relationship took up a lot more than she likes to admit. I mean, it took her almost two years to get over him—"

"Wait, what does this have to do with her crying the other night?" Michael felt his chest getting heated. "What happened? Is she still not over him?"

"Not exactly," Harper tried to explain.

"Okay, then— Why did she cry? Did he do something to her?"

"Not exactly," Harper continued to stay cool and collected, contrasting Michael's uncomfortable state. "He was..."

A tint of sadness washed over her pretty face. She looked worried. Guilty even. "I'm sorry, you know what? I probably shouldn't have said anything." Harper sighed anxiously as she ran both hands through her hair. "This is all very complicated and I shouldn't be the one to explain it. This should be coming from April."

Harper stood up, apparently deciding now was the best moment to finally join the food line.

"Wait, Harper, you can't just end it like that." Michael quickly stood to his feet and followed the worried girl. He was more concerned than angry. Michael needed answers. "Harper, wait," he quickly rushed behind the sister. "Why bring up this guy in the first place?"

Harper hushed him. "Michael, you really should be having this conversation with April."

"What's going on? Am I missing something here? Is she still talking to this dude?"

Harper froze. She genuinely took a second to think about his question. A hint of concern was painted across her fore-head. "I don't think she's talked to Preston for a few months now, actually." Michael watched her face as she thought about it some more. "He still reaches out to me sometimes. Scarlet. My dad. He's constantly trying to get a hold of April. But it's best for her that we don't let the messages reach her."

Harper thought for a while longer. Her eyebrows furrowed as she processed some more. Michael felt so confused. There was so much new information all at once. He never really bothered to even think about any of April's past boyfriends un-til now.

"She never tells us when they're talking again because she knows it's a bad idea. But you can tell," Harper nodded her head at the wall. "She gets this weird vibe whenever they've been in contact. A heavy sadness. It's just a side effect of Pres-ton Schuyler."

Michael was trying to understand all that Harper had said in that past several minutes. More than anything, he was trying to understand what any of that stuff in the past had to do with right now. This was not the conversation he had been expecting. Michael had so many questions still. And at the same time, he was afraid to ask many of them. He was afraid of what the answers might be.

"Should I be worried?" He finally forced the words out.

Harper crossed her arms and smiled painfully. Her eyes searched his for a moment. He thought for a second she might tell him this time.

"Michael, I'm sorry. But this is a conversation for you and April."

Chapter 14

The screeching of chair legs dragging across the fake wooden floors gave April goosebumps on her arms. It was an unpleasant sound to her sensitive ears along with the clinking of forks against plates, spoons falling on the ground, and the noisy chatter of graduated high school juniors and seniors. The aroma of warm food excited April, and she quickly found herself in front of the 'Ethnic food' line in the back of the cafeteria.

Unfortunately, however, nothing about the bland quesadilla looked ethnic to April. The white flour tortilla: way too squishy. The tiny pinch of yellow cheese in the center: underwhelming. Questionable chicken that smelled as if it hadn't even been seasoned with anything more than light salt: slimy.

It didn't matter that much in the end, though. April would have rather taken the sad quesadilla over a hamburger that looked just as depressing. Standing in the middle of a group of people was not pleasant for April, especially when she was trying to decide whether to hide her face in her phone to keep from looking lonely, or take the risk and attempt talking to someone next to her. There was still the risk of ending up in a very awkward and boring conversation about absolutely nothing with a stranger, though. It was too much for April to worry about at the moment. The quesadilla would just have to do.

The dining hall was quite large. Just one massive square room with light grey walls and white crown molding all around. The cold setting may have looked more like an insane asylum if it wasn't for all the glass windows surrounding the front third of the building. The stale room felt somewhat fresh even with all the chaotic mixture of noises echoing from every which direction. April wondered how the room might feel with fewer people. Maybe more like her ice cream shop back at home. Or the sports club after dark when most members had wrapped up their workout for the day to go home and rest. Quiet. Peaceful. But not today.

"Hey," the deep voice startled April, causing her to jump the slightest bit. She glanced over her shoulder to see a tan, tall boy smiling down at her. His jawline was sharp, his fiery blue eyes were piercing but full of interest. His white, fitted t-shirt clung to his torso like it was his own skin. He was attractive, but the backward flat-bill hat was a real turn-off. "Aren't you in my business class?"

"Oh," April tried to think for a second. She felt awkward as she tried to remember his face. "I'm sorry... I don't really know."

The out-going boy had a welcoming grin. His vibe was chill and exciting at the same time. "Hey, don't worry about it.

It's only the third day of classes. No big deal if you didn't recognize me as the guy who sits at the table behind you in Dr. O'Conner's class," he teased playfully.

April chuckled lightly. "I'm sorry, really."

"No, don't worry about it," he shrugged his shoulders. "You're much easier to remember seeing that you're the only girl here with purple hair. Kinda hard not to notice you."

"Ah, yes. One of the many perks of having abnormally colored hair," she nodded.

The boy flashed another friendly white smile. His teeth were surprisingly pretty. Maybe he wasn't as scary after all.

"Skylar," he extended his hand. April's body tensed like an icy breeze had just run down her spine.

Schuyler. She hesitated before coming back to earth.

"April," she smiled politely and extended her hand. Skylar returned the gesture with a firm handshake and nodded as the line moved up closer to the plates of food. April assumed that was the end of their conversation. She wasn't exactly in the mood anymore to be making friends with this guy, anyway.

"So, what's your major?" He persisted.

What's your major?

The most uninteresting, basic question everyone used to start a conversation when it came to college. That question was always the worst for people like April. The ones who were told they were going to need a 'real job' in order to make money. Always such an uncomfortable conversation to have with adults.

"Um, I'm an artist, actually," April crossed her arms feeling slightly judged. Not that Skylar had given off any indication that he was judgmental of her dream, but April had become accustomed to people being very turned off by her career path.

"Ah, that explains the hair." He moved in front of April to grab them each a plate as they stepped forward in the line. "Okay, so then, what schools are you interested in?"

April accepted the plate as Skylar handed it to her. They both made their way over to grab a glass for soda on the opposite wall.

"I actually was just recently accepted into SCAD... in Savannah, Georgia?"

Skylar did a double take. "Wow, that's impressive! I've heard SCAD looks amazing on a resume."

"Yeah, that's what I've been told," April nodded her head as she pinched her lips. She didn't really care about this conversation, but she didn't want to come off as a jerk. "What about you? What's your plan?"

"Uh, business," Skylar served himself a dark soda from the fountain dispenser. April poured herself water and picked up her cup to follow the boy to a nearby table. He nodded towards a big group of maybe 14 students, all cramped and cluttered around a table only meant to seat ten. "I want to open a tech business with my brothers one day."

Why was April not surprised by his major? He seemed like the type.

"Hey, April!" Ethan happened to be sitting at the far end of the table. "You guys can take those two seats. They were just leaving."

April carefully placed her food and drink down in front of

the now-empty chairs. She ran over to give her friend from home a hug from behind his seat.

She sighed with relief to see him. "Ethan, where have you been? I haven't seen you since we got here."

Ethan held on to April's arms for a second to keep her from going anywhere. "You making friends?"

April felt a little hollow in her stomach for a moment. She knew Ethan was just checking in on her, trying to make sure she was okay. He wanted to know that she was adjusting well. But she still felt uncomfortable. Slightly upset even that he would ask her something like that.

"I'm being social. I've been talking to lots of people," she forced a smile. She wanted to go back to her seat now.

"Talking to people isn't the same as making friends, Purple Hair. It's okay to make friends," he spoke sympathetically, patting her arms as he released her from his grasp. April stood tall and sighed through her nose as she thought of all the things she wanted to say. All the things she wished she could explain but didn't feel like anyone would care about.

"What's the point?" She shrugged at Ethan. "We'll all be gone from here in two weeks, anyway."

"April," Ethan sighed as she walked away.

What did it matter? He knew she was right. She could have buddies, and people to talk to. But was 'making friends' super necessary to her survival here? No. April knew how to be on her own. She would be perfectly fine with just mingling with people until it was time to go. Like this new Skylar guy she was walking back to sit with. What was wrong with him? He was nice. A lot nicer than any of the girls on campus had been to her.

April was used to it, though. Making friends with girls was always difficult for her in the beginning. It took most girls some time to warm up to her friendliness and realize she was genuinely being nice and perfectly not a weirdo just because of her hair. But by the time these girls would figure that out for themselves, it would be time to head back home. There was no point. Except for maybe her roommate, Nia. She was pretty fun. Bubbly. Exciting. Sometimes she could be a bit over-whelming, but if April tried hard enough, maybe she could have at least one girl to keep her company.

"You're back," Skylar smiled as April pulled out her chair to sit down.

"Yeah, I just went to say hi to my friend from home. I mean— Georgia. I mean— his name is Ethan and he's from Georgia, not home. Home is Indiana. But... I'm also from Georgia." April froze, feeling very embarrassed for her awk-ward moment. She closed her eyes and let out a laugh. "I'm sorry, that was really confusing."

"Don't say sorry," Skylar flashed another bright smile. "I thought it was actually pretty cute."

April blinked, feeling suddenly disappointed. Apparently, she had been wrong before. She was now down to zero new friends. A milk chocolate skinned girl practically pranced her way past the table on her way to the salad line. April immedi-ately recognized her beautiful roommate and raised her hand to get the pretty girl's attention.

"Oh, Nia!" She called out. The bright girl spun around with her eyebrows raised. When her eyes finally landed on April, she seemed more disappointed than excited. "Hey, do you want to sit with us?"

"Oh, um. No. That's fine," her green eyes scanned the room as if she were looking for any other table besides the one April was at. "I have friends at another table."

Nia turned back around without even a head nod. No 'thank you.' No 'maybe next time.' Nothing. April bit the inside of her lip as she felt yet another sting of a person who she felt like was avoiding her. She watched as Nia skipped over to a small table on the opposite side of the room.

The roommate hugged a tall, white boy. He looked friendly. Confident. Maybe cocky? April tried to read him from where she sat. Nia pointed over to what seemed like to be directly at April. Quickly glancing away, April poked at her soggy quesadilla with her finger. She wondered what Michael was doing at camp.

In her moment of loneliness, she slid her phone out of her pocket to shoot Scarlet a text. She didn't really know what the message was supposed to accomplish or why she felt the need to send it now, but for a moment April just wanted to hide in her phone.

April: Hey. No matter what happens, I love you.

"Who you texting?" Skylar pried with a mouth full of food.

April wondered why she was even at this table anymore. Even the idea of sitting with her creepy twin suite mates sounded better at this point than this guy who wouldn't stop asking her questions. Although, April had a strong feeling that she had messed up any chances of being even sort-of-friends with Thing 1 and Thing 2. They had also been avoiding her since the day they moved in. Then again, April hadn't made the best first impression there anyway.

"My best friend," April sighed and crossed her arms on the table.

"You guys in a fight or something? You seem upset." Skylar crammed another bite full of food into his mouth. Where were this boy's manners? And why did he have to ask so many questions?

"No, we've both just... been busy that's all." April took a swig of her glass of water.

She held the gulp in her mouth as she stared at the clear cup for a long moment, trying to see if anyone else could read the word 'LIAR' that was spelled out in bright red on her forehead. Thankfully, not a signal person here nor in Georgia knew April that well. No one except Harper, whom she had also been avoiding. She swallowed her swig of water as she set the glass back on the table.

"It'll be fine," she forced a smile. "I've got everything under control."

Michael

Chapter 15

A blood-orange glow illuminated the dusty blue clouds above the wooden picnic tables. A fresh breeze blew over Michael's face as he patiently waited outside his team's cabin. It was almost time for the night's service. Three of his kids had spilled taco ingredients all over their clothes during dinner and had asked to go back to the cabin to make a quick wardrobe switch before their camp crushes had a chance to see the embarrassing accident.

Of course, Michael had agreed to walk them back as long as they promised to change in under three minutes. Although, they were pretty messy. Michael figured it wouldn't hurt to give them a little buffer time. There wasn't that much of a rush to get back to the other building yet. He just wanted to minimize the amount of goofing-around-time to prevent any injuries or rolled ankles.

The little bit of quiet time Michael was getting to enjoy during this quick intermission had been unexpected. He hadn't realized how much he needed a breather before. The last day of camp was always the best. The best worship set. The best message. The best small group time after. It was the night everyone felt ready for more. Whatever last laughs and games they could cram into their tight schedule. Soaking in all the spiritual benefits of the life-pivoting sermon to come. This went for more than just the campers. Even leaders felt the same way.

As exhausting as camp was every year, there was nothing else like it during the summer. Thankfully, Michael would be getting to do this same routine all over again next week, too. This time with elementary schoolers. Blue team. The future winning team, of course.

Michael was excited to get back home for the weekend. No plans. No major responsibilities. Just chilling in front of his TV with Isaac and his dad. Where was Isaac right now anyway? He hadn't seen his middle school brother at camp since yesterday morning during breakfast. He just wanted to make sure he was okay.

The crisp sound of footsteps crept up behind Michael, pulling him out of his thoughts for a moment. He glanced over his shoulder to see a small student strutting over. However, the aggressive sound of keys clinking with each step made Michael do a double-take. That wasn't a middle schooler making his way over to the picnic table. It was a short, Italian high schooler ready to chat up a storm.

"Aye, Michael!" Jimmy held out his hand to dap up the newly graduated senior. The kid looked ridiculous, completely dripping in red sports gear. Red bandanna, red face paint stripes under his eyes, a tight, dark red tank top to show off his slightly muscular arms, red swim trunks and high, red socks that came halfway up his calves.

"Your shoes don't match," Michael sighed as he offered his hand back to return the lazy greeting. Jimmy leaned back on his heels to get a better look as if he forgot what his shoes even looked like in the first place.

"They're black. Black goes with everything," the poor boy replied defensively. He was so easy to get fired up.

"Still doesn't match."

Jimmy's light green eyes went wide. He stared intently at Michael as if he was trying to figure out if he was stupid. "But they're black and black goes with—"

"Black. Black goes with all black and red goes with all red. Come on, Jimmy. You gotta keep up with the trends," Michael shook his head playfully as he proceeded to stand to his feet, suddenly back to being a whole two heads taller than the child. "You know, before today, Jimmy, I used to think you actually had pretty good style. But now..."

The outfit was so typically Jimmy. Over the top, on the verge of being a costume, and yet still comical to look at. Michael pinched his lips together and shook his head in disappointment. "I'm sorry, Jimmy! I just lost so much respect for you."

Jimmy's jaw practically dropped to the floor. Most likely in shock to think Michael even once had respect for him before this moment. Now, it had just slipped from his grasp without even knowing. Panic flooded his face.

"No, no, no! Wait, Michael!" Jimmy frantically threw his

hands as he raised his volume even louder than before. "Camp doesn't count! Okay? Let's make an agreement. *This*— doesn't count!" He swiped his hands up and down to display his outfit further.

"Nah, I'm sorry man," Michael continued shaking his head as he made his way across the grass to the boy's cabin. "I just— I can't unsee it."

"Michael, please! This is just for the kids. You know how they get," Jimmy begged. The walking chili pepper was talking faster than his brain could keep up. "They practically made me wear this outfit. No, no— they *forced me* to wear this outfit, you know? I had no choice! Michael, you gotta believe me. This was *not* my fault!"

Michael smirked to himself as he listened to the kid ramble on and on. It was funny to listen to him frantically compose stories on the spot thinking this was somehow helping his case. It never was. Typically, April would be the one to interrogate the freshie at this point in the game. She would immediately find any holes in his plot and bombard him, asking questions like:

'They forced you? I'm so sorry! That must have been so scary for you to be tied up and threatened by a gang of Christian middle schoolers! What did they do? Hold you at gun-point? Try and force-feed you peanut butter when they know *you're deathly allergic? Oh, wait, I know what it was… They held you hostage and played One Direction on repeat for hours straight until you caved! You poor child.'*

Michael had to hold his breath to keep himself from laughing. This would be so much more fun with April right now.

Not only was she a second antagonist, but an audience to entertain through all of this as well.

"Black. Shoes." Michael cringed. "Red. Outfit." He pinched his eyes closed as he winced in pretend pain. "Can't. Look."

"Michael! Please! Pretend you never saw me!" Jimmy was acting as if this was life and death. So dramatic. 24/7. Must be exhausting.

"Well... I guess... If I didn't see you for the rest of the day, I might be able to wash this memory out of my mind," Michael knocked on the wooden door in front of him.

"Yeah! That's exactly what I was thinking!" Jimmy's face brightened with enthusiasm. "Pretend this never happened. Okay? Let's just, go back to the way things were before. Michael? You hear me? Deal? Say deal. Michael."

Michael made a deep thinking face. He didn't say anything for a long moment, leaving Jimmy in suspense. The sound of boys laughing and sliding suitcases back under their bunk beds rustled in the background of the silence.

"What were we talking about, again?" Michael's eyebrows popped up with surprise. A sly grin spilled across Jimmy's face as he started to back away from the door.

"Exactly," he nodded before sprinting off back in the direction of the gym-style chapel a little ways towards the center of camp. Michael shook his head once again as he popped the cabin door open and stuck his head in.

"Come on, guys. Time to go," he knew how to speak with authority without sounding bossy. "Service starts in 10 minutes."

All at once, the three 5th grade boys came crashing through the door. They ran out chasing each other in the grassy area in front of the cabin. Looping around the set of picnic tables, they screamed at pitches only a dog could possibly hear.

"Alright, alright. Come on, guys. Let's stay together," Michael led the way to the chapel, following the same direction Jimmy had just left in moments before. It took a minute before the rowdy boys added 'following Michael' to their current route of tag.

"Tag, you're it!" A curly, redheaded kid rammed into Michael at full speed. Gary was a sneaky child. Mischievous but full of fun.

"You're it," Michael tapped the kid on the head before he even had the chance to run away.

"No... You're it!" Gary giggled as he quickly hit Michael again.

"You're it," Michael tapped the kid again. He saw the excitement in the kid's freckled face fading, instead now being replaced with a more competitive spirit.

"You're it!" Marquis, who was the tallest of the three boys, pushed Michael aggressively.

"You're it," Michael tapped his dark hand so fast, Marquis only had to blink to miss it. Finally, the third boy, Nicholas, joined in on the game. Back and forth each boy would hit Michael as quickly as he tapped them back. The symphony of 'you're it's' sung loudly as they made their way to service. The sky had already darkened in just the past several minutes.

The dark orange tint was instead being replaced by a deep purple shade.

"Okay, okay, that's enough, Gary. You're getting too aggressive," Michael held back the skinny little boy.

"Michael, what grade are you in?" Marquis asked with innocent eyes. His chest rose and fell heavily as he tried to catch his breath once again. He adjusted the placement of his glasses that were now starting to slide down the bridge of his sweaty nose.

"Um, I just graduated," Michael watched the sky as they approached the tall, grey building up ahead.

"Graduated? I need to graduate." Nicholas ran his fingers through his short, black hair. What he really needed was some deodorant. "My brother graduated. He's in college now. He went to the Bulldogs."

Michael huffed, correcting the boy. "UGA."

"Hey, my dad went there too!" Gary's squeaky voice chimed in. "Where are you going to college, Michael?"

Gary meant no harm by the question. Curiosity wasn't an attack. Why did some of the simplest questions have such complicated answers?

"Um, I don't know yet, bud," Michael gulped lightly. He stuffed his hands in the front pockets of his khaki shorts, feeling put on the spot. "I'm still looking at my options."

Gary nonchalantly shoved his index finger up his right nostril without any shame. He dug around for a few seconds before examining his now shiny finger only to see that it was completely clean. Well, not totally *clean.*

"That's okay," Gary wiped his wet finger on the side of his sky blue shorts. He shrugged his shoulders, speaking to Michael as if he had everything figured out at the age of 11. "You have a lot of time to pick. I think you should go to Yale, though. That's where my mom wants me to go. But I don't know yet."

Michael smiled to himself, finding it cute that a younger person would be talking with more confidence about college than Michael, who was 18. Michael wished he had the same, easy-going attitude about the whole situation as Gary. Unfortunately, unlike what the kid was preaching, Michael didn't have much time left.

The four boys walked up to the heavy doors of the building. The hum of pre-service music was already bumping through the walls, exciting the overly-hyper boys before they even walked through the doors. Michael held the door open for them with one hand, smiling down at the redhead.

"I'll be there in a minute," Michael nodded before Gray smiled back and ran inside, leaving Michael alone again in the quiet of the outdoors.

The chapel sat on the top of a grassy hill, alone from the rest of the camp. As Michael made his way toward the edge of the hill, a dark green, still lake sat peacefully at the bottom of the green slope. One of his favorite things used to be rolling down this hill like a wheel barrel with Ethan and Nick back when they were campers. They'd race from the top of the hill all the way to the bottom, seeing whoever could get up first and run to the edge of the lake while still dizzy. Nick would usually make it first, and throw the other losers into the lake as playful punishment for losing. That was back before the camp became stricter about their life-vest policies. Back when goofing around to kill time wasn't a big deal. Life was just fun back then.

The tired boy sat down on the edge of the hill, watching the sun as it slowly descended behind the fence on the other side of the lake. The setting looked so peaceful. The water barely rippled in the distance, free to follow whatever pattern the wind conducted for it without hesitation.

He pulled out his phone and began composing another message for April. He still had no signal out at camp, but it would send tomorrow on his drive back to normal civilization. That was all that really mattered.

Michael: Hi. Today is Thursday. The last night of camp number one. In a few minutes we'll find out the official winner, but everyone knows it will be Green. We've been in the lead all week. Purple will probably come in as a close second though. Your sister's team put up a good fight. I thought about you a lot today. But then again, I think about you a lot every day. Jenni and I talked about you for a while, and that made me really happy. Also, I had this really funny bit going on with Jimmy tonight that you really would have gotten a kick out of. I'll tell you about it when you get back from Alabama. I hope you're doing okay there. Ethan better be looking out for you. You're doing great. God's got your back and so do I.

Okay, that's it for today. I'm proud of you. 9 more days, Bandkid. We've got this.

Within minutes of sending the message, Michael's phone vibrated with a notification letting him know the message failed to deliver, which he already knew of course. He shut off his phone before taking a deep breath. It was time to go inside for service. The silence couldn't last forever.

Chapter 16

The black needle of the depressing clock on the wall seemed to tick in slow motion. Each minute that went by felt like an entire five minutes. The dull, mono-toned voice of Dr. O'Conner acted as some sort of hypnotic spell the entire business class was trying to fight against. The past hour and twenty-minutes had been nothing but a struggle to keep from falling asleep.

Five more minutes, April. You can push through for five more minutes.

Her black pen tapped her wrist rhythmically as it followed the pace of her obnoxiously bouncing leg. She knew it seemed rude, annoying, maybe even disrespectful to not be able to sit still in front of her professor, but how else was she supposed to control herself in this uncomfortable situation? She was an anxious soul, but then again, most artists were.

"Alright, this weekend's homework will include—" The symphony of backpack zippers and jingling keys flooded the intimate classroom until none of the students could even hear the professor. April slung her backpack over her shoulder and quickly untucked her long, straight hair from out underneath its weight. She followed the stampede of teenagers who all forced their way out the door and down the quiet hallway.

Campus during the summer seemed haunted, ghostly even. There was something about it that made April feel insecure, unsafe sometimes. She just wanted this Friday to be over so she could enjoy the weekend to do nothing but hide in her room and mope. She wanted to be alone. To shut off her phone and hide in her dorm sleeping. She wasn't especially tired; she just didn't want to be awake. Then Monday would come around and she'd force herself to relive this whole week all over again.

Get over yourself, April. You have no reason to be sad. Stop finding excuses to be sad. What is wrong with you? People have real problems. Stop being sad.

As April stepped outside the chilly building, her cool skin was met with the striking welcome of the hot sun that toasted her goosebump-covered arms. She liked the way the sudden contrast felt. It warmed up whatever was wrong with her body that always kept her unsteady hands at an icy temperature. It made her not have to think about how little oxygen her body was receiving on a bad day.

The glass window of a blue Jeep Wrangler rolled down. Literally, rolled down. April could see Skylar's arm cranking the handle of the window around and around, slowly inching its way down to the halfway mark. He pulled the Jeep up to the curb of the sidewalk, across the green patch of grass separating the concrete from the School of Business building.

"April," he shouted. "Want a ride to the cafeteria?"

"No, I'm good," she half-smiled, slinging her practically empty backpack over her right shoulder.

The past few days had been interesting with Skylar. He was constantly watching her, waiting for opportunities to steal her attention. As if claiming the chair to her right in business class hadn't been enough of a statement the day after they officially met in the cafeteria, he also found it necessary to make comments to her the entire 75 minutes of class as well. April was not a fan.

"You sure?" Skylar persisted, seeming perfectly friendly. "It'll just take a few seconds."

April heard the swing of the door to the business building opening behind her. She wished at that moment she had made at least one friend in class that could save her from the awkward encounter. But of course, the only 'friend' she had made so far was her roommate Nia, who inconveniently happened to be taking the same class as Ethan in the nursing building halfway across campus. April carefully brushed her long, straight hair over her right shoulder as she tried to come up with an excuse.

"I know, but it's really nice outside and I was just sitting in that dark, cold classroom for so long." She heard the footsteps of the last trail of students behind her. The patter was making its way towards the tall bell tower. Away from her. "I'm just going to walk with everyone else."

Skylar watched the herd of people walking down the concrete path, thinking, slowly gliding his thumb across his razor-sharp jawline as if he were debating something in his head.

Please don't say you'll walk with me. Please don't say you'll walk with me.

Why was Skylar being so persistent? April didn't want to be rude to him, especially since now they would most likely be sitting with each other every morning in business class for the last week of classes. But she wasn't interested in him. Even if she weren't dating Michael at the time, April knew better than to go for a guy like Skylar.

"I'll walk with you," he flashed a smile and reached out to shift gears to park his car in a parking spot again.

Dang it.

There was no escaping it now. April wondered how rude it might be if she sprinted to catch up with the other group before he could find her. She needed an out. An emergency plan. Anything at this point would be better than this.

"That's okay, Skylar."

April almost jumped at the sudden voice that had sneaked up behind her. A soothing baritone voice. The southern Georgia accent was different from Tennessee and not the same as an Alabama accent. It might not have seemed that different to her Indiana friends, but April had learned the difference by now. Even if it was subtle. "We're actually walking to pick up Nia from the nursing building right now. But I mean, you could tag along too if you don't mind the pit stop."

The mysterious voice behind her had to be Nia's friend from the cafeteria the other day. He sounded tall. Like his voice was singing from above the top of her head. Who else would have known to comment about Nia?

April already knew Skylar wasn't a fan of the popular teen. She was obnoxious and had a ridiculous obsession with his muscles. She also had no problem with showing Skylar how excited she felt whenever he came around. It was completely reasonable for him to want to avoid the crazy girl at all costs. From the bothered look on Skylar's face, his distaste for her seemed to be coming in handy for April at the moment. Skylar sized up the boy still standing behind April.

"No, it's fine," he looked pissed off all of sudden. Shifting the gears of his car again, Skylar popped his head out the window one last time before speeding off. "See you later, April," he winked, pretending Will was no longer standing there.

The Jeep whipped around the corner and zipped down the street. The rumble of the engine faded away and instead was being replaced with the distant laughter of students walking in the same direction. April let out a long sigh. She hadn't realized before that she had been holding her breath. How long had that been? Probably since the Jeep startled her. 30 seconds ago? 45? How much longer could she have held it before realizing her lungs were burning?

April spun around on her heels to face the friendly voice. But of course, with April's luck, she spun right as he was stepping around to face her. Her shoulder collided with his chest.

"Oh, I'm sorry!" April laughed nervously. "I didn't mean to— I was trying to—" her cheeks felt hot with heat.

The tall boy chuckled. Now standing directly in front of April, he seemed even taller than she remembered. He had to be at least 6'3. Maybe even 6'4. April had to tilt her head the slightest bit to find his dark green eyes. A black ring traced around the perimeter of his pupil.

"It's fine," he smiled. "I've seen him bothering you the past few days in class. Thought you could use a little backup."

April pinched her lips and nodded her head. She tucked her long, straight hair behind her right ear and furrowed her brows. "Thanks. Sorry about that. I'm April."

"Will," he extended his hand for a handshake. His grip was firm and strong. Like he had just wrapped up negotiating an important business deal. "Nia's told me about you. You're her roommate."

Great. Considering she seems to run from me any time she sees me, I wonder what kind of wonderful things she's been telling you about me.

April started inching her way towards the direction of the bell tower. Will immediately followed. She assumed the two of them must have been heading towards the nursing building to actually pick up Nia. It was only about half of the way to the dining hall. A two-minute walk. Maybe three minutes if they were to walk slow enough.

The two continued their walk in silence. The awkward tension brushed their shoulders like the cool afternoon breeze of the summer morning. But she couldn't place where the tension was coming from. April tried to keep up with Will's pace. He was a fast walker. It didn't help that his legs were so much longer than hers. She felt like she was getting a quick morning workout in trying to keep up with his pace.

"My girlfriend's name is Sara."

April didn't respond at first. She just kept up with his stride, not sure what to say. Not sure where that comment even came from.

"Okay," April tried not to chuckle. After a brief moment, she peeked over at him. "Is that your way of telling me you have a girlfriend?"

Will nodded, still smiling. "Yeah, pretty much." He glanced over at April again. "I just don't want you to mistake my friendliness for flirting."

April smirked, wondering if he had been trying to think of a way to say this the whole walk so far. She chuckled, adjusting her bag strap once again to stay on her shoulder. "Okay then. Since we're just blurting out personal information, I'm in a relationship too."

"With a boy?" He asked.

April came to a halt in the middle of her speed-walk. "What?"

It took Will a second before realizing he was no longer being followed. He stopped to look back. His fitted navy-blue shirt made him look broader in his chest than before.

"Was that supposed to be a joke?" She half-smiled again, eyebrows furrowed.

Will looked around for a second, kicking his foot out like he was suddenly slightly uncomfortable. "Well, you know... with the purple hair I just thought..." He smiled when he started to realize she wasn't actually seriously offended. "You know... Maybe."

April scoffed and rolled her eyes playfully. Crossing her

arms, she shook her head in disapproval. "You thought what? Because I have purple hair, I must be a lesbian?"

"Or bi," he shrugged confidently.

There's a fine line between confident and cocky, and yet Will had seemed to figure out how to dance right on the edge of that line. He carried himself with his shoulders back, yet still relaxed. He moved with purpose. Made eye contact like he wasn't afraid, yet still seemed welcoming, not intimidating. It was like with each gesture, April wanted to label him as cocky until he would do something to step back behind the line into 'confident' again. It was impressive, really.

"Wow," April's mouth dropped, but the corners of her lips still tugged upward. "Way to stereotype me."

"What?" Will smiled wide. "This can't be the first time this has happened, am I right?"

April pinched her lips tight. She knew he was right, but part of her was disappointed he had been one of those people who automatically assumed he knew her before she had the chance to even get more than three sentences out. He hadn't come across as the type until now.

She pinched her lips and squinted once again. "Well, for your information, I am very much into boys,"

"Okay, fair enough," the blonde boy turned back to keep walking, this time slowing down his pace so April could catch up to him. When she reached his side once again, he continued to pry.

"Alright, so you have a *boyfriend*," he nodded without looking at the girl. His deep voice and sweet accent was the type that demanded attention. "What's his name?"

"Michael," she smiled.

"Michael," he nodded. "Sounds like a decent dude."

The red brick School of Nursing building was coming up on the path. April could already see the clutter of sociology students stepping out onto the path up ahead. This slightly awkward conversation with Will would soon be interrupted by Nia. Thankfully.

"Is he anything like Skylar?" He blurted out.

April lost her train of thought for a second. She had forgotten what they were even talking about before. "What?"

Will turned to April but did a slight double-take when he saw the look on her face. "Skylar? The guy who tried to kidnap you less than two minutes ago?"

April blinked. "Right, sorry." She closed her eyes and shook her head for a brief second. "I thought— no."

Will scrunched his brows together. He seemed slightly amused by her sudden baffling moment. "Geez, how many Skylar's do you know?"

April noticed that he seemed to be slowing down his walking pace even more than before now. Their stride turned more into a stroll as they continued to approach the upcoming building.

"Skylar is... okay, I guess. Not my type." She ignored his previous comment, her mood now slightly thrown off.

"Yeah, he's kind of a douche," Will said so matter-of-factly.

April huffed with amusement. "Wow, didn't expect a guy like you to use words like, 'douche.'"

"Oh, so now you're going to assume things about me, huh?" He smirked playfully.

April shrugged as she turned away. "Well from my first assumption about you, I figured you were mister, 'I'm a perfect Christian.'" She pursed her lips and mimicked the boy's deep accent. "'I don't drink or swear, and I never stay out a minute past my 9 pm curfew. My momma wouldn't be pleased. Those things are of the devil.'"

The bright-eyed boy seemed amused by her sudden change in mood. She was antagonizing him, her sassy Latina attitude making its way into the conversation. Her filter was slowly unraveling and coming undone across her mouth.

"Oh, and you don't curse Miss Purple Hair?" This was fun for him. April could tell by the way he tilted his head up every time he glanced down at her. She spun on her heels again, arms crossed, chin up so she could better see the tallboy's light face.

"No, believe it or not," she raised her eyebrows as she explained. "I don't curse, I don't vape, I don't have any unusually placed piercings, I don't listen to 'emo' music and I'm not into girls like that." She huffed playfully. "Any other stereotypical assumptions you need me to clear up for you?"

The handsome guy just smirked, making her wait a few seconds in silence before asking one more. His eyes glimmered with curiosity. "Tattoos?"

April hesitated before responding. "Nope."

There was a long pause as he watched her nervous reaction. "Would you?"

April bit the inside of her lip. "Maybe," she shifted her

weight from one foot to the next. "Would you?"

His smirk split into a full smile. Both their head snapped in the direction of the door that busted open to their right.

"Will!" Nia squealed. She did a double-take when she saw April standing beside him. "April! My two favorite people together!"

April scratched the back of her neck with one hand and brushed her hair out of her face. Will peeked at her before responding to Nia.

"Skylar was stalking her," Will shrugged. "Again."

She watched the tallboy proceed to nonchalantly explain their sudden partnership. He had a vibe to him that could make any person feel comfortable.

"Just thought she needed some backup," he explained.

"Oh my gosh, Skylar is so hot," Nia fanned herself with one hand and gripped April's small bicep in the other. "How could you reject Skylar Price? Every girl here is dying to get his attention."

"I guess he's attractive... somewhat. But— no," April chuckled as she peeked back at Will.

Nia rolled her eyes as she led the trio back in the direction of the dining hall two minutes away, completely oblivious to the way the other two teenagers had been getting along right before she interrupted.

"You're at a summer program," Nia tried to argue. "Everyone has a 'camp crush.' Your boyfriend is two hours away. He'll never know." She had a slight skip in her walk as she proceeded ahead. "It's just harmless flirting."

"Yeah, no thanks." April's shoulders felt tense.

"I agree with Purple Hair," Will chimed in. "Do you know how many girls have asked for my number in the past three days?"

"One?" April teased. "And if it was that thirsty old grandma who stands behind the salad bar in the caf; that totally doesn't count."

Will laughed as he shook his head "I was going to say 'six.'" *Cocky.* "But I can tell you guys that because you're my friends." *Confident?*

"We get it," April rolled her eyes. "Girls are into you here on campus. No need to brag."

"I'm not bragging," he shrugged. How was it that what he was saying should have come off as douchey, and yet, somehow didn't? "I'm telling you that four out of those six girls told me they were also in relationships. I hate that there are people who act like that in relationships. You have a girlfriend or boyfriend but flirt like crazy with everyone else? Just grow up. Or don't be in a relationship. I don't know. Sorry. I just get really bothered by that stuff."

April crossed her arms and inhaled deeply through her nose and exhaled through her mouth. Her chest felt slightly tighter than its usual chains this afternoon. This sudden shift in conversation was making her uncomfortable. And right when she thought she had a chance before to laugh a little.

Unexpectedly, April's phone chimed. It chimed for a second time. And a third. And fourth.

"Someone's popular," Nia smirked back at April who still

felt confused. What was happening? Why was Nia out of nowhere being so nice to her all of a sudden? Also, who in the world was spamming her phone?

She slid her phone out of her pocket and glanced at the glowing screen. She felt her tense face break out into an uncontrollable smile as her heart lightened up.

Will hesitated as he watched her reaction for a moment. "Boyfriend?"

"Yeah," April forced her eyes away from her phone to find Will's. "He, um..." she glanced briefly at her phone again. "I didn't know he was sending me good morning and goodnight messages every day while he was away at camp. He didn't have signal, so I guess they're all just coming in right now."

April went back to scrolling through her phone. Her face was hot with heat. She didn't usually feel this shy. Ever.

"That's really sweet," Will grinned. "Church camp?"

It took April a long moment to process what Will had just said to her. She was too distracted by the excitement she tried to suppress.

"What?" April dragged her eyes away from her screen. "Sorry," she giggled bashfully. "Um, yeah."

"You should call him," Will politely suggested. "He'd probably be really happy to hear from you."

April peeked up at Will one more time. Her lips finally were able to close again, but the corners of her mouth still refused to turn down. "Okay, yeah. I will."

"Good," Will nodded as he looked around for an exit. "I'll see you around then."

The tall boy waved as he spun on his heels to leave. Nia quickly followed behind him without making any sort of comment, which was unusual for her.

April paced slowly as the phone rang in her ear. What if he was busy? Maybe he was on one of the church buses and still couldn't answer. It was probably too soon for her to call. She probably should have waited an hour or two before jumping on the phone and just calling him out of—

"Hi," a cheerful, calm voice spoke through her phone speaker. April felt her heart immediately start to slow back into a steady rhythm just by the trigger of that sound. She almost forgot what that felt like for a while there. What it felt like for her brain to stop racing for even just a few seconds.

"Hi," she sighed. "I've missed you."

Michael

Chapter 17

"But mom said you have to," the spoiled little boy pouted his big red lips. Arms crossed. Angry eyebrows. Stubborn eyes. This kid was not giving up.

"Mom did not say that," Michael rolled his eyes and sighed heavily. All he wanted to do was watch his TV show in peace for at least one full hour without any interruptions. Why couldn't his family understand that? "I am not driving you all the way to the mall, Isaac. Just go to the store with mom and find a present for your friend there."

"What am I supposed to get Nicholas there? A potato? 'Oh, here Nicholas. I got you a ball of lettuce from the vegetable spot.'"

"It's called a *head of lettuce*, not a 'ball.' And *produce aisle*, not 'vegetable spot.'" Michael shook his head annoyed.

"Fine, I'm getting Mom," Isaac marched all the way upstairs to the master bedroom. His pounding footsteps boomed the entire way to the room, paused, and then stomped back into the hall and down the stairs. This time, a less angry Isaac reappeared in the living room with his mother following close-ly behind. She carried a basket of laundry on her hip and cell-phone in her opposite hand.

"Michael, honey, I need you to take your brother to the mall," she spoke without glancing up from her screen.

"Mom, I can't today. Dad and I are planning to watch the game as soon as he gets back and that's like," he checked his watch. "Twenty minutes from now."

"Oh, perfect," his mother plopped her basket on the seat next to Michael. She sighed heavily, exhausted from a day of house chores. Saturday's were her cleaning days. "That gives you just enough time to take your brother and get back before baseball even starts."

"Mom," Michael pleaded.

"Michael," she looked directly at him. "I really need you to do this favor for me."

The frustrated boy sat in silence, staring at the TV as he tried to convince himself to just get it over with. He wasn't going to win this argument. Why even go through the drama of protesting anyway? She won, like always. Michael dragged himself out of his seat and walked to the other side of the sofa to put on his tennis shoes.

"Thank you, Michael," Mrs. West went back to scrolling on her phone, still standing in the center of the living room. "I'm trying to find a picture of the thing you're supposed to get Nicholas. It should be in that video game store but if not, I think I know of a different place you can get it from too."

"Mom," Michael tried to be patient. "Remember, I'm trying

to get back in time to watch the game with dad."

"Oh, right, right!" She nodded understandably. "Hey, here's an idea. What if you pick up April and take her with you guys?"

Michael blinked. How would taking April somehow help speed up the errand? If anything, it would take more time to go out of their way to pick her up and drag her along.

"Um, April's still in Clanton for another week." His mom should have known that. She did know that. Why did she even mention the idea, then?

"Oh, shoot." The curly-haired woman snapped her fingers. "Never mind. I forgot. That's fine."

Michael felt pretty confused, but right now he had to grab his keys and go take his brother on this stupid errand as quickly as possible. That was his priority at the moment.

"Okay, well, just send me a picture of the video game and we'll grab it for him," Michael quickly swerved into the kitchen to grab his Jeep keys. But they suddenly weren't in the kitchen drawer they were usually kept in. Only one set of keys for their mom's car was left chilling in the corner of the junk drawer. Where had Michael placed his own?

"Now listen, Michael, it's very important that Isaac picks out the game himself," she shouted from the other room. Michael opened every drawer and cabinet nearby, shuffling through pencils and paper clips and chip bag holders. His keys were nowhere to be found. "I want Isaac to be able to feel empowered by picking out his own gift for a friend, but it's your job to make sure he doesn't pick the wrong one."

"Mom, do you know where my keys are?" Michael called from the kitchen.

He continued to look through the drawers. Gum. Chapstick. Quarters. No keys. Maybe he had misplaced them in the dining room. It was very rare that Michael went into that messy room. The table was always cluttered with papers of bills and mail that needed to be taken care of, but he felt he vaguely remembered dropping off the food he picked up from his mom in there just yesterday on his way back from camp.

"I'm giving you my card to pay for the gift, Michael," the high pitch voice continued to yammer on. "Please do not pay for it unless you have approved of the game."

Michael walked up to the cluttered, circle table as his eyes scanned the piles of papers for his pair of keys. How had his mom managed to hoard so much crap? There couldn't possibly be this many—

The corner of a gold and blue envelope caught Michael's attention. It was only barely peeking out from a pile of white paper, but it was the colors that made it stand out against the others. Was that— No. That would have come in months ago. But then again, these papers had been sitting here for months. Michael felt a pinch of suspicion rise in his chest as he wrestled with the idea in his head.

He leaned over the glass table and pinched the corner of the envelope with two fingers. He carefully tried to inch it out with one hand while the other did its best to balance the foot-tall stack of folded papers on top. There was nowhere to put them. No time to organize this chaotic mess. As he revealed the envelope from underneath, he noticed how much bigger it was than the others. Slightly heavy. One by one the white letters emerged with the rest of the page. Michael's heart began pounding. What was this doing here? Why was it hidden?

GEORGIA SOUTHERN UNIVERSITY
Michael West
3805 Peachtree Ln
Atlanta, GA 30339

When did this get here? How long had it been here? Out of the handful of schools Michael applied to in the winter, GSU had been the only one he hadn't heard back from. Until now. He carefully ripped open the large envelope and slid the paper out.

Michael West,

We are pleased to inform you...

Michael's brain cramped up with confusion as he tried to understand. How had he not known this was here? How had his mom forgotten to mention this to him?

Michael's thoughts hit a wall. A slow heat of anger started to bleed through his body instead, growing from his chest to his arms to his feet. Michael gulped as he quickly turned back to walk into the living room.

"Mom," Michael stood blank faced at the door frame of the kitchen. "When did this get here?"

The woman was still obliviously scrolling through her phone, looking for who knew what.

"Mom," Michael snapped.

"Michael," Mrs. West whipped her head around to give an ugly glare. "Do not snap at me like that."

The sass in her face instantly melted away the moment her eyes landed on the envelope. Her eyes danced back and forth between the blue and gold paper and Michael's own green eyes. Her mouth was parted open as if she was going to say something, yet no words came out. Worry was all Michael could see in her face. The confirmation only made his heart pinch tighter.

"Honey," the nervous woman placed her phone down on the couch next to her and crossed her arms. "I'm sorry, I forgot all about it. It came in the mail and it just got lost with all my other papers."

"When did this get here?" Michael persisted. He watched his mother bite her lip anxiously.

"A few months ago," she mustered. "It got mixed up with my other junk mail and I was going to give it to you whenever I found it—"

"You couldn't have even mentioned it to me within the past like 9–10 weeks that you had known about it?" Michael tried to keep from yelling, but the frustration in his body was struggling to keep his volume down.

"Michael," the lady sighed, looking disappointed. "You

have to believe me. I was just—"

"What?" He finally snapped. "You were just what? Go ahead. Say it. You were just deciding for me. You handed me whatever acceptance letters *you* thought were acceptable and hid the one you didn't agree with. Right?"

All previous emotions faded from the mother's face. The corners of her mouth twisted downward. The tone in her voice, however, was still stern. One of motherly authority.

"I just want what's best for you," she spoke slowly as if her next words were so matter-of-fact. "I know you only applied there because April is going to school in Savannah, and son, let me tell you, that is not a good idea."

Michael huffed as he ran his hands through his hair. Michael bit his tongue as he tried to control his tone.

"I applied to GSU because my *school* made me apply to three colleges, mom. My *school*," he hissed. His entire body felt like it was overheating. "I also applied to Georgia State. Why didn't you hide that one?"

"I just didn't want to confuse you," she begged. "You're so young and this is such a big decision."

"Yeah, *my* decision," his voice cracked. "All I wanted was to be able to finally make my own choice, and you couldn't even let me do that without manipulating the situation somehow."

"Michael," the woman's eyes dropped with sadness. "You'll understand when you get older."

"I'm done," Michael shook his head dismissively as he tossed his keys on the sofa. His feet pounded up the carpeted stairs to his room where he slammed the door shut as hard as he could making the walls rumble around him. It felt childish, Michael couldn't lie. But slamming the door right now was all he felt he could do to be heard in this house at this point.

Chapter 18

The Band Camio blasted through the car speakers at full volume, so loud April felt she could barely even hear the lyrics to the song. Squished to her right was Nia, screaming and dancing like a madwoman who had never even heard music before this moment. Ethan, along with a new redheaded girl, Caroline, squished against April's left side, laughing and yelling at the slightest turn the car would make to cause Ethan to be squished even closer to the door than before. The four of them crammed in the back three seats of the Honda was not ideal, but definitely added to the fun.

Will was a careful driver, however, having his cousin in the passenger seat seemed to be more of a distraction than a help. He was trying so hard to out dance Nia, being a complete goofball trying to make fun of popular TikTok dances.

"You know way too many of these dances for someone who claims to not have the app," Ethan yelled from the backseat. April and Nia exploded with even more laughter. The excitement of the whole event had April on an emotional high. Her head felt dizzy with happy feelings as her stomach became sore from laughing so much. The roads were almost dark, and the lack of lighting inside the car seemed to only add to the hysteria.

"Oh my gosh!" Nia cupped both hands around her nose and mouth. "Will, was that you?"

The commotion of the car began to fizzle out for a split second as everyone looked between Nia and Will with confused glances. That was when it hit. Like a tidal wave of foul odor, heavy and inescapable. April gagged as she tried to plug her nose.

"Will! What did you eat?" Will's cousin, Gavin, screamed like a little girl as he aggressively jerked on the door handle like he was going to jump out of the moving car. April tried to catch her breath, but every time she laughed she only inhaled more of the horrid fart.

"Roll down the window!" Caroline squawked.

April felt thin streams of tears seeping from the corners of her eyes. She didn't know if it was from the laughter or the stench. Probably a mixture of both. She leaned forward and tapped Will on the shoulder over and over.

"Roll the windows down before we die in here," April wheezed. She better have had abs by the next morning from all this pain of laughing tonight.

"I'm rolling them down! I'm rolling them down!" Will screeched. The strong gust of humid air forced its way through the cracks in the car, spilling and pouring, taking up all the other air in the car. It blew April's hair back against the seat as the little streams of tears quickly dried up as if they had never been there. After a few seconds of chaotic wind, the windows made their slow way back up, allowing a bit of calm to reign in the car again.

"You guys?" Will finally spoke up. "For the record, that wasn't me who farted."

Nia's head jerked back as she thought for a second. "Wait, if it wasn't you then who—"

April noticed the faint sound of giggling on the other side of Caroline. She leaned forward to see a red-faced Ethan chuckling to himself slightly as if he couldn't hold his giggles much longer.

"Ethan!" April gasped.

"Push him against the door!" Nia demanded. "Lean on three! One, two—three!" The girl jammed her shoulder against April's trying to use all her body weight to cause the other two girls to fall like dominos.

"Ouch! Nia!" April yelped as she tried to lean into Caroline.

"I wouldn't do that if I were you," Ethan wouldn't stop giggling. "I have another one locked-and-loaded."

"Stop, stop, stop!" Nia gripped April's arm and jerked her back.

"Ouch!" April winced again. "Seriously, Nia. Chill out. You're hurting me."

"Oh suck it up," she rolled her eyes and adjusted her seating. "You're being a baby. You're fine."

April gently massaged her bicep in the spot Nia had just grabbed her. Why was she being so aggressive? She thought she could feel her skin barely inflated in the sore spot. It was too dark in the car to see if there was a scratch mark, but her skin stung as if there was one.

The maroon car pulled up in front of the girls' dorm. They still had three more hours before curfew, but after the hour drive out into the mountains only to miss the sunset, the gang didn't have much else to do in Alabama. Besides, April still had homework due before her business class tomorrow. Skylar had asked if she wanted to study with him tonight, but thankfully Nia saved her by inviting her out with Will and Gavin instead.

Caroline had been a surprise, and Ethan was a personal invite by April. It would have been so much more fun with Michael. Right now he was probably struggling to get a group of obnoxious 3rd graders to go take showers on their own. April did not envy Michael at that moment. She did, however, wish he could have been here tonight chasing sunsets in a car of strangers. Dancing to The Band Camio. Struggling to breathe in the backseat next to Ethan as he released the hounds. She wished he could be part of all these fun moments with her. Was it going to be like this when they went to college? Living completely separate lives, with separate friends, without each other?

Nia hopped out of the car and waited for the other two girls to do the same.

"Bye guys," Will waved from his seat. "Thanks for coming on our failed adventure."

"It wasn't a fail!" April giggled as she stepped out onto the sidewalk. "Watching the sunset? Yes, that was a fail. But the entire past two hours were still an adventure regardless."

"Oh, hey April," Gavin leaned back to try and see her outside the open door. "Can I get your Snapchat?"

"Yes!" Nia practically threw herself back into the car. What was wrong with her? She was acting out of control. April popped her head back into the car and smiled shyly.

"Sorry," she smiled politely. "I don't give my Snapchat to guys."

Snapchat. Shoot!

April suddenly remembered she hadn't logged into her sister's account today to keep up with her streaks. Harper was at camp with no signal for five days straight which left April in charge of keeping her streaks alive. She pulled her phone out of her back pocket and began the process of logging herself out of her snap and into her sister's account.

"Don't worry, Gavin!" Nia was practically screaming at this point. "I'll send you her snap later."

"Nia," April scolded. "What is going on with you?"

"G'night, y'all!" Will shouted. He seemed to also be getting pretty tired of this game Nia was playing. If anyone should know what was wrong, it was Will. But he didn't seem concerned about her even in the slightest.

"Goodnight!" The three girls waved back and walked into the front lobby of the girls dorm they were staying in. Nia was practically skipping her way down the hall singing some Lizzo song at the top of her lungs. She bounced off the walls like a child who was on a sugar high.

"It was really nice meeting you," the redhead began unlocking her door at the beginning of the other side of the hall.

"Oh, bye, Caroline," April smiled happily as she waved. The somewhat familiar stranger smiled back. She was beautiful. Fiery, straight red hair. Beautiful, icy blue eyes. Freckle sprinkled white skin. The contrast between colors was stunning. The smiley girl opened her mouth to sneak in a final comment before popping her door open.

"You're really pretty, by the way," she smiled.

April giggled awkwardly. "Oh, thank you. So are you. I'm honestly so jealous of your natural hair. I could never pull that off."

"Thank you," the friendly girl laughed. "Yeah. I hear that a lot too. Maybe we can hang out again before we all leave?"

"Yeah, totally!" April shrugged, excited. "Goodnight."

Caroline waved as she walked into her room and closed the rickety door behind her. April opened her phone again to finish her Snapchat chore for her sister. She took a basic picture of her forehead with the word "streaks" typed out on the screen.

April personally hated the trend of sending streaks. They felt so artificial to her. So forced and impersonal. If she had more than 5 streaks to keep up with on her own phone, April would have to drop someone. She hated the clutter of notifications. The idea of trying to keep up with so many people each day sounded exhausting. But her sister liked the challenge. April only had four more days of this. No biggie.

She clicked the little blue circle with a white arrow pointing right. She tapped every name with a little red flame emoji beside it. There had to have been at least 16 names. Maybe even 20. What was even the point of this?

Once all streaks had been replied to, April tapped her sister's bitmoji character to log back out. But as she went to do so, her eyes flashed over a blue message waiting to be opened. Her heart skipped a beat when she read the name.

Preston Schuyler.

April felt a faint punch to her gut. It felt like all the oxygen in the room was disappearing along with April's sense of self-awareness.

What is Preston doing talking to my sister again? Does Harper know about this? Why of all weeks did Preston choose this one to message her? When I have her account? He doesn't have a flame next to his name. They don't have a streak. What is he trying to do?

April didn't even hesitate. She didn't wonder if it was any of her business. She didn't bother to let her sister read the message when she got back and hopefully tell April what they talked about all on her own. April lost all sense of respect of privacy. She didn't care at all. This message now belonged to her, no matter what the contents were. April tapped the message and began to read right in the middle of the now-empty hallway.

Preston: Hey, Harper. I know we haven't talked in a while but I've been thinking a lot and felt like you were the only person I could talk to about this.I was just thinking that I missed you. And your dad. Your whole family, really. I've been thinking about everything that happened, and if I'm being totally honest with you, I have a lot of regrets.

No kidding.

Preston: My biggest regret though has to do with your sister.

Good, April laughed to herself. *Because you really screwed up. And there's nothing you can do about it. It's been two years. Whatever apology you have is not going to change anything.*

Preston: I know she's with someone else now. That... boy. I know that I've been with someone else for a while now, too.

Going on a year, now. Right?

Preston: But all I keep thinking is...

What? You're jealous? You think you're better than this guy I'm with? So, it's totally fine for you to move on but the second you realize I've moved on too, now you have a problem with it? What? Go ahead. Say it. I don't care. None of it matters to me anymore. Anything you say at this point will make me just laugh out of pity.

Preston: I wish I had kissed her when I had the chance.

April had been anticipating to laugh at whatever nonsense Preston might have said then. But instead, she felt anger rising within her body. Hot and intense, April felt her chest tightening to an uncomfortable level. Like a volcano getting ready to explode, she felt her hands becoming jittery all over again. Worse than their typically subtle dance.

Of course, Preston would say something so pathetic. So selfish. So completely unrelated to the real problem at all. If Preston could go back in time to any point in the past five years, he wouldn't choose to fix anything. He wouldn't wish to make better choices. He wouldn't think to find a way to make the five-year rollercoaster they had been on less painful for the both of them. No. Instead, all he would want to do was steal her first kiss.

That's why you're so jealous? Everything was fine when I was single. You could get a new girlfriend and get serious with her and act like you two are married but the moment someone might have something from me that you didn't, you have to jump in and interfere. Really?

April felt hot tears rushing to her eyes, but she was only left with blurry vision as she tried to hold them back.

If you could go back and change anything, that's what you'd pick? You wouldn't choose to take anything back? All the pain you caused me. All the emotional turmoil you put me through— put us through? You wouldn't take any of that back...

April took in a shaky breath. She wanted to scream. She wanted to punch something. To break something. She wanted some way to release the overwhelming emotions that were attacking her all at once without resorting to tears. No more tears. April swore last year that she would never cry over Preston again. She spent too many years crying over that stupid boy. Too many months drowning in her tears over someone who didn't even know she was hurting so badly. No more tears. Never again. He didn't deserve it. April wouldn't fall backward. Not this time.

Why are you even shocked right now? You weren't actually expecting him to apologize, were you?

April stood in silence. Her heart felt so heavy and yet so hollow at the same time. How stupid was she? She had told herself a year ago that she would never let Preston hurt her again. And here she was. Graduated from high school. About to leave for college. And still feeling the repercussions. Why did she have to feel anything for him? She had been able to go numb for so long and now here he was, finding his own sneaky way to take another jab at her heart. But really, maybe it wasn't his fault at all. It was April's for even still caring.

Preston: I had so many opportunities, and she just never let me. Will you just tell her that for me? That I wish I had been her first kiss? Thanks. Love you, sis.

What? That's what this message was? To tell me you wish you kissed me. Of course, I couldn't kiss you. How could I get myself to kiss you when you constantly turned it into some sort of twisted game? You let girls crawl all over you and tug on you, and you'd smile right to my face. You said it was my fault. Every time I said 'no': it was my fault. Every time you touched her skin: it was my fault. Every time you found someone else to get back at me: it was my fault. You'll never know how sick that felt. You'll never know the way my stomach twists to this day because of it. You'll never understand the way I flinch and squirm and hate my body— I hate myself for it. I wish I didn't have to be like this. I hate myself so much some days, Preston. And I wish I could hate you for it too.

'Don't cry, April. Don't cry, April. Do not cry or I'll hate you forever,' she hissed at the voice in her head.

The tears were building in her eyes. She quickly used the hem of her shirt to absorb the liquid anger before she blinked. As long as the tears didn't fall down her cheeks, it didn't count. As long as she held her breath and didn't exhale completely, it didn't count as crying. As long as she held as much as she could together. Her body was tense, her lip being bit so hard she feared she would draw blood, her thin fingernails dug into her palms due to her hands that had cramped up into fist so tightly it hurt.

She felt her fists going numb with pain. Her arms and legs were tingling, the way it feels after your foot has gone to sleep and starts to vibrate awake with electricity. She felt dizzy. Out of control. Like her body was going rouge and acting however it wanted without her consent. The least she could do was not cry. She could at least try to fight her body and keep herself from crying.

What is wrong with you, April? You're a psychopath for crying like this over a boy. Look at you. You're acting crazy and crying over nothing.

'I'm not crying!' April screamed back at herself. 'I'm not crying. I'm not crying.'

You're 18 years old and still crying over the same crap that you've been crying about for years. Admit it. You're broken.

'Shut up. I'm not broken.'

April squeezed her eyes tightly shut as she took the punches. She saw a blurry galaxy of purples and blues with each hit. She thought for a second that she might pass out. She didn't want to pass out. She tried to fight against her own body but felt as if her sad soul and physical cage were completely separate arenas. And she was losing in both.

You're weak. You're going to be trapped by this forever. You know that, right? You're never going to escape this feeling.

'Shut up.'

Hit after hit, the blows kept coming. April wasn't holding her breath by choice anymore. She physically had lost the right to make herself breathe.

You're forever going to be broken. You're never going to stop being hurt by this.

'Stop it!' The echoes in her head were getting louder and louder. Her head was pounding with blood. Like a hammer smashing against her skull.

He doesn't love you. He never loved you. No one loves you.

April felt her throat running dry. It burned as she fought to hold back the flood of tears trying to escape. The least she could do was not cry. If there was anything she could control at this point, it had to be her tears. She wouldn't let those win too.

'I have Harper. I have my mom. I have Scarlet and my family—' Her lungs screamed for air, but none came. Her vision was becoming blurry and faded.

No guy could ever love someone like you. Preston doesn't care about you. Michael doesn't care about you. If Michael knew how badly bruised you were, he would throw you out. He would look at you with disgust and leave. You don't deserve someone 'good.' He's going to find out. Soon. You're too broken. You'll always be broken. That's the truth. Wake up, April. This is who you'll always be. Broken till the day you're finally dead.

April's legs suddenly buckled under her before she knew what was happening. She felt her body aggressively collapsing into itself as she stumbled out the back door of the dorm, dying for air. She dropped herself next to the nearest pile of bushes. She leaned over with her clenched hands trying to hold back her purple hair. Her stomach forced her to pump out whatever bit of pizza it still had sitting in it from dinner. The darkness of the night hid April's out-of-control episode well enough that she hoped no one would be able to recognize her if they did happen to pass by. She couldn't even imagine what her mother would be saying to her if she were right there.

You're being dramatic. Stop acting crazy. There are bigger problems in the world, April. You don't even know the kind of life I had to live. Pull yourself together. You don't know what real problems are. People are starving. People who don't have houses or clean water to drink. Stop being dramatic.

April closed her eyes and tried to catch her breath, still leaning over her knees. She felt exhausted. So mentally and physically beat up. She just wanted to lie down and sleep for a few hours. But she knew her brain wouldn't grant her such peace. Her heated brain was quiet now but alive with electricity. Like tv static. Saying nothing, but still restless and loud.

April waited for the tingling in her legs to go away. She felt her cramping, clenched hands slowly starting to loosen as the collection of minutes passed by. She didn't know how much time had gone by when her legs had finally gone back to normal. She forced her exhausted body to walk back through the doors of the dorm and straight into her suite. She walked past the creepy twins who seemed to be baking cookies in the simple kitchen.

"Hi, April," Lauren stared without blinking. April smiled politely and waved.

"Hi, Lauren. Hi, Lynn." She walked right into her bedroom where Nia rested on her bed, scrolling through her phone.

"Where'd you go?" Nia peeked up. Her mood had completely switched. From 100 to 0 from one encounter to the next.

"Oh, I was on the phone with Scarlet," April lied nonchalantly as she went to her drawer to grab pajamas. "I'm going to shower."

Nia didn't even respond. She was typing away at her phone and thankfully didn't ask any more questions.

April turned the squeaky handles of the shower and let the sound of steaming water patting against the shower floor fill the room. White steam swirled and danced through the air, completely consuming every corner of the bathroom. The thick fog around her became her blanket, comforting her in her isolation. The soothing rhythm of the artificial rain against her scalp brought a sort of ordered chaos to the pounding of her skull.

The warmth of the water on her skin allowed her muscles to relax somewhat. And the silence. The silence allowed her to process all the thoughts she had just gotten back from war with. Fatigued. Drained. April had no timer. She would leave this bathroom when she decided she was ready.

Half an hour later, April found herself lying under the cool covers of her temporary bed. Hair still damp, fresh-faced and even slightly chilly. She stared blankly at her dull, white wall lacking in any personality or style. She wasn't sure where Nia had gone or when she would be back, but April was thankful to have the room to herself at the moment.

Maybe the voice in her head was right. Maybe April didn't deserve Michael. She knew it the night he held her hand in the movie theater. He squeezed her palm and all April could think was 'He's going to leave you. Don't get too attached. You'll only end up hurt.'

It was probably true. Michael was eventually going to find out how broken April really was. He didn't love her. He couldn't. No one could. Michael deserved someone less dramatic. Less emotional. He deserved someone easier to love than the mess April tried to hide. She should just stick to what was familiar. Stay comfortable in what she knew best. Even if it was painful, pain sounded more like something April was used to than the fear of whatever Michael offered. She still didn't know exactly what that was. All she knew was that she didn't deserve it. No one deserved to live like this.

The sound of the phone ringing played in April's ear as she waited for an answer. She didn't know if he would answer her call, but she knew she had to try. The phone clicked on the other side. There was a long pause before she mustered up the courage to speak.

"Hey," April spoke softly, timid even. She felt so many emotions flooding her heart. Fear. Anticipation. Sadness. After a prolonged moment of silence, April gulped. There had been no response for so long, she feared maybe he had hung up. This was a mistake. She shouldn't have called.

"Hey, April," Preston sighed heavily. "You don't know how much I've missed you."

Michael

Chapter 19

"**M**ichael!" Sara shouted from the other side of the soccer field. For a 3rd grader, her athletic skills were impressive. "Come play with us!"

Michael was not in the mood to be running around in the scorching hot sun right now. The pink sunburn on his face was still trying to heal from last week's camp. But he supposed that's what baseball caps were for anyway.

Michael sighed as he put his phone down in the grass next to Jenni's fanny pack. He jogged over to the small cluster of elementary schoolers where Nick, Jenni, and Anne were all fighting over who was on what team. The kids weren't listening much. They argued over who got to kick the ball while the big kids made the real decisions of the game.

"I say we do girls against guys," Jenni placed her hands on her hips. She stated the idea as a suggestion, but her body language said that she had already made up her mind. Anne looked around at the group confused. Her mouth was still full of the granola bar she was chewing on as she spoke up.

"Wait— I didn't agree to this," Anne's blonde, wavy ponytail bounced side to side as she shook her head. "Nick and Michael will destroy us if they're on the same team. You have to separate them."

"Yeah!" A child growled his way into the circle. Derik. The most entertaining little kid to ever live. Nick's favorite child out of all the campers. "The boys are going to kick your butts!"

"Alright, alright, Derik." Anne patted the overly excited child on the head a few times before taking another bite of her granola bar. "Take the sass down a few notches."

"Deriiiiik," Michael nodded teasingly. He crossed his arms and slightly smirked at Anne. He knew how much this was going to get on her nerves. In the most fun way, of course. "Picking the winning team. I like it."

"That's not fair!" Anne threw her hands up in defense. "You and Nick can't be on the same team. That's a total disadvantage for us!"

"Boys against girls! Boys against girls!" Michael cupped his hands around his mouth and called for all the kid's attention. "Let's go! Game's starting!"

"Nick!" Anne panicked. "Michael!"

Michael smirked back at Anne finding her concern of losing so badly humorous. It was true. Michael and Nick were totally about to beat Jenni and Anne. But that was what made it so fun. Well, not for the girls.

"Three, two, one— go!" Michael kicked the ball out from under Derik's foot straight to Nick who readily ran with it to the nearest goal and kicked it right into the center. The black and white ball flew through the air and collided with the net inside the frame.

"Goal!" Nick jumped up and down screaming like a mad man. Michael yelled as he and Nick ran at each other at full speed, jumping into a dramatic chest bump for all the kids to laugh at.

"Wait! We weren't ready!" Now Jenni was starting to freak out a little. She stomped her way towards the middle of the field, ready to argue. "You can't just start like that! We didn't pick a goalie. At the bare minimum, we didn't even pick a *side* of the field!"

"Keep up, Capri," Nick patted her shoulder as he ran to the opposite side of the field with Michael. "You're about to get your butt kicked."

The four teenagers ran the field back and forth, hooting and hollering. The sound of children screaming with laughter and arguing over who got to the kick the ball was obnoxious. They drowned out the noise of simple conversations some of the less athletic kids were having while playing with ladybugs. The sun was beating down like a hot oven while the humidity kept the outdoors feeling like being trapped in a sauna.

The competitive game of soccer lasted for only ten minutes before the entire field gave up. The boys were outscoring the girls by a long shot. It helped when Nick and Michael practically took over the entirety of the scoring on their team while Jenni and Anne focused on group participation by giving the girls some opportunities to score. The question was simple: Did they want to share the ball? Or did they want to win? Michael and Nick already knew their answer. And so far, it worked like a charm. Finally, Sara tugged on the hem of Anne's shirt to get her attention.

"Can we stop now?" Her squeaky voice was raspy with exhaustion. "I'm getting really tired."

"Yeah, of course," Anne placed her hands on her knees and tried to catch her breath. "Why don't you go over to that building with Mrs. Caprio and she'll give you some water, okay?"

Jenni wiped her sweaty forehead with the back of her hand as she walked over beside Anne. "That's a good idea," she nodded her head while trying to gulp down the little bit of saliva still left in her mouth. She shouted so that the rest of the kids on the field could follow Sara to the cafeteria on the other side of the fence. "Hey, everybody! Go to my mom in the cafeteria and she'll give you water. Everyone needs to drink at least one cup of water, okay?"

The faint replies of 'okays' were only scattered throughout the crowd of children as they made their ten-second journey to the cafeteria. Michael followed his three friends who walked sluggishly over to a single tree out on the other side of the field. Jenni sat down at the trunk of the tree and leaned her head back with her eyes closed, trying to decompress.

"Water, anyone?" Nick took a swig of his steel water bottle as he leaned his shoulder against the tree. Without hesitation, Anne reached her hand out to Nick who immediately handed the bottle over. She sighed as she plopped herself down in the shade on the prickly grass. After a few chugs, she handed the bottle to Michael who proceeded to sit on the ground next to her.

"My gosh," Anne sighed as she leaned back to lie down on the grass. "I'm never playing soccer in the middle of June ever again."

Nick snatched his water back from Michael after he finished taking a few chugs. "Yes, never again...Until tomorrow when it's time to play soccer again."

"Exactly," Jenni laughed, still looking more nauseous than tired. She opened one eye to scan Michael's face briefly. "You good, Michael?"

"Huh? Yeah." Michael positioned his feet near Anne's face as he also stretched out on the ground. He was hoping getting out of Jenni's direct line of sight might help hide him from her unnecessary concern.

"You sure?" Jenni chuckled. "You've been in a bit of a funk all week."

What was that supposed to mean? Michael was fine. He was here at camp, being present and participating with his team. He was even goofing around with his friends. Everything was normal.

"Did you decide yet?" Nick chimed in on the interrogation as he slid down the tree trunk to sit next to Jenni. The sudden quietness of the group was very unlike them.

"Nope," Michael stared at the tree branches above him. They laced and tangled into one giant maze of leaves. The sunlight barely poked through a few cracks in the canopy here and there.

"Woah, Michael," Jenni took down her hair and began to redo her ponytail. "It's the middle of June. You've gotta pick one, like... now."

'No. Really? No one has told me that yet,' he thought.

"What's the big hold up?" Nick picked at his teeth. "You can't decide? Or is it something else? Or *someone* else?"

Anne swung a loose hand at the nosey boy's ankle. "Nick, leave him alone."

"What?" He threw his hands up in protest. "So you're saying Purple Hair has nothing to do with this?"

Michael sighed slowly, still staring up at the greenery above him. He wasn't sure if he wanted to talk about any of this. Jenni, Nick, and Anne were some of his closest friends. He grew up with them. But that didn't make talking about what was going on inside his head any easier. Expressing how he really felt about things was a real struggle for Michael. One he felt not many people would even understand.

"I just keep thinking," Michael finally forced the words out. "Is this what it's going to be like?"

This: As in, not seeing each other for weeks at a time? Missing her all the time? Of course, when they went to college they would both have phone service and be able to FaceTime and text and Snapchat and all that, but that wasn't the same. Michael wanted her around. He wanted to be doing life with her, hanging out with the same friend group, finding some new kid similar to Jimmy to antagonize and keep them on their toes. All of this without her just wasn't the same.

None of the three friends said anything. Instead, they all exchanged subtle glances with each other.

"Is it even that serious between you two?" Jenni finally asked. "I'm not trying to sound insensitive. I'm genuinely asking."

Michael sighed heavily. He didn't even know the answer to that question. He knew he liked April. A lot. How was he supposed to view their relationship? It was all still new in a way. Michael didn't even know where April stood on this topic herself. He found himself plucking strands of grass out of the ground next to him.

"I don't know. I mean, I think it could be. One day, I guess. I just..." Michael felt like he was physically straining his body to force the words out. He felt incredibly out of his comfort zone sharing his inner thoughts out loud. "I don't want to lose her."

More silence. Michael felt the awkwardness of feeling emotionally exposed stretching out across the four of them. Like taking a mask off and now everyone was staring. Gawking, even. Nick would be jumping in to make fun of him any second, probably calling him too sensitive for being so mushy about his feelings. Michael shouldn't have said anything.

After what felt like an hour of silence, Anne finally sat up. "I think you should talk to April about this."

Much to Michael's surprise, Jenni responded similarly. Nodding and verbally agreeing with Anne. But Michael huffed out of frustration as he sat up to face them again.

"You guys don't understand," he shook his head. "It's not that simple."

"Sure it is. Tell her exactly what you just told us. Just like that. Simple. To the point," Jenni shrugged.

Anne nodded in agreement as she pointed to Michael. "Exactly. It'll help you so much if you know where you guys stand."

"Guys," Michael released an awkward chuckle as he rubbed his forehead with his hand. He felt the tension of the topic increasing as the conversation continued. "It's not that easy."

"Why not?" Jenni smiled. "It's April. You should be able to talk to her about these things."

"I know that," Michael propped his elbows on his knees as he rubbed his eyelids in a circular motion. "That's just... not me. I'm not good with words."

"Then don't say it to her," Nick finally chimed in. He had been quiet the whole time up until now. "Show it to her. 'Actions speak louder than words.' It's cliche but... I mean, come on, it's true."

Michael was genuinely surprised by his friends' reactions. He had become so used to the way they usually spoke to each other with the constant teasing and inside jokes, he hadn't realized how supportive they really could be. They didn't make fun of him. They didn't make him feel bad for even thinking about April when it came to college. From what Michael could tell so far, they were actually offering him some solid advice. He started to wonder how many other things his friends could have helped him through in the past if he had just dared to open up.

"So... What do I do?" Michael finally felt less awkward. Still worried about the whole situation, but more comfortable talking about it to his friends.

"Make a gesture, I guess," Jenni stood up and held her hand out to Nick who returned the gesture with a look of disgust.

"Get that hand away from me," he pushed her elbow. Anne giggled at their sudden playful banter that helped break the ice. Michael reached out his hand to Anne who took it as they pulled themselves up together.

"I don't know, Mikey," Jenni smiled to herself as she watched Nick struggle to get up. His legs were probably still sore from last week's camp. "Do something that says, 'Hey, I want to make this work' and see how she responds."

Nick winced in pain as he stretched his legs. "Buy her a wedding ring! Nothing says commitment like a wedding ring."

Anne rolled her eyes as she shook her head at Nick in disapproval. "Yes, at 18 years old. They should get married. Great thinking there, Nick."

"Woah, woah, woah. Engaged isn't the same thing as married," Nick protested as he chugged the last bit of water in his bottle. "Obviously, I'm joking guys. Chill out, geez."

Michael smiled as he shook his head. The idea of leaving him, all of them really, made Michael sad at the moment. These were his people. Plus Ethan. He had grown up with them his whole life. The time was coming for all of them to split in their separate directions. How weird would that be? And right when he felt like they were all getting closer than before.

These guys had been with him forever. And Michael felt confident that they would be even during college. Even on breaks. Even in the summer. All the way up until after college.

He'd always have them. But right now, the one he was afraid of losing was April. He knew they were happy together. So why was he so nervous?

Suddenly, Michael felt silly for even worrying about it in the first place. The two of them were going to be fine. He had nothing to be afraid of. More than anything at the moment, Michael wished he could just get in his car to drive and see April wherever she was. All this talk about her was making him miss her more than ever.

Chapter 20

Purple waves. That was the hairstyle April was going for: beautiful purple waves. She used her black hairbrush to smooth out the fat, uniformed curls she had just achieved with her curling iron half an hour ago before she did her makeup. The final night of Clanton University's summer program was celebrated by the school with a simple banquet to end the two weeks.

Simple?

April chuckled to herself. None of these girls had packed anything *simple* to wear tonight. From the handful of girls she had talked too, three of them were wearing their homecoming dresses from last fall, and the other four had packed cocktail party dresses. April could only imagine how overdressed the pretty group of girls would be dressed for such a lame event.

April used a few bobby pins to pin the front layers of her hair back, creating the illusion of a half up half down look. April scanned herself in the mirror. Her long hair rested in full, natural-looking waves over her shoulders. The best set of clothes she had packed for tonight had been a long, black beach skirt with a slit up to her knee on the side, along with a white, v-neck tee shirt that was decorated with silver jeweled flowers on the loose sleeves.

She felt completely underprepared for tonight. If she had been given the heads up beforehand that people were going to be taking tonight so seriously, April would have upped her game a few notches. Instead, she tried to compensate for her lack of glam with a bit of glitter in her eyeshadow.

Her makeup looked nice. Really nice. She was an artist. How could it not be? Most people didn't expect her to be so good at the natural glam look simply because she rarely wore more than a few swipes of mascara and clear eyebrow gel as her daily routine. But that was okay. April enjoyed being full of surprises.

She walked barefoot into the shared walk-in closet and skimmed over Nia's three pairs of heels she had left. Last night when April had mentioned not bringing any dressy shoes for the banquet, Nia had pursed her lips almost with pity at the unprepared girl. She offered April whatever shoes she decided not to wear tonight.

April strapped on a thin pair of white heels. They were the shortest out of the three, maybe only three inches, but April liked the style best. She snatched her black purse off her still cluttered desk as she left outside to meet Ethan. As April locked her dorm door behind her, her phone suddenly rang with a FaceTime call.

"Hey," April giggled at the boy on the other side of the screen as she attempted to stuff her keys back into her purse.

The hazel-eyed boy's jaw dropped before he responded. "Wow, you look... Stunning."

April rolled her eyes, annoyed. He knew she hated it when he said that. It didn't matter too much though. It wasn't like she cared that much what he thought anyway.

"You like my shoes?" She spoke in a silly, high pitch voice as she stopped to show the camera her feet.

"Yes, I do," Preston laughed. He was so handsome. Dark lashes, thick eyebrows, big hazel eyes and a full set of lips. More than anything though, what got April was the sound of his voice. It was like music. It did things to her heart that no one else could. Like a cello singing the richest version of Ave Maria the human ear had ever heard. She had missed that song so badly.

"Hey, I have to go because I'm meeting a friend to drive over to the venue. I'll call you tonight, okay?" April smiled.

Preston bit the inside of his lip and smiled back. Wow. That smile. Undeniably gorgeous.

"Okay, April," he shook his head. "Just a little heads up though, if any of those guys there cause you problems, you just call me, okay?"

If April were going to call anyone to protect her, it would not be Preston. What was he going to do? Chew them out through FaceTime while April held the phone up for him? Unfortunately, she knew Preston was only half-joking. He actually would fully expect her to call him if a boy were bothering her. But April didn't need Preston, or anyone else to take care of her. She would be just fine on her own.

"Mhm, sure," April's tone was thick with sarcasm. As she walked up to the glass doors leading outside, April could see Ethan standing on the other side looking more dapper than usual. "Okay, talk to you later, bye."

"Bye," Preston grinned as he hung up the phone. April pushed open the door and smiled as Ethan's face brightened.

"Purple Hair," he took a step back to scan her outfit. "Look at you all nice and whatever."

April pursed her lips as she swayed in her long skirt. "Thanks! I actually tried today," she danced around some more to be goofy. "And look at you! I don't think I've ever seen you in a suit before." She dropped her jaw as she walked up to tug at the edge of his jacket sleeve.

"I have lots of suits," Ethan posed with his hands in fists at his sides. "I have this black suit, I have a grey suit, another grey suit, my birthday suit—" April burst with laughter.

"I knew you were going to say that!" She hit his arm with the back of her hand. Ethan chuckled back at her as he walked her toward the passenger seat of his car. The two friends rode the brief drive over to the event hall the dinner was being held at.

The entrance of the pastel brick, one-story building was swarming with high school upper-classmen. There were dozens of fresh-faced boys in suits, and even double the number of girls in skin-tight Kardashian dresses. This was starting to look more like a club than a banquet.

April took a deep breath as she opened the passenger door and stepped out onto the black asphalt of the parking lot. She only had to cross the street, but the feeling rising in her gut was making it seem like an entire raging river that she inevitably had to conquer.

"Hey," Ethan startled April when his finger tapped her elbow. "You good?"

What are you doing? You might as well have shown up in pajamas. You would look just as stupid.

"I look dumb," she bit her bottom lip. "They all look so dressed up and I'm wearing a skirt and t-shirt— I look ridiculous."

"April," Ethan placed his hand on her shoulder blade to comfort her. "You look great. Come on." April held her breath, wishing Ethan would never have to see her the way she saw herself right then. "There's something you're going to want to see... Come on."

April took in a deep breath as she forced her feet forward.

Fake it. I can fake it. Act confident. I just need to pretend to own it. If I just act confident, they'll think I am. I can fake it. Come on, April. You can fake it.

Her originally tense arms were forced to loosen and sway at her sides. She clutched the edge of her thin black purse with one hand as she dropped her shoulders back and held her head up. Her clenched jaw did its best to ease up, and she knew to slightly drop each hip as she took her graceful steps. Even though she felt so uncomfortable she wanted to jump out of her skin, she knew how to exude confidence in moments like these. April could fake it. She learned to fake these things a long time ago.

As she followed Ethan across the street, April was already starting to forget her original fear. The number of eyes that were suddenly following April didn't frighten her anymore. Both boys and girls glanced and watched from their circles of friends. Only a few whispered, but for the most part, the teenagers stared without actually verbally acknowledging the purple-haired girl who had shown up late. This wasn't so dangerous. April could handle this.

A gorgeous, dark girl with blonde braids suddenly approached April in a gorgeous green cocktail dress. Her false lashes were bold, her perfect pink smile stunning.

"Awe, April!" Nia smiled, but it looked catty and fake. Her eyes scanned April from the white shoes to the long skirt to the white t-shirt to her hair. Her words were sweet, but her eyes and lying tone sent a different message. "You look so..." she tilted her head to the side. "Cute."

April quickly bit the inside of her lip to keep from verbally swinging back. Seriously? April was over here admiring the stunning girl's beauty and here she was coming to take a petty jab at April's self-esteem. April held her breath as she tried to keep her face from adjusting in any way to the snarky girl's comment.

Just be nice, April. There's no need to be petty back. Don't even think of punching her in the face. Be the bigger person and be kind.

"I think you look beautiful."

Confusion hit April as she realized that those words had not just come out of her mouth but actually belonged to a familiar voice behind her. She quickly spun around when her gaze landed on a sparkling pair of ocean-blue eyes. Before her stood a handsome blonde boy. He smiled proudly in a black suit with no tie, but an open collar instead, and in his left hand he held a humble bouquet of purple and white daisies just waiting to be gifted away.

Michael.

April felt an unexpected pit growing in her stomach. Uncomfortable and hollow. Guilty and embarrassed. The complete opposite feelings she had always used to feel when with him.

The bright-eyed boy's smile broke into a full-on grin, beautiful and bright. He ducked his head and watched his feet as he took two more steps closer to April. When he lifted his eyes to find her's again, April felt her heart tingle. She didn't know if it was from happiness or the beginning of a tearing heart.

He smelled like his car still. A clean, deep forest smell. The warmth radiating off his body was usually supposed to put April's heart at ease, calm her down and make her feel at home. But this time, she felt terrified.

"Hi," Michael watched the floor and smiled bashfully before finding the pretty girl's gaze again. April gulped ever so slightly before forcing a smile back. At least the one thing she didn't have to fake was how shocked she truly was.

"Hi," April whispered back as her eyes fell to the bouquet.

Why would you bring me flowers? Do you not know me better, Michael? They're fragile and frail and only plucked out of the ground for selfish people to display for themselves until the poor things wither up and die from thirst. They should be left alone in the soil where they belong. Do you not know me at all?

"Um," Michael licked his lips as he broke into another uncontrollable smile. His eyes were glowing with excitement.

April could feel his overwhelming happiness bouncing off his entire body. She felt she had never seen him this happy before. "These are for you."

April's heart dropped as Michael handed her the raw bouquet. The green stems were still cold and tied together with a thin string of yarn. The array of delicate purple and white petals was no bigger than the size of a cantaloupe. And the smell. They smelled like the dirt fresh after rain in the spring. April's absolute favorite smell in the world. She dragged her sad eyes from the beautiful arrangement back up to Michael who still smiled at her with care.

"You look really pretty," Michael huffed with relief as he leaned forward. April slowly closed her eyes as he gently pressed his lips against her forehead. Her eyebrows slightly scrunched together in emotional discomfort as the warmth of his kiss affected her heart the way it always had. It made her want to sink into that feeling he gave her. That feeling of being safe and happy and protected. But this time, it hurt.

It hurt just like the way it hurt the night he kissed her. She felt her heart screaming at her to run. Get away before it was too late and she became too attached. If she let her heart go where it wanted when she was with Michael, this was going to be more painful than anything Preston had put her through.

With her eyes still shut, April took a slow, deep breath in through her nostrils as the boy stepped back again. She blew out through her nose heavily as her eyes fluttered open again.

"Let's go inside," April pinched her lips together and forced a soft smile, trying to redirect the attention of the moment to something that didn't have to do with the two of them. Her eyes were slightly glossy now, but not for the reason Michael might have guessed. The sweet boy held out his hand for April to take.

As she did, she noticed the small audience that had formed during their encounter. It was the curious stares of girls, especially, that seemed to be most viewers. Maybe admiring the couple. Secretly burning with envy for the romantic moment. April tried to keep her head down, wishing the gawking girls around her would stop wishing they had what she and Michael had. If they really knew the truth about it all, they wouldn't envy April the same way anymore.

Slowly, the couple walked up to the tinted doors of the venue. April's brown eyes lifted to meet a tall boy's stare. Will gave her a slight nod, motioning to the flowers she held close to her chest.

"You got a good one," he forced a smile, his comment referring to Michael.

April felt her heart twist a little as her eyes fell to the concrete floor, breaking their eye contact.

I know.

She walked past Will without a reply and followed her boyfriend through the glass doors into the mysterious event room.

A simple wedding reception was how April could have described the style of the room the two of them stepped into. The two dozen round tables that were crammed on the right side of the room were draped in white tablecloths with simple, sunflower centerpieces in the centers. Bubble string lights dangled in a zig-zag pattern across the entire glossy wooden dance floor.

There, a handful of teenagers were already dancing, each paired up with a partner as they swayed to the music of a popular song by The Temptations. The dim space sparkled with digital lights that subtlety reflected off every surface. The warmth and simple dazzle of the room felt welcoming. Beautiful, even.

Michael swiftly reached for April's bouquet of daisy's and placed them on the nearest table.

"What are you doing?" April panicked.

Michael smiled warmly as he took both her hands in his and began to lead her onto the dance floor. Was he really about to make her dance with him? Right now? When there were barely even any people still on the dance floor? To this song?

"Just come here," Michael chuckled as he placed both hands around the middle of her back and pulled her close. April awkwardly placed the palms of her hands on either of Michael's shoulders who immediately laughed and corrected her.

"Just hug me, and when you pull back, that's what it should look like."

April blinked a few times, oblivious. "What?"

She couldn't even focus. She was usually the one teaching Michael how to dance. She felt like she was having a ghostly out of body experience. Her body was here but her mind was on a completely different planet. Michael's head dropped as he sighed with laughter. He lifted his face again to search her confused eyes.

"Okay, so, hug," Michael wrapped his arms the rest of the way around her waist, pulling her body close to his. Her arms awkwardly wrapped around his neck as her body tensed up. As Michael released his grip, April began to slip away. Her fingers now softly clutched the back of his neck, right underneath his hairline as her feet followed his lead in a simple sway.

April watched Michael's ocean eyes as they danced to the sweet song that played in the background of their quiet moment. She studied his face as her brain came up with a million questions she had for him, including what he was doing here. Had Ethan known about this the whole time? Or was this more of a spontaneous idea? Where was he planning to stay tonight? Was he driving two hours back home after this was over? What about his parents? What did they think about this? Why was he here?

"What?" Michael finally cut through the silence between them with his patient voice. "What are you thinking?"

April held her breath as she tried to pick one thing, just one thing she wanted to say. One out of the million and one thoughts she was coming up with at the moment.

Just tell him. Get it over with. Say what you really think.

April opened her mouth to tell Michael the truth of all the ideas she had in her head. She wanted to tell him about Preston. She wanted to explain to him why he wasn't going to want to be with her anymore very soon. But out of all the truths to pick from, something unexpected came out instead.

"Your eyes," she blinked slowly, dazed and confused. April tilted her head slightly to the side as her eyebrows furrowed.

She spoke slowly, softly, as if she were sleep talking. She didn't understand what was coming out of her mouth.

The truth, April. Tell him the truth. Not this crap. Tell him what you're really thinking.

April stared for a while longer, trying to get the courage to open up her mouth and let her truths spill out. But instead, her mouth continued to speak for itself.

"Some days I'm staring at you and think, 'Yes, his eyes are for sure ocean blue. I'm 100% certain.' And then the next day you're looking at me and I'm telling myself, 'No wait, they're deep, sea green. No question about it.'" She breathed slowly as her lips spoke without her consent. "And it's like this back and forth game in my head where I try to figure out which answer is right. But the truth is, no matter how long I study them or what my conclusion is each day, in the end, they're still your eyes. And… they're beautiful."

Michael's face started to flush a slight shade of pink as he felt put on the spot. April could tell that was nowhere near what he had been expecting her to say. It wasn't what she had expected either.

What is wrong with you? Tell him your actual truths. The ones about how messed up you are. Tell him he's stupid for even showing up tonight for a girl he can't have. Tell him the real truths. Stop getting distracted.

"I'm sorry," April closed her eyes and shook her head with embarrassment. She felt shame flooding her body. "That was not what I meant to say. I shouldn't have even—"

"No, it's okay. Really." Michael blushed at his feet.

The two continued to sway slowly together. Their feet were barely taking any real steps to the slightly upbeat rhythm. Neither of them spoke, but April couldn't even look at his eyes anymore. After what she had just said, she felt they were now suddenly too personal to connect with. And if she did, she would only be hurting herself more.

"April," Michael's face was flushed with worry. "Are you okay?"

April had to talk herself into finding his gaze. She didn't want to be looking into his eyes. She needed sunglasses. Or even a blindfold for her outfit would be nice. At that moment, she realized it wasn't looking at Michael's eyes that was actually the problem. It was him looking into hers.

"Yeah, I'll be okay," she forced a smile as she peeked at him.

Her heart felt heavy. Like a 50-pound bag of bricks had replaced the once beating organ in her chest and dragged her whole body down, ready to collapse. Michael studied her. His gaze was steady and full of questions. April could have sworn she saw a hint of hurt in his eyes. She wondered if it was her causing him a little bit of pain, or something else.

"April... I came here tonight because..." The handsome boy seemed to be having second thoughts about whatever he was planning to say before. His mouth adjusted as he tried to remember how to speak. April gulped, unsure of whatever he was about to say. Finally, he flinched before spitting out his next phrase. "April... I don't want to hurt you. I hope you know that."

Silence.

April's mind went blank for a second. She didn't even blink. She looked as if someone had just said something to her in a foreign language and the phrase hadn't even processed through her head yet. She replayed the words over and over in her head for a few moments, feeling vulnerable as the words finally started to sink in.

"I really like you. More than I've ever liked anyone. And I just..." Michael took in a shaky breath as he forced his final words out. "I really don't want to mess this up."

April felt the previous sadness in her body melting away. Not with relief, but instead with guilt sinking in. It didn't matter. That wasn't the point. Soon this would all be over with and she wouldn't have to worry about anymore hurt between the two of them.

"It's okay, Michael. You're not going to mess this up," she barely even smiled.

April felt so guilty. So ashamed and embarrassed and angry with herself. She wished she could admit to Michael right then and there that she was the actual time bomb in this relationship. She had triggered her own countdown the second she called Preston the other night, and soon enough, no one would be able to save her from what her heart really wanted. By the time anyone figured it out, it would be too late. And Michael? He would only be a small casualty in the wake.

"You're...You're different, April," Michael's eyes cut right to her soul. "I've never... The way I feel about you..."

"Shhh," April pinched her lips. She shook her head trying to hold back her tears of shame. "You don't have to say anything,

Michael. Let's just dance, okay?"

Michael released his breath before chuckling at the ground with relief. "Alright. I can do that." He smiled while scanning over her face once more. "Whatever you need, Bandkid. I've got you."

Michael

Chapter 21

Top-down, stereo up, My Girl blasted through the black Jeep that cruised the backroads of Vinnings, Georgia. The air was fresh with the gush of the midday breeze. Only partly cloudy outside, it was a perfect day to meet Ethan for a quick game of casual golf at the entertainment center nearby. Michael sang along as he drummed with his fists on his steering wheel. The song had been on repeat for the past three days now.

The loud Jeep pulled into the parking lot and drove around a few times before finding Ethan's white car on the front left side of the building. He left his top down and jogged into the empty place. Wednesday afternoons weren't ever busy at this location.

Ethan played like such a goof when it came to this version of golf. He wasn't a very skilled golfer, so instead of aiming for the targets, halfway through the round, he would always challenge Michael to see who could hit the golf cart that drove underneath the platforms to collect all the missed shots. Out of the ten times they had played this version, only a handful of times had Michael actually hit the cart. Ethan was still yet to make it even close.

"And then one of the nights, we all went driving to go see the sunset with this girl named Caroline— dude. Caroline." Ethan pulled an iron club out of its socket and hovered the end over the button to send a ball to his platform. "She had this red hair and— man, she was just so funny. I was laughing the whole night. I think she kinda liked me too."

The ball rolled out from its little hiding spot and Ethan set it up on the golf tee in front of him.

"Well unfortunately with your luck with girls, you'll probably never end up seeing her again," Michael teased his friend.

"No! I'm serious, dude. She gave me her number and everything," he slowly stretched his arms back and pivoted his hips back. With one swift swing, the club hit the ball sending it flying up and over the speedy golf cart zipping around under them. Another miss. "Actually, a lot of guys asked April for her number too. You would have hated it, not gonna lie."

Michael watched as Ethan called for another ball. Another swing. Another miss. Ethan was on a roll.

"Did she?" Michael finally asked. He tried to act casual as if he wouldn't care either way. "You know... like, give her number to any of them?"

"Not that I know of," Ethan waited for his third and final swing before it was Michael's turn to play. "Honestly, she didn't seem to have any interest in those guys. You honestly have nothing to worry about. April's not that kind of girl."

Michael stood up to pick out his club of choice. Unlike his friend, he decided to take a driver to use for this particular game they were competing in. Ethan's ball barley even made it over the edge of the platform this time.

"Did something happen in Clanton? With April?" Michael didn't even know if he was asking the right person. Ever since they had got back from their separate summer programs, April had been acting... different. He couldn't quite figure out what was off or what might have happened between them to cause the slight shift. But things didn't feel the same.

Ethan returned his club back to its holding compartment. "What do you mean? Like something bad?"

"I don't know," Michael dragged the little white ball with his club to his foot. He didn't even use the tee. "I feel like she's been acting kinda different. Like... I don't know."

Michael lined his club up with the ball. He looked out to follow the trail of the little golf cart that twisted its way around the enclosed course, trying to predict the exact spot it would drive across next. Timing was everything.

"You know what? Never mind. It's probably nothing." He swung his arms back and knocked the golf ball with a crisp 'clink' sound. It arched through the humid air, gracefully flying out and over, barely missing the tail end of the incoming golf cart by inches. He was only a second too late.

"Speaking of which," Ethan took a swig of the cold glass of soda sitting on the booth behind them. "Have you put any more thought into UGA?"

Michael pinched his lips as he focused heavily on the next

ball in front of him. Another calculated swing only to miss and reveal his calculations had been off again. This time about a second and a half too early.

He didn't bother to respond to Ethan. He was tired of everyone asking him about stupid college every time there was a conversation happening. The only person he wanted to talk to about it now was April. He wasn't sure how to bring it up or when, but the next time he talked about college at all, it would be with her.

Michael swung one last time. This time he kept all his focus only on the ball and the cart. He imagined a dotted outline in front of him of exactly where he wanted the ball to fly. He waited patiently as the miniature car came speeding by this time.

The sharp clink sound was music to his ears. Both boys watched as the ball flew gracefully up through the air and zipped back down, perfectly timed to hit the tin top of the little cart and bounce out into one of the net-lined holes.

Michael: 7
Ethan: 0

"Sucks to lose doesn't it?" Michael smirked playfully at his tall friend. Ethan bit his tongue as he shook his head in annoyance.

"You know what? One of these days, you're going to see what it feels like to lose. And it will not be fun for you, my friend."

Michael chuckled to himself as he put his club away. He wouldn't ever have to worry about losing a stupid golf game to Ethan. After all, it was only golf.

April

Chapter 22

"We're breaking up."

The phrase kept repeating in her head over and over and over again. Like a broken record stuck on repeat. The rough, natural-based bristles of the paintbrush scrapped across the grey-blue base coating of the canvas. She dragged the brush over the heavy, storm-like waves that she created with her fingers. Her heart pounded as she let her emotions of anger, fear and frustration bleed messily all over her artwork.

She felt the tears surging behind her brown eyes. Her unsteady hands struggled to keep total control of the brush. The poetically conducted paint seemed to smear with little to no focus. She was stupid for even painting today in the first place. Another pointless ocean. Another waste of expensive material and precious time that she could be using to do absolutely anything else.

Her phone buzzed on the glossy, wooden floor beside her. She didn't even bother to pick it up and check. It was probably

Michael messaging to check-in on her again. She already told him today wasn't a good day. She wanted to be alone. He could tell she was upset, but April figured it was best that way to make sure he stayed away. She couldn't see him today. Not like this. Too messy and pathetic.

She looked down at her blue and white splattered hands. Glossy and toxic smelling. The contrast of colors on her skin made her feel like a piece of art herself for a sad moment. She stood up from her floor pillow to rinse her hands in the sink of her connecting bathroom. She watched as the paint that climbed up her arms tricked and spilled into the drain with the stream of hot water that ran down her skin.

As she looked back up into the mirror, she saw her sloppy, messy bun on the top of her head. She wore the blue and green and white stained grey t-shirt that she always wore when it was time to create. And then there were her eyes. Her puffy, swollen eyes. Pink and painful looking. Raw from a full day's worth of crying.

She heard her phone buzz again in the other room. Maybe it wasn't Michael after all. Maybe it was Anne. Or Scarlet. Or Preston. It didn't matter. No matter who it was, April did not want to talk to anyone today. Especially not Preston.

Her mind sunk as she remembered the conversation they had last night, where Preston told her that he and his girlfriend of over a year were breaking up officially. He didn't really explain why, no matter how many times April asked. Did it really matter though? Having dated Preston herself in the past, April was sure she could think of at least a dozen reasons why this girl she knew nothing about would break away from a guy like Preston Schuyler.

"We're breaking up," Preston had whispered over the FaceTime call. It was past midnight by then. The droopy effects of sleep had already started to kick in for April as she lied sideways in her bed. "I just find the timing so strange."

"What do you mean?" She closed her eyes, trying her best to stay awake.

"I mean, just weeks before me and my girlfriend break up, you and I start talking again?" He didn't sound sleepy. He sounded serious. "And both of these things happen just two months after you graduated high school? I mean, that can't just be a coincidence, April. It's like finally, everything is aligning for us. The way we always wished."

Although April was dozing off, she refused to wake up and acknowledge his suggestive comment. There was absolutely no way she was going to have this conversation with him. The best thing for her to do then was to just let sleep take its course and knock her out for the night without even having to hang up.

The thought had been running through her brain all day today, though. It was strange that all three of those events had lined up so evenly. What were the chances? And the fact that it was all happening months after April graduated high school? The timing was shocking. Scary even. Almost undeniably—

Three solid knocks come from the other side of April's bedroom door. Harper's voice rang from the hallway. "April, there's a package for you downstairs."

The artist dried her hands on a hideously bleached grey and brown towel, specifically designated for drying her painted hands only. April sniffled as she wiped the bottom of her nose with her wrist. "Okay, thanks. I'll get it tomorrow."

She turned on the faucet again to rinse her hands with soap. After a few seconds of scrubbing, the reflection of her sister's figure in the mirror startled her. She jumped as he turned around to face the rosy-cheeked girl.

"What the heck, Harper?" She gasped as one of her wet hands hit her pounding heart. She rolled her eyes in frustration as she tried to regain her focus. "You're going to give me a heart attack. Geez."

"Sorry, but you turned the water back on and couldn't hear me," Harper shook her head in defense. She scanned her sister's ever-changing shirt as she searched for new marks of cool colored paints.

"I said I'll go down and get the package tomorrow, okay?" April splashed her face with warm water, trying to get rid of the puffiness of her eyes before her sister could see how awful she looked.

"Actually, I really think you're going to regret not getting it now," Harper persisted.

April quickly made her way down the wooden staircase. Paint stained shirt, black sports short, messy bun and all. She hated surprises. But more than that, she hated suspense. She opened the backdoor of the house that was already cracked open to reveal a much bigger surprise than she was prepared for.

A handsome, blonde boy lifted his face to see the messy, colorful girl in front of him. In his hands, he held a large, brown paper bag of some mystery food. April felt her heart skip a beat as she stared at him, confused.

What is he doing here? I told him today wasn't a good day. He knows I'm upset. That's supposed to make him want to avoid me at all costs. Not be an invitation to come check up on me or whatever he thinks he's doing.

Michael squinted the slightest bit as he took in her messy look. "Hi. I know you said you weren't feeling well, but I just wanted to drop this off."

April stared blankly as the shy boy took a step up to place the bag in her arms. He was pleasant and calm. April tried to come up with every reason in her head why he shouldn't be here right now. He didn't even look nervous.

"Um, so I brought you chicken nuggets and large fries because I thought you might be hungry. Oh, and I got you mayo and ketchup packets so you could do that weird Puerto Rican thing where you mix them and dip your fries in it or whatever... Which, you know, I personally think is absolutely disgusting. But clearly, it makes you happy, so..." He sighed before smiling softly again. "Yeah. That's it."

Michael smiled pleasantly, but April didn't show any expression of emotion. She glanced down at the gifts she had just received. She was starving, with an odd craving for blueberry pancakes. But on days like this, she typically refused to feed her body anything as punishment for being upset in the first place. Why would he do this? What was he trying to get from her?

Clearly, he had to be doing this expecting some reward in return. What was his game?

"Alright, well, I'm going to go now. 'Cause I know you said you didn't want to talk about it. And that's okay," he smiled humbly. His green eyes sparkled in the sunlight. "Remember you can call me anytime if you change your mind."

April watched as Michael quickly walked over to his car and hopped in the front seat. She looked back at the food she held, now feeling more confused rather than angry.

What is going on? Michael couldn't have just driven all the way over here to buy me food I didn't even ask for and drive fifteen minutes back home for absolutely no reason. Where's the part where he pressures me into talking to him, promising it will make me feel better? Why didn't he even try to exchange the gifts for something more obvious like a kiss or uncomfortably long hug? What's the catch? Why would he do this?

She noted how the Jeep engine had stayed running the entire time he was standing at the door. She noticed the way he dropped off the food without even asking to come inside and intrude in her space. And most importantly, she watched in awe as his Jeep began backing its way out of the driveway to leave without expecting any sort of immediate reward in return. The act of kindness was almost unrecognizable to the young girl's warped vision.

"Michael, wait!" She closed the house door behind her as she jogged out to the moving car barefooted. She made it to his window just as he rolled it down.

"Yeah?" Michael waited with a look of worry on his face.

April stared at the bag again, still trying to figure out what she was secretly agreeing to by accepting these gifts. There had to be hidden strings attached. There was no way he could do something this selfless for her and not have a hidden agenda. Right?

"You look sad," Michael glanced down at her unique shirt. April thought for a moment, unsure of how she still felt. She was trying to read him. She wanted to know what he was secretly trying to gain from this moment.

He reached out of the car and placed his hand on hers as he carefully stroked her wrist. April watched his finger glide across her skin. He was always so careful with her. So gentle and patient. It was almost like he was actually paying attention to her, trying to figure out what she needed in these moments. Not what he wanted.

"Michael?" Her frail voice broke its way to the surface of her throat. He barely scrunched his eyebrows. He looked worried. Not manipulative. He stroked her hand. He felt comforting. Not pushy.

"Yeah?" He half-smiled.

Her gaze jumped around as she tried to get up the guts to tell him the truth. What had really been on her mind all day. It was better if he knew now so he could decide to stay today or not.

Tell him the truth.

April fidgeted as she tried to muster up the courage to speak up. She did need to tell him the truth. He had the right to know the truth. April opened her mouth again and let her deep, inner thoughts speak for themselves.

"Will you hold me?" April felt her body freeze.

She wasn't sure where that came from. That was not the truth she was supposed to tell him. One of the last things April wanted to do was have any sort of physical contact with anyone at this moment. She wanted to be alone. Isolated. Far away where no one could reach her or use her or try and use her vulnerability as leverage. Touch was the last thing she needed right now.

Don't do this, April. Don't get too comfortable. You're being a burden. You're going to get too attached. What happens when he leaves you and you have to go back to taking care of your own heart without him? You're going to regret this. You're setting yourself up to get hurt all over again. You're only making things worse, April.

The two of them spent over an hour by the pool that evening. Michael told April lots of stories from his time at camp while she shared her french fries with him. And April just sat there listening. She knew he was intentionally picking his funniest stories, mainly because they all included Jimmy in them.

Michael's storytelling sent happy hormones dancing from her brain all the way down to her feet as she couldn't help but laugh at his humor. His impersonations of Jenni and Nick triggered feelings of nostalgia as she realized how much she was going to miss her friends in a few months when she left. Her mood had changed since the girl who first stood at the door a few hours before. Still mellow, slightly sad. But less closed off then she had originally tried to be.

After a few minutes of peaceful silence, Michael took her hand and led them to the beautiful dogwood tree that patiently waited in the backyard of April's house. The calm boy sat in the grass, leaning his back against the thin trunk of the green and white decorated tree. He scooted closer to April's side as she wrapped her arms around his torso and rested her head on his chest. Her thin fingers gripped his sweater tight as she listened to his steady heartbeat.

Michael leaned his cheek on top of her head and sighed. She breathed in sync with the slow rise and fall of his chest that her head was on. Her confusion slowly melted away. His arms around her made her feel safe. What a strange feeling for a girl who constantly felt fearful.

He just held her. Totally patient. Incredibly selfless. Her heart calmed down. And her mind shut up. Completely enveloped in the smell of his sweater.

A minute went by. Then a few more. Neither of them moved. April eventually lost track of the time that melted by. There was the occasional squeeze Michael would give her every few minutes. He'd take a breath in as he slowly tightened his arms around her. Her eyes would shut as her whole body was compressed for a moment. Her heart felt warm. Then he'd release her and carefully dance his thumb across her bicep.

She wished she never had to leave. She wished she could just stay wrapped in his arms forever with a quiet mind and resting heart. It was like she got to leave her anxious body for a moment and become a whole other girl. One who wasn't bruised or scared, but instead safe and calm. The person she always wished she could be but didn't believe was possible.

The incoming clouds whispered that it was getting late.

Michael had to go home soon before it got dark. As much as she didn't want to move, April knew this couldn't last forever. It was time to go back to reality.

She sat up slowly and turned to his sleepy face. He blinked slowly as he studied her for a long moment. He was trying to read her. She closed her eyes and smiled softly, reassuring him she was fine. But when she opened her eyes, he was still studying her, carefully searching her eyes. His eyebrows rested with a hint of concern. Slowly, Michael leaned his face into hers. Naturally, the purple haired girl closed her eyes, expecting a kiss.

I told you. This was the real reason he showed up.

A few lonely seconds ticked by. But nothing came. A few more seconds passed. Nothing. April fluttered her eyes open to see Michael's dark green eyes staring into hers. He was hesitating. Why?

Michael's eyes moved to her lips. He watched for a moment, and then barely leaned in again. April closed her eyes a second time. But nothing happened.

What is happening? Isn't this why he came here? To kiss me and pretend to be the hero and leave feeling good about himself? Just take your reward already and leave. I don't know what else you want from me.

Suddenly, April unexpectedly felt Michael's nose press against the side of her cheek. His forehead leaned into hers. And he didn't move. April closed her eyes as she tried to understand. He just held her for the longest moment, his sturdy arms holding her small body like that was all that mattered.

Finally, April turned her face to his and this time, he did kiss her. The softest kiss in the history of kisses. So gentle and calm, April didn't even have the opportunity to kiss him back. It felt like a sweet flower petal brushing against her upper lip. Delicate and airbrushed. Careful and beautiful. There one second. Gone the next. Just like a raindrop.

April's eyes fluttered open as Michael watched her. She felt seen. She felt vulnerable.

"Please, tell me the truth," Michael whispered. He stared deep into her eyes, his gaze so sincere. "What's going on, April?"

The truth was that right there, at that moment, under the tree and being held by Michael, April really did feel okay. She felt safe and secure and cared for. The best feeling in the world was being able to sink into someone's arms and not have to worry about anything else in life for a few short seconds. Not college or money or family situations or even the person holding you.

"I'll be okay," April whispered. Her heart felt so overwhelmed. This moment wasn't forced. It was real. It was raw. "You're a really good guy, Michael."

The boy blushed and shook his head at the ground before gently running his hands over the messy flyaways of her bun.

"I just don't like seeing you upset," he smiled softly. "You don't have to be scared of me, April. I hope you know that by now."

April closed her eyes and nodded slowly. She wanted to believe his words. He probably meant them. Or at least Michael probably thought he did. But he didn't know anything about April. And if he did, he wouldn't be able to handle her hurricane of her constantly aching heart anyway.

She smiled painfully as she sunk back into his arms so she wouldn't have to look any deeper into his ever-changing eyes.

Michael

Chapter 23

She just sat there. Quietly picking at her fries. It was an odd thing for her to get quiet. Everyone knew April was a talker. Whenever her mouth shut for long periods, something had to be off. But even though her lips weren't moving, he could see the wheels spinning in her head. He could feel the vibrations of all the loud gears turning faster and faster as the minutes went by. Her jaw was clenched, and her shoulders were slumped. She looked disconnected from her environment for a few lonely moments.

Michael wondered how loud it must have been in her head. Maybe it was chaotic, like pots and pans banging together so loudly that she couldn't even hear the sound of the crying baby screaming and bawling in the booth next to them, desperately calling for his mom to give him the pacifier she held in her hand. Or maybe it was more subtle, he wondered, like the sharp sound of her ears ringing at such a piercing pitch that there was the possibility it could somehow cause permanent damage to her hearing.

"What are you doing?" She snapped out of her daze. He was holding up his phone, camera aimed right at her.

"I'm taking a picture to send to Ethan," he started tapping his screen with his thumb, typing something to their friend.

"I wasn't ready," she barked defensively. Without saying a word, Michael turned his screen to face her. A dazed and confused looking girl stared off at whatever might be distracting her on the wall behind the lens. She examined the picture for a moment as if she saw the resemblance but still didn't recognize the purple haired girl displayed before her. Embarrassed, her eyes fluttered to the table.

"Please don't send that to anyone. I'm sorry," she finally forced herself to make eye contact again. "I didn't realize I was doing it... again."

Michael lightly pressed his lips together and gently breathed through his nose, the way he always did when he got slightly annoyed. He placed the phone face down next to his half-empty glass of sweet tea and stared at the drink for a moment. He noticed the way the tiny beads of condensation collected in a uniform pattern halfway down the surface of the cup. The contrast between the dark sugary liquid and the clear pellets kept him distracted for a few seconds. Only a few seconds.

He couldn't help but feel frustrated with her. He wanted to be sympathetic and sensitive towards April, but in a lot of ways, he felt the tiniest bit of resentment clinging to his chest instead. Resentment towards the fact that this wasn't the first time she had done this during one of their dates in the past two weeks. Zoning out was becoming a reoccurring pattern.

"Was it something I said?" He broke the awkward silence. Michael genuinely wanted to understand what went wrong. Somewhere between the two of them poking fun at her brother and the waitress coming to bring back the check, there had only been a two-minute window for something to have happened to cause her mouth to zip shut.

"No, no," she shook her head while poking her fries with her finger. He could almost swear he saw a little grey rain cloud floating above her head sprinkling a mood-changing mist on her scalp. As if it was shifting the once cool temperature of the room to a now uncomfortable warmth. Even though they had just acknowledged her new little friend, the rain cloud didn't seem to get the hint that it was no longer welcome to stay for the rest of dinner. "It's not you. You didn't do anything wrong."

April reached across the table and rested her naturally tan hand on top of his light skin. Her dark brown eyes searched his face as if she was considering telling him something. Maybe whatever was rattling in that head of hers. Instead, her lips parted and closed again. She glanced down at his pale hand and gave it a gentle squeeze.

"I promise. It's not you. You're great," she smiled lightly, scanning his blonde hair with her eyes.

She was always telling him that. 'It's not your fault. I promise. You're great. You're the best.'

But if he really was so great, then why did it always feel like he was doing something wrong? Why was it that some days, without warning, something inside this girl would switch like the power going out of an art museum? All the perfectly illuminated displays suddenly hidden and kept secret, no longer available to be studied or interpreted. How could they go from joking and laughing to all of a sudden complete silence without any explanation?

She had been imitating her brother before, reciting cheesy romantic movie lines in his continuously deepening voice. She was cracking herself up while trying to do his signature look: right eyebrow cocked, slightly squinted eyes, half-smirk. Considering they already had similar features, she did a pretty accurate 'Christopher' impression.

"But I mean, who am I to judge?" She had giggled before. "Some girls buy that stuff."

"He's such a player," Michael smiled. Less at the idea of Chris and more with amusement that April was getting such a kick out of teasing her brother without him being in the room to defend himself.

"But I mean, what are you supposed to do, right?" She sighed, putting her glass back on the wooden table. She shook her head at the basketball game playing on the flatscreen TV propped on the wall behind Michael. "He's gonna break some girl's heart."

"Lots of girls," Michael corrected. April had tilted her head to the side, still not taking her eyes off the screen ahead of her.

"Well, yes. There will be more than one. But Chris? He's not your average player. He'll take quality over quantity."

Michael just stared at the booth next to him in confusion. He had noticed a baby boy with blue eyes starting to fuss in his uncomfortable wooden high chair.

"Some guys are like that, ya know?" She had continued. "They don't necessarily care about how many girls they can get. They just want the *best* one. They pick a girl and say, 'That's her. That's the one I want.' They stroll into the room like Prince Charming to sweep a helpless girl away with all the cheesy lines and promises we are force-fed through magical movies and dramatic books. All he has to do is follow the script and the girl believes this is what love is supposed to be. It takes a special type of guy to take pride in how *deeply* he can get a girl attached. Not how *many* girls. I see some of that in my brother sometimes. If I'm being honest, it scares me some days."

That was when the waitress had popped in to interrupt their conversation. Even after replaying through their conversation in his head, Michael still couldn't find where he had gone wrong. Did he miss something?

The stroke of her smooth thumb against his hand brought him back to the present.

"I'm sorry, it's not your fault. I'm okay now. I promise." April sighed. Exhausted. From what? Michael did not know. She forced a sympathetic smile. "I'm ready to go now if you are."

He could still see the little rain cloud dancing above her head. Taunting him. Taunting her. He wanted to know how to get rid of it. He wished he knew how to keep it from showing up uninvited altogether.

The drive back to April's house was a quiet one. She didn't

hum to the usual 80's playlist they listened to. She didn't dance or sway or sing at all. The precipitation that collected on the windshield cluttered up the glass until the mist turned into sprinkles, and the sprinkles turned into showers. The steady cry of the clouds beat down loudly against the glossy glass as the windshield wipers swiped back and forth slowly across their views. The gloomy clouds above seemed to be sick from their own sadness.

Michael didn't know what to do. He didn't know what to say or offer to somehow make this uncomfortable situation any better for the two of them. He wished she would just talk to him. Why couldn't she tell him what had been going on with her lately? He wished he could reach her where she was. He just didn't know how to.

Without saying a word, Michael's warm hand reached out to take April's cold hand that was sitting limply in her lap. She blinked hastily as her brown eyes made their way from the watery window to her fingers that Michael now laced his own through on her lap. He sighed heavily as he watched the incoming bypass they were about to drive under.

The rain cut off as the Jeep flew under the safety of the concrete structure above them. For a few short seconds, there was complete silence. No music. No thunder. No rain. And for a split moment, Michael could almost swear he felt April begin to release the breath she had been holding.

'It's okay, April,' He thought and gave her hand a gentle squeeze.

Immediately, the splashing of heavy rain came beating back

down on the Jeep as it emerged on the other side of the bypass, pouring even harder from the grey sky than before. Just like that, the moment was gone.

"I'll wait with you in the car when we get there," Michael whispered as he took their exit. "You don't have to rush out into the rain."

April nodded silently in agreement.

The two quiet teenagers sat patiently in the driveway as the clouds continued overflowing all over the neighborhood. Both their hands were still intertwined, both kids still sat in silence. Michael didn't mind the untimely situation. He was thankful to be able to sit with April in her silence for a few minutes.

His eyes wandered to the hand that he held. Her tan skin looked more bronze than olive in the summertime. Her miniature nails were bare but well-groomed. Michael could still see the faintest specks of blue paint under the tips of them. His gaze landed on the black and blue bracelet April always wore, now that he was up close and still, he was able to make out the shape of the three turquoise beads on her wrist. They were dolphins.

Michael had spent so many weeks when they were just friends trying to figure out what was on that black bracelet that never left her wrist. The waxy band was thin but intricately braided all the way around. Michael used his free hand to take the piece of jewelry between his fingers as he studied it further.

He brushed his thumb over the glossy sea creatures. They were roughly shaped, made of some sort of turquoise rock or stone. Now that he could easily see the details of the piece,

Michael thought the bracelet looked slightly exotic. Maybe a souvenir from an island her family had gone to on one of their recent summer vacations.

April's wrist unexpectedly slid away from his grasp. He noticed how small and tense her body had gotten in the past few seconds. Before he knew it, she was ripping the bracelet off her wrist and cramming it into her thin black purse sitting on the floor of the car.

April closed her eyes as she tried to find the words. Her mouth hung open. Her eyebrows furrowed. Her head barely shook side to side as if she were saying 'no.'

"Michael," she spoke softly. Her voice became louder as she started to ramble with her eyes closed. "I'm so sorry. I'm so... awkward and weird and confusing and that was weird— what I just did was super weird and I'm sorry I didn't mean to just make things weird by taking off the bracelet I just— I don't know why I do this..."

Michael felt bad for wanting to laugh... But he did want to laugh. The entire moment was to the point of awkwardness that it was almost comical. So out of nowhere and unexpected and weird that he felt he might not be able to hold in his laughter.

Michael pinched his lips together tightly as he tried to hold back. April slowly peeked over at the boy. When she saw the way his eyebrows were raised and lips were sealed shut, her face grew bright as a messy flood of giggles exploded from her. Michael practically spat all over the car as his laughter came tumbling out of him.

"I'm sorry!" Michael hid his face with his hands as he flipped out still. "I couldn't help it. I laugh when things get really awkward."

"Thank goodness you laughed!" April belly laughed as her hand gripped his shoulder. "I was over here literally dying of embarrassment. I was like, 'Oh my gosh, April. What have you done?'"

They both laughed even harder as she exaggerated her responses. April's face was bright red with embarrassment, but at least she was laughing. A real laugh where her eyes squeezed tightly shut and her mouth cracked open as her voice boomed throughout the car.

Michael leaned into her arm as he chuckled loudly still. He rubbed his face with his hands as he tried to get his laughter to settle down some, but his stomach wouldn't let him just yet. Out of nowhere, the faint sound of a phone ringing barely got both of their attention. April reached for her purse and went digging for her device before checking the incoming FaceTime call on the screen.

"Oh," April's giggles began to fade. She stared at the phone for a long second as Michael's chuckles naturally drifted off as well.

He watched her phone before speaking up. "You can answer it if you want."

The rain had only calmed down a little, but the chances of April making it from here to her door without getting drenched still wasn't looking too great. The skies would have cleared up in at least another ten minutes according to the weather app.

"Um… No. It's fine." April started to strap her bag on her shoulder and readjust herself in her seat to get out of the car. "I was going to go inside soon anyway."

Michael looked at the windows all around them. Was April seeing something he wasn't? "April, it's pouring outside."

"Yeah, I know. I'll be okay." She quickly shrugged and leaned across the seat to plant a quick kiss on his right cheek. "Thanks for dinner. Goodnight."

"Wait, April," Michael stopped her from opening the door by gently grabbing her arm closest to him. She froze before slowly turning to face him. The blonde boy hesitated before taking a deep breath in. "There's something I need to talk to you about."

April studied his face for a second. Her expression was completely blank with emotion. She glanced back down at her phone that was still buzzing in her hand. She watched it for a second before silencing the ringer.

"Okay," she leaned back in her seat and watched his eyes, cautiously. She crossed her arms and searched his face as if she were the one that was defensive all of a sudden. Michael felt a pit rising in his stomach. He knew what he wanted to say, he just hadn't figured out how to say it yet. It had been three weeks since they got back from their camps and he still hadn't figured out the right way to address the subject. His time was practically up already.

"So, I got all my acceptance letters back," he tried to act casual, but the knot in his stomach was only twisting itself tighter and tighter by the second. "Well, actually, I got all of them back a long time ago. In the spring, actually. My mom had just been hiding one of them this whole time, which is crazy. But it's fine now. I called them and they said everything was fine, and I was still able to enroll."

Michael paused for a second, waiting to see if April had any questions or comments that could redirect the attention off of him for even a moment. But April only sat there, still staring blankly. He wondered if she could even hear him. Had he said anything this whole time? Or was this entire conversation happening in his imagination and in reality, he was still sitting here trying to get up the courage to speak?

"Which college?" April finally asked, dryly. She looked more annoyed than curious. Michael took a deep breath before spitting the words out.

"Georgia Southern."

Once again, there was no reaction from April. Not a facial expression, not a sound, not even a blink. Michael wanted to make a joke to lighten the mood, but even he felt the tension in the car was too heavy for such a thing.

"You know, Georgia Southern?" Michael repeated. "It's pretty close to Savannah."

Michael couldn't tell how April was taking this. So far, she was acting as if he were a stranger on the street.

"Why would you apply there?" Her tone became more defensive the longer she spoke. "I thought you wanted to go to UGA?"

Michael sighed through his nose as he pressed the back of his head against his seat. This conversation was already becoming much more difficult than he had originally anticipated.

"It's not my dream school or anything. I don't really care that much *where* I go," he sighed.

"Well, I know you don't care that much about *which* school it is because you honestly don't even seem that excited about any colleges in the first place, but UGA is obviously your best option." Why was she getting so aggressive?

He squinted his eyes. "Yeah I know, but—"

April interrupted him before he could even finish his thought. "Then I don't even understand what the point is of even considering Georgia Southern. What? Like, do you even *know* any friends who go to that school?"

Her face now scrunched up with frustration as her volume crescendoed. Michael didn't understand why she was getting so unbelievably triggered. She was ranting to him as if she were his mother or something. April didn't even look at Michael anymore, instead, she ranted to the bottom of the steering wheel across from her. Michael felt his entire body tensing as her level of overreaction continued to increase. He had never seen her act like this before.

"You got accepted into UGA," she ranted. "Ethan is going to UGA and you said that was why you wanted to go there, right? Isn't that what you've been saying this whole time? Is that why you won't just pick a college already because suddenly Georgia Southern is, like, some random option for you? Why in the world would there be any other options for you? I just don't get how you could even—"

Michael finally exploded. "Gosh, April! Will you just chill out for one second?"

The only sound that could be heard now was the faint dripping of water all around the outside of the car. Peaceful and quiet. But not happy. Michael sighed heavily. He hadn't meant to get so frustrated with her. This was not how the conversation was supposed to go at all. This wasn't even a conversation anymore. It wasn't even an argument either. Michael didn't know what to call it, but whatever it was, he hated it.

The awkward silence between them grew bigger and bigger. It kept bleeding as the seconds passed, taking up all the space in the car, completely crushing their bodies like the uncomfortable water pressure of diving too deep in the ocean. Michael sighed heavily as he wiped the edge of his brow bone with his fingertips. He felt sadder than any other emotion now.

Michael noticed the rain outside the windows had stopped. It must had been at some point during their loud discussion of sorts. He watched as the green leaves on the tree closest to his window dripped with leftover water from the previous rain shower. The colors were vibrant and saturated even under the cloudy sky.

"You shouldn't even consider me in this," she finally whispered. Her voice was low, dripping in insecurity and sadness. "It's not like we're even that serious anyway."

April popped the passenger door open and stepped out of the Jeep before Michael even had the chance to respond. Like a thunderclap, the car door slammed back shut. The black interior was lightly misted with cool water. He stared blankly at the door handle as he felt the previous tension in his body melting away. His bones slowly started to grow heavy.

There it was. There was his answer his friends had said he so badly needed. Michael hated to secretly admit that he was not completely shocked. He felt deep down he had secretly known April's answer all along. He just hadn't had the guts to admit it to himself until now.

How could he be this surprised, though? She had been keeping herself hidden from him emotionally since the night she hit his head with her car trunk. He couldn't keep lying to himself anymore. April had one foot out of the water since the beginning. And Michael needed to stop lying to himself.

Chapter 24

Cleaning the sticky, sugary substance that was spilled on the cold, black marble countertop was the least favorite part of her job. The squishy rag wiped back and forth as her hand glided across the cool surface of the counter. Closing the shop on her own wasn't part of her normal routine. At this time of night, the windows brought in no light. The bubbly music of the store that typically kept her company was absent this time.

She needed the silence. She craved loneliness. Her head was pinched tight with a headache that even her pills of aspirin had lost their fight to. How much more medicine could she force herself to swallow without accidentally harming herself? Her family probably didn't even own any medicine to deal with this level of tightening in her skull. She would just have to deal with it the way she always forced herself to: shut up and get over it.

A dozen tubs of colorful ice cream each were capped with a large, plastic lid. April lifted the half-empty gallons out of their seats and stored them in the massive freezer in the back of the shop. One by one, she walked the cumbersome containers to their temporary homes for the night. The coffee machines had already been cleaned out. All the snacks and fruits were prepped and ready to go for tomorrow morning. All that was left to do was turn out the lights and lock up for the night.

April looked around at the little space. So empty and alone. She had spent the past six months working at this hidden gem in Vinings. Only six more weeks at BitterSweet and she would be off to her dream college down in Savannah, Georgia.

Savannah.

April felt a heavy tug of weight in her heart. She closed her eyes as she roughly massaged her forehead with the palm of her hand.

'Shut up. Shut up.' She told herself. 'Stop thinking about it. It doesn't matter.'

She clicked on her phone to distract herself from the uncomfortable thought.

3 missed calls. 4 new messages.

All from Scarlet. April had been avoiding her best friend for the past two days. She knew she wouldn't be able to talk to her without bringing up Michael. Which would force her to confess about Preston. She couldn't do it. She had already dug her hole too deep. She wished she could fake it with Scarlet the way she attempted to fake it with everyone else around her.

4:45 pm: Missed Call from Scarlet

4:45 pm Scarlet: Hey! Are you at work?

6:21 pm: Missed Call from Scarlet

6:22 pm Scarlet: You can't avoid me forever, Chica.

7:57 pm Scarlet: You better be at work... That should be your only excuse for ignoring the LIGHT OF YOUR LIFE right now because I am a DELIGHT!

7:58 pm: Missed Call from Scarlet

7:59 pm Scarlet: ANSWER THE PHONE, DINGUS!!

April thought about how she should be calling Preston. He had told her last night he was going on a long car trip after he got out of classes today at Indiana State. She couldn't recall if he had mentioned where he was driving to, but it was 10:30 on a Friday night. He should have been at whatever party he was headed to already. Or at least close to it. He most likely wouldn't need April to keep him company on the trip anymore. She would talk to him tomorrow. Or whenever she assumed would be the most convenient time for him.

The little grey typing bubble popped up under Scarlet's messages. April panicked the slightest bit when she saw it bouncing for a few seconds.

10:32 pm Scarlet: Well now I KNOW you're ignoring me... you have your read receipts on, genius.

Dang it.

April forgot about the read receipts. Her fingers hovered over the digital keyboard as she tried to think of some crappy excuse to blame other than her cowardice spirit. What should she say? That it had been a long day? Her phone died before she could respond? Maybe she could text her friend tomorrow morning and say she had been planning on responding tonight after she got home but magically forgot all about it by accident.

A new message appeared.

10:33 pm Scarlet: Okay, so clearly you're not in the mood to talk, and that's fine. I won't push you anymore. But just know that I'm here when you're ready. You're obviously upset about something and have been for a while now. I just want to make sure you're okay so you don't do something stupid like call Preston or get in a fight with Michael or something bad.

April pinched her lips together. Scarlet knew her all too well. She was only a bit too late to save her this time. That was part of why April couldn't bring herself to respond. Or talk to anyone for that matter. It was too humiliating for her to admit.

10:33 pm Scarlet: Anyway. I love you. I hope you're just taking some time to think through whatever you're going through right now (and making good choices.) I'm here whenever you're ready. Goodnight. I love you.

April stared blankly at her phone. After a few moments of heavy silence, she shut the screen off and let it hit the countertop. Her hands slowly ran over the surface of her face as she held her breath. Her knuckles pressed against her forehead like a rock to a brick wall. When she lifted her eyes again, they met with a messy girl in the distant reflection of dark, glass doors ahead. Shoulders slumped. Lips drooping. Forehead slightly scrunched. Loose strands of hair falling out of her messy braid.

This wasn't the beautiful, confident girl she had presented herself as to Michael five months ago. Look at what he was stuck with now. A mess of a lonely girl who refused to take help from anyone, no matter how desperately she might need it. No one else would understand. No one else would actually be able to help the way they thought they could. Everyone made it seem so simple. "Just be happy." "Stop worrying so much." "Pray about it." But all those phrases only seemed to make April feel more alone than before. Like with each time those words were said, they were pushing her one inch further away.

"Time will help. You'll get over him eventually. Don't beat yourself up. It'll be fine."

Why did people always say that? "Time will help." How much time? It had been almost two years. Why couldn't she just "let go" the way people told her to? As if she hadn't tried that before. They made it seem like she was just holding onto this empty silhouette of a person. Knuckles white, eyes squeezed shut. As if it was a choice. As if she was the one holding onto this feeling of emptiness.

But that wasn't how April would paint it if she could. This burden felt like being trapped at the bottom of a lightless ocean. Covered and laced and tangled in heavy chains that wrapped around her body and kept her tied to the floor of the sea. It wasn't about her choosing to let the feeling go from her hands. She wanted this feeling to let go of her heart. She wanted to be free.

Her thin fingers snatched the cold keys off the shiny counter and locked the front door behind her. She hopped into the driver seat of her little green car and began her brief drive back to her house. With one elbow propped up on the window beside her, she ran her fingers through the edges of her fading purple hair under the pattern of streetlights that lit up the car every few seconds. She hadn't touched up her hair dye in several weeks, making the usually vibrant purple look more grey, lavender. Faded and dull.

She tried to plan in her head how she was going to do it. More importantly, when she was going to do it. How much longer would she and Michael be able to not talk before he tried to break it off first? April hated that idea. The idea of him dumping her. She would avoid it at all costs. She had to push him away just enough to make him think he couldn't stand her anymore, and then right as he was ready to break, she would be the one to say she was done. It would hurt her less that way. It would hurt Michael too, but he would be fine. He wasn't as attached as she was anyway.

April pulled her little car into the stone driveway of her family's house. Turning off her engine, she sat for a moment staring off into the darkness, soaking in the silence of her safe space. She didn't want to go inside her house. The sound of her stomach growling snapped her out of her daze.

It's fine. One day without food isn't going to hurt you. You'll survive.

April rubbed her face again, trying to somehow press the pressure out with her fingertips. She didn't want to be awake right now. She didn't want to cry. She wanted to massage her arms until they stopped feeling sore the way they did tonight. She had no choice but to go inside.

April lazily got out of her car and swung the door shut. She slowly followed the little porch lights beside the garage that glowed like captured drops of sunlight in the darkness of the pitch-black sky above. If the stars had been showing tonight, she might have considered staying out. Watching the stars always helped her think better. But the thick, dark clouds cut off the girl from her usually favorite season.

The sky didn't sparkle tonight the way it usually did in the summertime. The air was cool. Slightly chilly even. Surprise thunderstorms raced their way towards her little neighborhood. Lonely. Dark. She was only halfway across the driveway when her stomach dropped at the sound of heavy footsteps racing behind her.

"Don't scream," a deep voice muttered from behind and grabbed her arm aggressively. Throat tightening, body tensing, panic overwhelmed the isolated girl. She wanted to scream. She needed to scream. But she had no air in her lungs to do so. Her mouth hung open, empty of sound. Her fate was decided for her.

The man tugged her backward as she crashed into the closeness of his stiff body. The frantic girl struggled to jerk herself out of his grasp. The man's second hand covered her mouth to keep her silent. Her chest felt like it was collapsing into itself. Her body shook as if it were going into shock as she thrashed around trying to free herself from his grasp.

"Shhhh! Shhh!" The deep voice demanded. A beautiful voice. Almost musical even. "April, stop it. Calm down. It's me."

Her terrified eyes finally connected with his. Long dark lashes. Thick eyebrows. Messy dark hair. His eyes may have looked brown without light, but April could've recognized that voice anywhere.

The one word barely slipped through her lips. "Preston?"

An icy chill ran through the current in her veins. A flood of emotions consumed April's frantic little heart as she tried to connect the years of memories to this stranger in front of her. This guy— this young *man*— was not the boy she last said goodbye to two summers ago back in the Bahamas. He was taller. Shoulders broader. Arms more defined. Jawline chiseled. More grown-up looking than she had ever expected. She had seen his scruffy face on FaceTime a dozen times in the past weeks, but this person standing in front of her right now? This was completely different.

"Surprise," he whispered sweetly. His intoxicating eyes were intensely locked into hers. The familiar face smiled slyly as his hand that covered her mouth slid down the side of her cheek. He held her face tightly for a moment as he watched her hyperventilating body start to calm down.

Who was this 20-year-old man holding on to her in the middle of the night in Georgia? Who was this stranger who stared so deeply into her eyes as if he knew her with all his heart? April didn't know. Where was the 15-year-old boy with shaggy hair who sent her an innocent bouquet of roses for Valentine's Day? Where was the confident 17-year-old boy who held her hand and told her he was in love with her for the very first time? Where was the passionate 18-year-old boy who promised her his whole future on that ship if she promised the same? This was not that boy. Where was that boy?

"What—what?" April squirmed. She struggled to carefully release her arm from his grip as she sluggishly tiptoed backward away from him. "What are you— when did you—?"

"You don't seem as happy as I thought you would," Preston chuckled light-heartedly as he took a step closer. April stepped back in sync with him to maintain their little distance between each other. Her eyes studied him, trying to see who she once saw years ago. "Geez, April. You look like you've seen a ghost."

April felt as if her beating organ was trying to jump out of her chest and run far away. She struggled to find words as her frantic brain tried to keep up with her pounding pulse. She needed someone to run outside and be the buffer between these two elements. Like playing with a match near a field of dry grass, Preston was a fire hazard.

"Preston," April fought to push the words out of her straining throat. Her hands felt clammy and raw. "What do you think you're doing?"

Preston blinked slowly, pretending to be completely oblivious to how uncomfortable and scared she looked. Maybe he thought if he pretended this was romantic, April would have to see it that way as well. His intentions were being masked. April knew it. But he was here for something. He came with an agenda. He always did.

"I'm here to see you, April," he blinked slowly. "I thought you'd be happy to see me." Preston smiled as he took another step closer but she stepped back in perfect timing with him, refusing to let less than three feet of space separate them.

A glimmer of recognition flashed over his dark eyes. He ever so slightly tilted his head down as he realized she wasn't going along with the script he had most likely been rehearsing in his head the entire drive here.

April crossed her arms and squeezed herself tightly. She stared into the darkness behind him as she tried not to think too much. She couldn't stand to look at him. It hurt too much. It brought back all her memories that she had spent years trying to shrink until they were dried and shriveled up only to feel like silly dreams. But that night, looking at Preston only sent an unstoppable wave over her hidden heart. It saturated all those forgotten dreams and brought them back to life. Real and intense. Alive and reckless. This wasn't a fair fight. It never was with Preston.

"I want you to go," April forced the words out without looking at his face. "I didn't ask you to come here."

"You didn't need to," Preston sighed with relief. "I know you. I know us. I missed you."

April bit the inside of her lip. Could he even hear the garbage coming out of his mouth? What movie did he think this was? What fantasy land was he trying to pull her into this time? She wanted him to drop the act.

"What do you want?" She snapped.

He paused, licking his lips as he shook his head at her feet. He looked so different than she remembered. Where was the 16-year-old boy who chased her around the amusement park until dark so many years ago? Where was the 17-year-old boy who used to build palaces with his words and pull her into his glittery version of reality? Who was this stranger she stared at?

"April, there's something I've been wanting to say to you. And I just couldn't wait any longer."

No. No. Don't listen to him. He's just trying to get in your head. He doesn't mean it. Don't listen to him.

The charming boy kept his eyes locked on hers, although she refused to look at his face. He spoke calmly, and deeply, knowing the exact things to say to make her heart run after him even when she didn't want to.

"You know, when you called me that night a few weeks

ago, I was so surprised. Hearing your voice again was just... it did something to me."

His voice sung to her like a crying cello, the familiar song bringing back heavy waves of nostalgia to her mind. The problem with April was that sometimes she only paid attention to how the music made her feel rather than what the lyrics were saying. Still, he continued to play louder. And still, she continued to listen only to the melody.

"You always do something to my heart, April. Something I've never felt with anyone else before. I don't know how to describe it." He knew exactly where she hurt. He knew exactly what to say to make her scarred heart burst out of its cage and go running back to him without her mind's consent.

"April, you're special. No one makes me feel the way you do." His tone was sincere and believable. His posture was tall and strong. April closed her eyes as she tried to keep a grip on the pain that wanted to show itself. He inched towards her again but this time she didn't move away. Her body felt too overwhelmed to even do so anymore. She kept her eyelids shut as he continued to use his words to persuade her the way he always did.

He shook his head. "April... I'm in love with—"

"Stop," she snapped. Her chest rose and fell as she fought to keep her eyes closed. "Preston, please stop."

She could sense him stepping closer again. Still, she didn't move her feet. She only slightly turned her head to the side, as if that would somehow help protect her heart.

"I feel like we're supposed to be together," he continued.

"I said to stop talking," she scrunched her eyebrows in discomfort. She could feel the broken strings of her heart whispering. That desperate, aching girl inside of her chest starting to sit up in the cage she had been locked away in for so long.

He stood only inches away. Her arms ached in pain as she hugged herself tighter and turned her face further away. She couldn't bear to look at him. He was a smoking cigarette coming too close to her gasoline drenched heart. There was no way to save her now. Her demons were banging on their cages, fighting to break loose.

"I've always believed that. From the moment I saw you," Preston grazed her elbows with his fingers, sending an awful electric shock through her aching bones. Her body involuntarily jerked back as she suddenly shoved his hands away. His sweet serenade was cut off, leaving instead a high-pitch ringing in April's ears.

The roaring silence between the two of them pierced the air like a knife. The young man's face went sour, taking a moment to let the reality of the moment sink in.

This was not romantic. This was not magical. This was not as easy as he had originally thought it would be. However, Preston wasn't a fan of losing.

"Wow," his eyes glossed over. "Why do you always treat me like this, April? Like I'm the bad guy?"

The girl's shoulders sunk as the shame started to sink in. She knew this song all too well. It always started sweet and intriguing but took a dramatic key change by the bridge. This was the part she liked the least.

"I want you to go," she spoke firmly.

"You want me to go?" Preston repeated back as if he hadn't heard her the first three times she had said it. He crossed his arms and shook his head at the ground. His eyes sparkled with sadness as if she had just seriously hurt his fragile feelings. "April, you're the one that wanted me here."

"What?" Her eyes started to sting with tears. He was up to something. She could feel it. Even the storm that was fast approaching in the city could feel it. His words were being laced together to form another trap for her. She clenched her fists as she braced herself for whatever he was preparing to hit her with next. "No, I didn't."

"Really?" He squinted his dark eyes, his body exuding authority. "Then why did you even call me in the first place?"

April felt her throat tighten. He was cornering her. She knew where this was going. His words were sharp and poisonous. She saw the pity in his gaze as he acted completely innocent.

"Who have you fallen asleep with on the phone every night for the past week and a half?" His irritated voice continued to rise. "Who do you spend all day texting and sharing your problems with? Who did you call crying last night when you and your dad got into an argument? Your boyfriend? Scarlet? Harper? No. Me. So you tell me, April," his sharp tone reeked with dominance. "Why am I here right now?"

The sad girl sniffled as a roll of thunder barley roared out in the distance. She couldn't remember the exact moment it had happened, but her arms were back to hugging her body tightly.

She sniffled again as the tears began to puddle in the corners of her eyes.

April didn't have an answer. She didn't know why she had pulled Preston back into her life again just when things had finally gotten good for her. She thought in the beginning that she had it all under control.

If she could just keep him in her phone, maybe she wouldn't have to officially move on from him for good. If she could just keep talking to him, maybe she would finally be able to know for sure if she made the right choice leaving him exactly two years ago. But now that he stood here in front of her, confessing his still present love for her, April felt trapped in the mess she had made. No one was there to save her. This was her fight alone, and her past ghosts had cornered her at her weakest. She wasn't going to win.

Preston shook his head at her car that was parked quietly beside them. He bit on the inside of his cheek. His palm wiped his mouth as he turned back to the small girl, studying her for a moment, calculating her level of vulnerability. She knew he could see the tears in her eyes, the cowardice posture she held. Weak. Vulnerable. Fragile.

He licked his lips before slowly walking over to her again. This time, he wrapped his arms around her, pushing a hug on her. He pressed her face to his chest with the back of his hand as his fingers scrunched up her already messy braid. Slowly, his lips kissed the top of her head several times as his hand barely moved further down her spine.

Her body tensed up as she felt the way he held her. She felt the way his hand was taking in the curve of her back. The way his fingers greedily scrunched her hair. His hot breath that was now breathing down on her neck set an alarm off in her head.

"April, look at us. This is what we always wanted. And now we're finally old enough to make happen." His hand slid down to her hip as her stomach flipped inside out in the worst way. Why did this feel so disgusting? She felt so uncomfortable in his arms that she could almost hear her skin screaming bloody murder. This felt wrong. Why did this feel so unbelievably wrong?

"I want us to be together," he whispered gently into her ear. Her insides squirmed at the tickle of his breath. "I love you."

The words rang in her ear like a church bell, echoing their way throughout her skull. She thought of the phrase over and over. She had waited years to finally hear Preston say those magic words to her again. The words she had so desperately been trying to keep him from saying tonight. The reason she needed him so badly.

Her mind suddenly took her back to the 13-year-old girl who first knew she loved Preston the moment he walked into her band room in Indiana. The way her heart felt like a semi-truck had crashed into it at full speed without warning.

She remembered the 15-year-old girl whose heart nearly exploded out of her chest the first time she heard a boy tell her those words. So shocked, so nervous, so scared that she couldn't even say it back.

Her brain collided with the memories of the 16-year-old girl left crying in her bathroom on the cruise ship, so sick and tired of all the lies and secrets and broken trust he put her through. The girl whose heart broke so deeply because she didn't believe she would ever be worth loving. She had spent so many years trying to prove that feeling wrong. She had spent years chasing this boy around, desperately throwing her heart at him, begging for him to prove her demons wrong— but all this time he had only left her feeling more broken and emptier than before.

All she ever cared about was hearing Preston say those words. Those eight letters that were supposed to mean something but never seemed to hold any real promises. And finally, he was offering her those words again, that idea, that feeling she craved so passionately in her chest. But this time when he said them, they didn't hit her the same. The phrase that used to make her heart run into his arms sounded like an empty shot. Like pulling the trigger on a gun only to realize it wasn't loaded.

April slowly stepped back from Preston, unafraid to look into his eyes anymore. Her breathing slowed down. She blinked slowly as her eyes searched his. Where was the familiar hazel color that instead looked black in the darkness tonight?

Finally, she whispered what her heart had been dying to say for so long. The walls she had spent years building and pushing to keep others out and away from her open wounds. April's lips softly parted to speak. She couldn't do it anymore.

"I love you too," she whispered. "But... I don't want this version of love anymore."

She felt her heart aching as she shook her head slowly. Her chest sunk. Her eyes stung as she watched a wave of sadness wash over the handsome young man's face. It hurt. She knew that. But it was the real truth that had been buried so deep within her, she didn't think it could exist.

"Preston," her voice cracked. She felt terrible for hurting him with her words that began to flow like a waterfall. But she had to tell him the truth. She couldn't bear it any longer. "I hate this. I hate working for your attention. I hate paying for your affection. I hate waking up every morning trying to prove to you that I am special enough." The tears pushed their way to her dark brown eyes. And this time, April didn't try to stop them. She let her heart speak freely, and her tears fell softly down her face without guilt.

"I hate walking around wondering why you don't value our relationship enough to protect it. I hate being the one who always feels like I'm somehow in the wrong. Like, I must not be doing enough for you to turn away from the things that harm this relationship. I hate being the person who is always struggling to forgive you, just to watch you go and screw everything up again. You don't know how badly this hurts. It hurts to be with you. It hurts so bad to love you. I feel so broken when I'm with you. And I hate it. I hate this version of love, Preston."

April waited for a long minute. She wanted a response, a reaction, anything from the boy. But he only stood frozen in shock, trying to process what she had just tried to explain. He bit his lip and ran his hand slowly through his messy brown hair. He looked more hurt than she had ever seen him before. The roles had flipped completely. For the first time in five years, Preston was the silent and confused one, and April was the one who got to speak.

"April, I've loved you since the moment I saw you." The tears now started to run down his face too. The sadness in his voice broke April's heart. "You give me this feeling like no one else. When I see you—"

"That's not love, Preston." April shook her head softly as her heart continued to bleed with emotions. She searched his face, looking for the boy she once knew hiding somewhere under all that scruff. "I don't want to feel broken anymore."

The hurting boy kept his head down as he sniffled a few times. Finally, he picked up his head to read her sad eyes.

"April, you don't understand. I do love you," his voice sighed heavy with grief. "I wanted to marry you. I still do. I told you that on that ship—I told you I wanted to spend the rest of my life with you because I love you. You were put in my life for a reason. I wanted to marry you back then, April. I still would. Right now. I love you."

April gulped heavily as she wiped the end of her damp nose with the edge of her jacket sleeve. It was like all the tangled stitches she had sown on her heart herself were now painfully being undone. Messy and exposed.

"I know, Preston. I know. And for a long time... I wanted that too." She reached out to take one of his cold hands in both of hers. She brushed her fingers over his knuckles as the puddle of tears started to slowly trickle down her face. "I left you on that ship when I was 16 because I couldn't do it anymore. My heart couldn't handle the pain I'm in whenever I'm with you.

For so long, I believed this was love. I thought it was supposed to hurt and that I somehow deserved it. And I accepted it. But… I don't want this anymore."

The two young adults stood together in the darkness as the trees around them rustled in the breeze of the cool wind that was kicking in. The air smelled like rain. A beautiful glow of lightning flashed miles out in the distance of the clouds above them.

"I loved you, Preston. I really did. And part of me is always going to care about you, no matter what happens." She used the tips of her thin fingers to brush off some of the tears that were gently streaming down her face. She sniffled a few more times before squeezing his hand once more. He dipped his head down and peaked up into her sad eyes. His broken heart was fractured underneath the surface of his pupils. April's heart hurt for both of them.

The sound of rain patterning against the leaves around them left a faint smile on her sad face. She lowered her head as she forced herself to wrap her arms around him for the last time. His body was large and made her feel tiny in his arms. Still, she somehow felt strong. She carefully squeezed his torso as he held on to her tightly.

"I'm so sorry, Preston. I really am. But I need you to go."

Michael

Chapter 25

Green, prickly shredding's of grass showered the lawn as the electric mower made its course around the front yard. Michael wiped his damp forehead under the heat of the melting sun. He hated being outside when the weather was like this, but at least he finally had something to keep his mind occupied. Away from his TV, away from his thoughts, away from his stupid phone. He was sick and tired of checking it every ten minutes for the past three days waiting to see if she had called. No texts, no snaps. Nothing.

He felt stupid for even hoping for such gestures from her. He didn't know what the point of looking at his phone was anymore. Every time it buzzed all he wanted to see was April's name. Even if it was bad news. But each time he was left in disappointment. He needed to give up on even hoping for a final conversation with her. She was gone. That was the end. He needed to let it go already.

Michael cranked the pulling mechanism back and pushed the cumbersome machine around the lawn again. The ground slowly began to reveal a beautiful, even pattern of lines going back and forth. He wanted to wrap this up quickly before the sun was finally in the middle of the sky. Late morning hadn't been as great of a time to do the lawn as he had originally thought. Once again, it felt like his timing was just barely off for yet another thing. How was he failing to pay that much attention? It was very unlike him.

Out in the distance, Michael heard the voice of one of his neighbors calling for someone over the loud roar of the mower. After a few more shouts, he vaguely made out his name being called.

"Michael!" A young voice shouted. He turned to see a little green car parked across the street of his house. A purple ponytail swung gracefully as the driver's door slammed shut. The girl spun around on her heels before urgently jogging her way across the street.

Michael felt his heart drop as he slowed down to recognize the pretty girl. He found it interesting how differently he viewed her now compared to when they first started going out. Back then when he would look at her, he saw his awesome friend, April. The girl who was cute and flirty and bubbly and fun. Now, he looked at her and saw a much fuller view of the girl. One who had a lot more to her than Michael could figure out. She seemed older through these new lenses. A girl he spent so long getting to know, but still felt like he knew nothing about.

"You weren't answering your phone," April sighed as she stepped into the grass. She kept some distance between the two of them as if she were afraid that stepping too close would only push him away further.

"I left my phone inside," he stated dryly.

He didn't want to come off as shocked or nervous or upset. The fewer emotions he showed right now, the better. He knew this was going to be a million times more difficult for him to get through than April. He just wanted it to be over with so she could leave already.

"Oh, yeah. Okay. That makes sense," she gulped awkwardly and placed her hands in the back pockets of her jean shorts. Her white t-shirt was the same one she had worn to the banquet a few weeks ago. The sleeves were decorated with silver beads in the shapes of little flowers. She continued. "Hey, so I've been wanting to talk to you."

Michael slightly rolled his eyes as he reached down to pull the gas line to start the mower again so he could drown her out. "It's fine, April. I get it." He began cranking the line a few times. He slightly struggled to get his words out. "I would rather not hear all the details. So— thanks for stopping by or whatever. I'll see you around."

She closed her eyes. "Actually, I wanted to tell you—"

"Seriously, April. It's fine. I don't need an explanation." He spat his words out.

April wouldn't take the hint. She blinked rapidly, looking flustered and nervous. "Michael. I just—"

"You just what?" He snapped, tossing the cord to the ground. His hurt was not something he was ready to be confronting right now, but if she was going to try and force him to listen to her tell him all the reasons why she didn't want him, Michael couldn't do it. "You wanted to come here and tell me there's someone else? Don't worry, April. I was able to put the pieces together myself."

April's face flushed with embarrassment. She didn't say anything at first. She just stared at him as if she was confused. "What?" She frowned. "What do you—"

"Yeah, April. I know you've been talking to Preston." He shook his head with disapproval. How stupid did she think he was? "And you know, in the beginning, I wanted to believe your sister was wrong. All these little things had nothing to do with some guy from your past who doesn't even live here. But when I saw his name pop up on your phone the other night..." Michael pinched his lips and shook his head at the dogwood tree to his right. It hurt to look at her.

He spoke softly suddenly. "To think that my girlfriend is practically leaping out of my car to run off and go spend who knows how long on FaceTime with her ex-boyfriend? I don't need you to tell me why, April. I just want you to stop dragging me along any longer in this weird game you're playing with me."

"Michael, wait," she stepped forward, but he only turned away from her. "I want to explain."

"There's nothing to explain. You want him, you used me. There. That's all you need to say. Are we done?" Michael scrapped his hands off on the sides of his shorts with a pounding heart. He marched past the embarrassed girl, making his way across the front yard towards the open garage to go inside his house.

"Michael," April followed him. Her voice sounded weak with tears, but she was determined to not shut up. "You're not listening to me. I want to explain everything to you. Please, Michael. Listen to me. It's not like that with Preston."

Michael spun around to look into her emotional eyes. His chest weighed heavy with hurt. His voice was thick with frustration. "Then why were you talking to him that night, April? Why have you been so sad the past few weeks? Are you telling me none of that has anything to do with him?"

He dropped his hands at his sides. His chest rose and fell heavily as he searched for his next words. "You know, it feels like every time I start to get close to you, you push me further away. And I keep putting myself out there for you and all you do is make me feel like a total idiot for even trying."

April sighed, exhausted. "You think you're the only one who feels like an idiot? Michael, I have been fighting myself for the past three months ever since you and I started dating. Every instinct inside my body *screams* for me to run from you. And not because you're bad for me. Because you're actually *good* to me and I don't even know how to handle that!" April watched Michael, waiting to see if he would interrupt. He didn't.

"Michael, you make being in a relationship with you look like the easiest thing in the world. And I manage to find every way to make it difficult for both of us." Her eyes were glossy. She shook her head as her eyebrows scrunched together. "I'm not going to lie. I'm a mess. A tangled, confused, broken heart of a mess. And my fears of trust and safety are rooted way deeper than just the years of damage Preston put me through.

And for so long, I have been trapped in this fantasy of what could have been. But with you… I don't feel like I have to be something I'm not. I don't have to win your approval or do anything to buy your affection. You treat me like all of me is enough. Even the sucky parts that I try to hide."

She took a deep breath before taking a few careful steps closer to him. Her dark brown eyes resembled the saturated dirt of the earth after a cool, spring rain. Swimming with emotion and life, he saw a glimpse of a different girl he didn't quite recognize. One who was hopeful. Not fearful.

"For years, I believed Preston loved me. You were… the exact opposite of everything I had been conditioned to be comfortable with. And that was absolutely terrifying for me. If someone who I didn't trust could hurt me so badly, imagine how much worse it would be for someone I finally did."

Michael glanced down at her fiddling fingers as she grew silent. She stared out into the street for a long moment. He wondered if that was the end. Maybe that was all she had to say. But then her mouth opened again.

"Some people think the worst thing is loving someone who doesn't love you back. But that's not nearly as painful as loving someone who doesn't know *how* to love you back. Falling for a guy that believes with everything inside of him that you're 'the one' for him but doesn't even know how to hold you. Seeing a man cry because it hurts him so bad that he's losing the person he loves. But still, he only keeps making mistake after mistake because he doesn't even know how to love himself. And at first, you hate yourself for loving someone who hurts you so much. But you feel much sorrier for them because they're so broken themselves. That's the worst kind of heartache. A rare kind that, fortunately, not many people have the tragedy of being a part of."

The pure melodies of birds faintly singing in the trees around the cul de sac filled the quiet between the two teenagers. Neither of them said anything. They just stood in silence together, listening to the sweet songs of nature keeping them company on this hot summer day.

Finally, April glanced over at the quiet boy. He wasn't sure what to say to the overload of emotions she had just spilled for him. Michael felt as if he had just seen more of April in the last minute than he had ever got to see over the past six months. It was refreshing in a way. A lot at one time, but real and raw.

"Michael, look," the vulnerable girl took another step closer. She had to look up to be able to see into his eyes this time. "I know, I haven't been very easy to be with these past couple of weeks. And you know what? You have every right not to want this anymore. But I'm asking you to give me another shot. Just, give me time to work on this. I want to get better. I want to get healthy. And even if we go our separate ways, I'm still going to work really hard to get healthy. And I'm still going to care about you so much. But I didn't even know what healthy felt like until you came along."

Michael stared at his feet as he thought for a while. He didn't know how he felt about the whole situation. How did he know April was being sincere and not tricking him to drag him along and hurt him even more than she already had? How did he know she was done talking to Preston for good this time? It wasn't as easy as she was making it seem.

"What about all those things you said about us?" He sighed. "You know, in the car the other night."

April shrugged softly, her eyes honest and sincere.

"I was scared," she whispered. "The truth about college is that I'm going to cheer you on no matter what you decide, Michael. Whether it's Georgia Southern or Georgia State or UGA or— community college," she chuckled faintly. "But I don't want you to base that choice on me. It should be about you. And only you. Don't worry about anyone else. Not your mom or dad or Isaac or Nick."

She smiled softly. "I'm going to be cheering you on no matter where you go. That's what I'm here for. Not to just, be your 'girlfriend' or whatever. I want to be good for you. I want us to be good for each other."

Michael barley licked his lips as he stepped closer to April, taking her hands in his. She wasn't wearing her black and blue bracelet on her wrist. For the first time, he surprisingly saw specks of purple and yellow paint scattered down to her elbow. Not her typical blue and white pallet.

"I don't think I fully understand," he said. "I want to believe you. I still… really like you. But ever since we've been together you've been so different. And if you're unhappy, I don't want to keep you trapped. I'm being honest with you, April."

"I'm being honest with you too, Michael. Really this time. You don't make me feel trapped," she blinked slowly. "You…

make me feel safe. And that's the most terrifying feeling in the world for me. And you're right. I am different. I feel different."

Michael watched her calm face. He didn't see the wheels in her head spinning. He didn't feel her hands shaking in his. He felt like he could see her for the first time since they met. All of her.

"You sure this is what you want, Bandkid?" He smiled lightly at her hands before meeting her gaze. She smiled back gently. Her hands steady and eyes calm.

"If you're patient with me, I promise I'll make progress. It might not always be perfect and I'll have days where I'll probably mess up, but I want to do this right. It just might take me a little while to get used to this."

Michael squinted his eyes as he scanned her face. She looked freer than he had ever seen her before.

"Getting used to what?" He asked.

Her chest rose as she took a deep breath in through her nostrils, and slowly exhaled through her mouth. He tilted his head ever so slightly, watching as she pinched her lips and closed eyes.

Her lashes fluttered open. "Breathing again."

Chapter 26

The dorm was charming, abundant with personality and dripping in creativity. The lavender painted lanterns hung gracefully across both sides of the room. A glow of natural light spilled through the paper-thin curtains that clothed the only window splitting the room into two. With bright white walls, a fresh, fuzzy grey rug laid in the center of the wooden floors. the space was clean.

The cardboard boxes packed the SCAD dorm room with items from home seemed to take up nearly every inch of April's side. Massive stacks of the boxes cluttered her desk, consuming the entirety of her unmade extra-long twin size mattress and invading all the space under her bed. Her new roommate had already unpacked and set up her entire baby blue and grey side of her room. A digital arts major alongside a painting artist. Their plans to decorate their room would be exciting. A creative opportunity even. But right now, April just needed to focus on unpacking one box at a time.

"Knock, knock!" A pretty girl with fiery red hair wobbled in with her arms full of her last round of fluffy pillows. Caroline had almost a dozen decorative pillows chilling on her bed already. She swore there was no such thing as too many pillows, even convincing April to bring a few more herself. But even still, April's handful was nothing compared to Caroline's overwhelming pyramid.

"Oh my— will you just let me help you, please?" April chuckled as she rushed over to take a few pillows off the top of the pile the short girl carried. She tossed them on the already crowded white and baby blue floral comforter. April thought the fabric pattern would make a really nice summer dress.

"Thanks," her icy blue eyes squinted as she giggled playfully. "I promise, that's the last of them."

April smiled as she attempted to help spread out the clutter of miniature cushions. She was taken aback when out of the corner of her eye she saw the flash of a third girl beside her. But when she looked to her left, she only stared back at a slightly unfamiliar girl in the circular mirror on Caroline's wall.

She looked like April. Tan skin. Big brown eyes and tinted full lips. But she was still trying to get used to her new hair. Shoulder length. Dark brown. Not a hint of purple in any strand. The girl in the mirror looked older. Happier. No longer needing her hair to distract everyone else from who she really was. It was a scary kind of new, but at this point, everything around April felt new. And that was okay.

"Hey, is this yours?" Caroline reached under her bed to pick up a black hair-tie. Except, it wasn't a hair tie she revealed in the light. It was a thin, black braided bracelet with three turquoise stones on the top.

April took in a deep breath as she sighed lightly. "I don't know where that came from." She was only half-lying. She didn't entirely know how it got into the dorm or when it was packed up with her things.

"It's so cute," Caroline ran the piece of jewelry through her fingers. "Oh, look. It has dolphins on the top. Awe, my little sister loves dolphins."

April brushed her short hair out of her face as she went back to unloading her box of books. "You should keep it," she smiled over her shoulder. "Give it to Shannon for her birthday or something. It's really pretty."

"Hey, that's not a bad idea." Caroline continued to look over it. "Okay, I will. But I need to seriously sanitize this before because—yikes. We have no idea where this thing could have been."

April chuckled. "I have a strong feeling it was kept pretty clean up until now…" She hesitated. "But then again, it was on the floor… Yeah, I would sanitize that thing before a global pandemic breaks out or something."

Caroline laughed loudly as she stuffed the bracelet into her tan purse. April let out a long breath as she picked up another book. It was small and yellow. A devotional book. April flipped through some of the pages, her fingers glided along the words. The spine still hadn't been broken in. It was brand new.

Okay, God. I'm ready this time. I'm all in.

She carefully placed the small book on the edge of her desk, separate from her collection of novels. The little sounds of shuffling items in the room was eventually interrupted.

"Hi," she heard a familiar voice behind her.

Both girls turned to the open door to see a handsome blonde boy peeking in before stepping further. He held a small yellow gift bag in his left hand. His blue Patagonia hat hid his shy face slightly as he smiled at the roommate.

"Hi! I'm Caroline," she immediately walked over and gave him a quick hug before Michael even really had the chance to hug her back.

"Michael," the friendly boy smiled. He looked over at April before adding a comment. "Ethan wanted to come too, but unfortunately, he had an on-campus interview and couldn't make it."

April held back a laugh as she crossed her arms and nodded her head. Of course Ethan would have tried extra hard to come see April today. Not because of her, but her pretty roommate who he had happened to be crushing on back at summer honors at the beginning of summer.

"Oh, you know Ethan too?" Caroline reached out to grab her keys from the desk beside April.

"Yeah, um... We both go to UGA," Michael nodded his head and smiled. He gave April a playful look. "Now that I think about it, the four of us should hangout sometime."

April rolled her eyes teasingly at Ethan's wingman. She truthfully loved the idea of all four of them hanging out, but she knew exactly what Michael was up to.

"Ooh, yes. I love that idea. We could all go bowling or something," Caroline giggled as she swung her white a blue striped bag around her arm. Her dad was still out waiting in the car to say his final goodbye. Caroline beamed at Michael before turning to leave. "Hey, it was so nice meeting you, Michael. I'll see you in a little bit, April?"

"Okay," April smirked and put her hands in the back pockets of her thrifted mom jeans.

She watched her new friend walk out the door and turn left down the hall. April tilted her head and slightly twisted her hips side to side as she patiently waited for the jingling of Caroline's keys to fade further down the hall. After a few seconds, she lifted her eyes and smiled bashfully at Michael.

"Mine?" She nodded to the gift bag he held in his hands. He looked back down at it before shrugging his shoulders.

"No, actually. I just thought it would look nice with my outfit. Really more of a statement piece to go along with my khaki shorts," he smiled playfully. He handed her the tissue paper stuffed bag. "You can't open it until later though."

"What?" April's eyes went wide. "That's so rude!"

Michael pulled the bag back and made her promise. His face was bright and smiley. "I'm being serious. Not until I'm gone."

April rolled her eyes and huffed with a pouty face. He could be such a tease sometimes.

"Fine..." she sighed. Michael walked past the girl to place the bag on the overcrowded desk. He looked around the cluttered dorm, taking in the scene around him. His eyes finally landed on the fluffy, stuffed elephant sitting on top of one of the piles of boxes on her bed. He smiled before leaning over to pick the sweet gift up and walk it back over to April.

"How do you feel?" He spoke softly, as if not to startle her. April took a deep breath and looked around her room. It felt small but homey. Once all her stuff was unpacked, she figured she would be able to relax a little bit better in her new surroundings.

She nodded slightly. "Not as scared as I thought I'd be."

"Roommate?" Michael went down the list they had come up with last week. She had been feeling overwhelmed, so they wrote each fear down to keep track. Once she saw the list in her hands, she realized how big her feelings were compared to how small the things actually were.

"So far, so good," she studied Caroline's side of the room for a brief moment. When she got the DM from the girl she only hung out with once in Clanton just a few weeks before school started, April was surprised to find out they were both going to SCAD. Even more surprisingly, Caroline presented the invitation for April to be her roommate. She didn't know how that would go for them, but it seemed better than being assigned randomly. Thankfully, she and Caroline were clicking really well.

"Class schedule?" Michael continued.

"Made a whole color-coordinated schedule in my planner and an extra-large one for my wall."

"That's good," Michael grinned. He placed Leo in her arms, preparing her for his final check on their list. "Did you decide on going through with what your mom talked about?"

April brushed the silvery fur of the stuffed animal with her fingers. She liked watching the way it glittered and sparkled just the faintest bit in the light. Her elephant was one of the most important things she had brought from home. He made her feel safe. Less lonely wherever she went.

"My appointment is set for next Thursday at 2," she smiled lightly.

The counseling and therapy center was right down the street from her campus. Only a five-minute walk if the weather was nice enough. Marissa Dawson.

April felt weird knowing she would soon be going to therapy. She had used to think it was a place for severely mentally ill people or those who couldn't function at all in public settings. But when her mom had finally suggested it, April had to be honest with herself. She did feel physically and emotionally exhausted from fighting her mind all day and night. April was unhealthy. She didn't want to cope anymore. She wanted to heal.

"It's going to be really good, April." Michael leaned forward and gently kissed her forehead. She closed her eyes as she squeezed the stuffed elephant close to her body. The blonde boy pulled back and ran his fingers through the tips of her short hair. The moving strands tickled her sleeve as they fell peacefully back against her skin.

"I keep forgetting it's short," she chuckled to herself as she lifted a hand to run through the other side of her hair. Michael did the same as he smiled big.

"I like it," he assured her. "You look different. Good different."

April felt different. Not like the same girl Michael had gotten to know when they first started dating. Not even the same girl she was back at summer honors when her and Caroline first met. April felt like she was still getting to know herself, too. She was learning to become comfortable sharing her same body with her new growing soul.

"You hungry?" He asked.

"Um, always," she rolled her eyes.

"Okay, well I parked in a bad spot and might be getting a ticket as we speak." Michael ruffled Leo's fluffy ears with his hand before leaning in and giving April a quick peck on the mouth. "I'll meet you in the car?"

"Yeah, okay. But, hey, you might want to start looking for places to eat on your phone now. If we can't pick a place for lunch when we're home, I can't even imagine how long it's going to take in Savannah," she laughed.

"Okay, okay. Fair enough," he smiled softly, giving her hands a quick squeeze of reassurance before walking to the door.

"Hey Chad?" April's voice stopped him at the door frame. The handsome boy turned around and smirked shyly. Today his eyes looked green. Deep green like dewy grass in the morning. A dark shade she hadn't seen them in a little while. "I love you."

His face broke into a full smile. "I love you too, Bandkid." Michael tapped the side of the door frame with his knuckles before smiling one last time at his brown-eyed girl. The second he disappeared around the corner April counted in her head as she imagined him walking down the hall.

5, 4, 3, 2…

Immediately, she dropped her elephant on her stack of boxes and snatched the yellow bag off the desk, the loud sound of tissue paper wrestled under her fingertips.

"Wow, can't even wait till I get down the hall," she heard Michael's voice tease from down the hallway. She froze jokingly when she realized he knew her better than she thought.

She shouted so he could hear her. "I waited a whole five seconds... Almost..." She paused, listening to him chuckle. The sound of the stairwell door opening and closing was her final cue that the coast was clear.

She plopped down on the grey rug as she simultaneously threw the tissue paper behind her. Her hand reached down into the bag and cupped around what felt like...

A bowl?

April lifted the mysterious object to reveal a little, white glass pot filled with dark soil and nothing else. She slowly brushed her thumb over the little, light green handwritten note that was attached.

Hi. This is it. This is your whole gift. I know it doesn't look like much right now but be patient. Take care of it. Water it. Give it lots of sunlight.

And don't rush it. Growing takes time and I know you're going to do great here. I'll see you soon, Bandkid. You've got this.

-Chad ♡

April's eyes stung. She knew her insecure side was supposed to be mad, insulted even, that he had brought her yet another flower. Weak, and fragile. Used for their beauty and nothing more. A symbol of delicacy. April was supposed to be mad, but instead, a few silent tears began to wet her cheeks as she found another truth she had been burying inside her all along.

April didn't hate flowers. She had secretly always been envious of them.

She wiped her face with her cool fingertips as she stood up to her feet. She walked the little pot over to the wall and placed it on the edge of the windowsill where the sun could feed it well. The quiet girl took one final glance around her new home.

You're doing good, April. You can do this.

She was scared, but in a new way. It wouldn't be easy, but she had to believe it would be worth it.

Her fingers suddenly ached for a paintbrush. Her heart was free to paint whatever it wanted. And at this moment, she just wanted to see what artwork would be created if she let her hands dance freely. Whatever it was, she was confident it would be beautiful. Maybe not to her mother or Harper or Scarlet or Michael, but to her it would mean something.

April looked into Caroline's gold mirror once more. She studied her short hair, her dark eyes, even her hands that were still slightly shaking.

"Hey, you're doing good, April. You're making progress." She smiled painfully at her reflection. She inhaled slowly through her nose and exhaled through her mouth one last time.

"I can't wait to meet you ten years from now. I'm really proud of who you're choosing to be."

Acknowledgements

The author would like to acknowledge:

Lynn Alexander, for inspiring me to sit down and write the title "Chapter 8" (because I can never start a project from the beginning.) Thank you for telling me I was an author before I even called myself one.

My friend, **David Brown**, for making my vison for this book cover come to life. Your talent and skill took my blurry idea and made it even more beautiful than I imagined. Your constant support and spiritual encouragement mean the world and I could not be more grateful. You are awesome.

My proofreaders, **Rachel Valderrama and Gavin Robyn**, who were my first readers of my messy draft. Thank you for your commitment and pouring into this project. Your support, feedback, and love has strengthened my belief in the anointing behind my message. Thank you again and again.

My mentors, **Corrie Henson, Kailyn Cowger and Raissa Kubandi**, who continuously see potential in me even when I do not. Thank you for challenging me spiritually, mentally and emotionally. Thank you for believing in me always.

My supportive college friends, **Gracie Foster, Marena Bedwell, and Erica Love** for jumping on board with my dream with love and enthusiasm. Unfortunately, the release party didn't time out with all of this, but the fact that you all planned one out for me will always mean more to me than you know. I love you guys.

My cheerleaders, **Emily McManus, Daisy Salinas, Abigail Clark, Anna Hobart, and Janet Philip.** Whenever I was having a moment of doubt, insecurity or just feeling completely overwhelmed and discouraged, the Holy Spirit would send one of you to keep pushing me forward. Thank you for cheering me on the whole way and loving me so well.

My sister, **Isabel**, for processing every chapter with me over and over and never once telling me to shut up. Thank you for being my moral compass and voice of reason always. Writing a book can be feel lonely at times, but with you by my side, I did not have to go through it alone. You are my rock. I love you so much.

My brother, **John**, for reading random chapters for me and letting me interview him constantly in order to get into the mindset of teenage boy. Thank you for sharing your creative insight always and constantly chasing me down tell me you are proud of me. I love you.

My youngest brothers, **Benjamin and Jason**, for all the jokes and always showing continuous interest in my work. I love you guys. "I want to read your whole book… it might take me a few years to finish it, but I will finish it one day." -Jason, age 12

My parents. Ben: the dreamer. Jasmine: that dose of reality we all need. Having both of you as parents balances me out so well. Thank you for loving me and supporting me on my journey towards healing and self-discovery. You are the reason I am who I am today, and I love you both with all my heart.

And finally, my Creator and Savior, who started writing this story long before I did. My words are meaningless without His anointing. My works are worthless without His greater purpose. I thank Him for giving me this story along with a gifting that He is using to bless me not only me, but other hearts as well. He is my closest companion and the greatest love I will ever know. I am blessed to follow the path He is leading me in.

Briana Swann

is a self-published author from Atlanta, Georgia. She is an award-winning spoken word poet and is known for her encouraging Christian videos on the popular TikTok app. You can find her on Instagram and TikTok (@briii.swann)